The Bassington Murder

The
Bassington Murder

CHARLOTTE HOUGH

Academy
Chicago

© 1980 Charlotte Hough

Published by arrangement with St. Martin's Press

First American Paperback Edition 1983

Published by: Academy Chicago
425 North Michigan Avenue
Chicago, IL 60611

Library of Congress Cataloging in Publication Data

Hough, Charlotte Woodyatt, 1924-
    The Bassington murder.

    Reprint. Originally published: New York:
St. Martin's Press, © 1980.

    I. Title.
PR6058.079B37   1983   823'.914   83-6392
ISBN 0-89733-077-3 (pbk.)

Contents

For Phyllis

1

On the train

On her sixtieth birthday Harriet Charles settled herself in a corner
seat facing the engine and opened *The Diary of a Provincial Lady*.
In the circumstances it seemed a suitable book for her to read, and
it was also a very old friend. Harriet was efficient; she had left
plenty of time and now she read slowly and nostalgically for
twenty minutes or more, amidst the banging doors and shouts of
departure. As her compartment filled she politely edged further
into her corner, but did not look up.

When the guard's whistle blew her eyes were on: *Bestow*
belongings in the rack, and open illustrated paper with sensation of
leisured opulence, derived from unwonted absence of all domestic
duties. What a nice way of putting it, thought Harriet. Leisured
opulence. Soon she herself might well be feeling something of the
kind.

When she started feeling anything. At the moment she felt ...
numb.

The train started to move. Harriet read *Unknown lady enters*
carriage at first stop, and takes seat opposite. She looked at no real
fellow-passengers, known or unknown, nor did she watch
London slipping past.

In an hour or so she would allow herself to start noticing her
surroundings as they grew more countrified. The country was the
future, and the future was what Harriet intended to concentrate
on. For the Kensington flat that she had shared with her mother
for so long was the past. The rather short lease, the more
cumbersome pieces of Victorian furniture, the elderly car, too big
and too expensive to run, but so eminently suitable – indeed the
only possibility – for an arthritic old lady to clamber in and out of,
all had at last been miraculously sold, and here was Harriet, free,
healthy, of modest independent means, the possessor of a new
bicycle, a few old friends and a good many memories, en route
for the country cottage of her dreams.

It stood, she knew, ready to receive her, in its wild, neglected
garden on the edge of the village green. Newly decorated and

sparsely furnished. Harriet meant to enjoy herself perfecting the whole thing. Tackling the green jungle with billhook and hacksaw. Making cushions and curtains. Keeping a dog, bees, bantams, anything she chose.

For she was going to have plenty of time.

Harriet stared unseeing at the familiar page in her lap. Time. Time to browse through all her old favourites. Never, since her Oxford days, had she had it as she had it now. The young teacher, the headmistress, the nurse-companion, all had been absorbing roles. But now, with all the girls she had known and guided grown up and scattered, her school, Maplehurst, in other hands, and turned into a different sort of school altogether, and finally her beloved mother's death, her world had changed. Harriet must take stock and, if necessary, change with it.

Coping with bees, cleaning out the bantams, learning to sew, training a dog, cutting herself to pieces with a billhook, a whole new life. Quite a different kettle of fish. Lovely, really, but the trouble was that she felt much, much too tired to contemplate any of it.

Tomorrow morning she would feel very differently. She would be settled in then, wouldn't she? Wouldn't she?

She sighed. It was this ridiculous business of the birthday that had dragged the whole thing down. The utterly trivial fact of nobody knowing or caring about Harriet Charles embarking on her seventh decade had actually managed to depress her.

It was this sort of thing that made her feel her mother's loss so sharply. A purely selfish pain, for the very old lady had been ready to go.

Harriet had just left her solicitor. He had a kind smile, and had wished her luck in her new venture. She might of course, on this her last visit, have casually mentioned the fact that it was her birthday, could easily have done so, and then he might, in his polite, punctilious way, have wished her many happy returns.

But she had not done so.

She had not done a number of things. She had not married and she had not had children. She had not achieved great honours or true elegance, nor any fortune to speak of. She had, she hoped, made a modest name for herself in the educational world, but for five years she had been out of all that, looking after her mother. Five quiet, happy, uneventful years in the familiar old home with its creaking lifts and shared television and friendly porter. But during that time she had missed the ever changing young faces round her. New ones. Five years of outside contacts not made. Five years of social change that had passed her by.

Her usually robust spirits sank still lower. Even the train had come blundering into it now, great noisy impersonal thing, crashing along the rails. *Nothing to do*, it rumbled scathingly, over and over again. *No room for you.*

Happy and free, glad to be me? Irritated, Harriet tried to make it change its tune. *Harriet who?* Wonderful me? *No room for you!*

Feeble and self-pitying as she knew herself to be, Harriet could hardly blame the train for refusing to cooperate. No wonder it despised her, and so monotonously carried on with its old refrain.

It was grief, that was it. Grief for her life-long friend and supporter. Now, suddenly, when all was done, the loneliness of bereavement threatened to engulf her. A loneliness made even more desolate by the fact of those five years spent in − Harriet faced it grimly − spent in being forgotten.

She read on, refusing to listen to the unsympathetic train. Another page and the Provincial Lady would be coming up to stay with Rose. Another page ... it was perhaps a mistake to bring a book where she knew so precisely what was coming next. Harriet kept her eyes down but the words swam before her. Another page and we'll be leaving London. Another page and we'll be out of the suburbs. Another page and we'll be starting on the country. ...

But now the train had relented. *Another page*, it was saying, more hopefully, even encouragingly, *another page*, as it rattled her headlong towards this famous new life.

Harriet gave a deep sigh, took off her spectacles and shut her eyes.

Another page, another page,
Another page in middle age.

*   *

Rather a long time later Harriet had a moment of bewilderment before she registered the crick in her neck, and the fact that she was sitting all slumped over to one side in a different sort of train from that on which she had fallen asleep. It had become a small, pottering, amateur sort of affair, which had lost half its carriages and most of its passengers, leaving only one other in Harriet's compartment.

A stocky, powerful-looking man in a shiny London suit sat opposite to her, absorbed in a crossword puzzle.

His face was undistinguished and uncompromising, his mouth thin, his dark hair short and shiny with Brylcream, and there was something familiar about him.

Harriet's interested gaze travelled down to his well-polished shabby shoes and then slowly up again, past the waistcoat, buttoned cuffs and sober tie, until she encountered a pair of small, clever brown eyes.

Caught staring, Harriet pictured herself asleep. She hastily smoothed back her grey hair, picked up *The Provincial Lady* and replaced her spectacles.

But the man in the opposite seat would have none of this. Extending a large square hand he said, 'Miss Charles? You won't remember me, I'm afraid. It's Ted Baxter.'

'Mr Baxter!' Recollection flooded back over fifteen years, to a newly widowed Detective-Inspector. 'Please forgive me. I hardly knew where I was! How *is* Daisy?'

The craggy face lit up. She was fine. She had married. She lived in Scotland. She often spoke of Miss Charles. 'Like a second mother, you were.'

'The best head-girl we ever had.'

'It was getting that scholarship to your place after Margaret died. I felt so inadequate on my own, understanding a young girl.'

The stalwart and masterful Baxter looked far from inadequate in any circumstances. He had a nice face. A reassuring face. Where was he living now?

After ten years at Loxley Baxter had retired, as Chief Superintendent. 'I'm lucky really, they keep me in touch. But I miss the work.'

'I'm going to Bassington,' said Harriet. Loxley was her nearest town.

'Doesn't that take the biscuit! I'm out on the Loxley Road, not far from you. It's a nice place you've chosen.'

'That's a relief, because I didn't choose it. I know nothing whatever about it.'

Harriet now told this excellent listener about how, on holiday with a friend after her mother's death, she had chanced upon the derelict Rose Cottage, which had looked both delightful and inexpensive. How they had poked about among the honeysuckle and peered in through the dusty glass. How Harriet had finally agreed to look in at the auction the following day. ...

'So it's yours.'

'Exactly. We stayed on for a few days, finding builders and so on. Then I had rather a lot to do. One way and another I've hardly been down since.'

'That's the way to do things,' Mr Baxter pronounced solemnly.

Harriet agreed that it was certainly a change from the way she had always done things before.

'You'll need some help with that garden.'

She was going to have hollyhocks, lavender, nasturtiums and pinks, and bees to go with them.

'I'll give you a hand with it if you like. I enjoy tackling the rough, and mine's done,' he said casually. Harriet imagined its immaculateness. 'You'll like Bassington. It's close-knit but friendly. There's a nice looking widow lives on the other side of the green with her family. The doctor has been there since the year dot, getting on a bit now. And then there's his wife. And a retired colonel, very Poona, in the cottage next to yours. Sporting fellow. Friend of the Kilmarnocks on your other side.'

'What a lot you know!'

'Second nature to a policeman, knowing things. Hearing things. The only people ...'

'Go on.'

Mr Baxter smiled. 'I was only thinking that as far as police work is concerned I'd reckon none of your neighbours are all that likely to show up in the local dock!'

'Except?'

'Just gossip. There's one couple that's a bit mysterious. Nobody knows their business and it's not for want of trying, in a small place like Bassington. They don't fit in. They're out of step, the sort I was trained to look out for. Force of habit.'

'What are they called?'

'If you haven't spotted them in a week I'll tell you. Ten to one they're white as snow. But I'll give you a clue, Miss Charles. Those odd-balls all have one thing in common. No past.'

'They sound most exciting.'

'I wouldn't say so. For my money your next-door neighbours at the Hall are more that way inclined. Mrs Kilmarnock's got what's-his-name, Charisma, and everybody round her just where she wants them as well, in a very nice way of course.

They slowed down. Mr Baxter was getting out one stop earlier than usual. 'Here's my address if you want me. I'll call on you if I may when you've moved in. See if there's anything I can do.'

The train stopped with a jerk. Harriet watched his sturdy figure swinging away down the platform and then settled back into her seat.

She was grateful. The cure had begun.

2

Enter Thomas

Harriet unlocked the yellow door, and regarded her new home with pleasure.

The reckless and unheard-of signing of one cheque for thousands had made subsequent signings for mere hundreds seem paltry in comparison, and these in her opinion had been spent to good effect. It had been a rather poky little cottage; now there were three coats of white paint throughout, and several precious feet added to the sitting-room where the great fireplace had been dug out and exposed. Tomorrow, Harriet promised herself, she would buy the special stuff you had to have for maintaining black iron and red brick, whatever that might be, and set to work doing whatever it was you were supposed to do. A faithful old housekeeper from her mother's youth had looked after the Kensington flat and Harriet, so busy and responsible, now looked forward at last to learning the ordinary womanly skills.

Haircord carpet had been duly laid, ear to ear, even in the tiny bathroom. The remaining family furniture had managed the change from Victorian urban to cottage rural very well, looking, thought Harriet, perfectly happy in its new role. Stout wooden shelves lined the walls, waiting for the boxes of books to be unpacked. Her mother's Persian rugs, glowing from the cleaners, were propped in rolls against the walls, together with the small pictures she had saved; a swirling green woodcut of swans on a

river, a little rustic landscape with cows, a sampler, some miniatures.

Carpenters, decorators, removal men, plumbers, electricians, deliverers of fuel, food, tools and other necessities, all had been and done what she had asked with ease and dispatch, having caused no single one of the catastrophes so generally predicted. Perhaps it was because this was the country and not London, thought Harriet, as she arranged the groceries in the larder and collected coal and kindling.

First, a fire, and then, a drink.

She was stooping over the hearth when a squeaky knock sent her hurrying out into the hall. Her first caller.

On the doorstep in the gloaming stood a silent, plumpish, detached-looking boy of serious aspect. Harriet could almost have imagined that some local tradesman had delivered him too, along with the sacks of coal and the bags of potatoes. Her visitor had such a solid, unbudging air of having been uncomplainingly dumped, and of now waiting for the lady of the house to do something about him; to store him in the linen cupboard, perhaps, stack him in the shed, or plant him in the garden.

Harriet's offers of 'Hallo,' and 'Can I help you?' went unheeded. The boy neither moved nor spoke, appraising her with a lack of self-consciousness that was curiously restful.

Just as Harriet was wondering whether to shut the door or invite him in, the boy opened his mouth. 'Your knocker. Needs oil.'

'Yes, I thought that's what it sounded like,' agreed Harriet. 'Can I help you?' she repeated.

Again the boy gave her a searing glance before stepping into the hall. 'Saw the taxi,' he said at last. 'It's t'other way about.'

Harriet considered this carefully.

'You mean you've come to help *me*?' she asked, following him into the sittingroom. 'How very kind. I haven't any matches.'

The boy fell awkwardly onto his knees, slowly and expertly relaid her fire, and then turned out his pockets. A dog-eared notebook, chewed pencil, various unfamiliar objects, plastic magnifying glass, plastic burglar's mask, plastic fried egg, plastic carton of Smarties and four plastic tops from previous Smartie cartons. All were laid out in rows on the new carpet and all were noted patiently by Harriet. Each Smartie top bore within a letter of the alphabet, and was arranged inside upwards to form together the word W A S P.

'What's in the new one?'

'M', said the boy with a frown.

'Swamp?'

'Ah.'

'How splendid!' she cried heartily after he had rearranged them accordingly, and the battered box of matches finally appeared, as she had known it must. 'What a useful person you are.'

Harriet was not quite sure what manner to adopt with her visitor. Was he a small sixteen? Or a very big eleven? 'I was about to pour myself a glass of sherry,' she said doubtfully. 'May I get you something?'

The boy examined her small collection beside the fireplace,

moving the bottles in the front the better to see the ones at the back, before finally selecting a bitter lemon and sitting down on an embroidered stool opposite Harriet's armchair, with his eyes fixed on hers.

'Here's to Harriet Charles!' said Harriet gaily. 'It's my birthday.'

The boy raised his glass obediently. 'How old?'

'Sixty.'

There was a short silence. 'Getting on,' he observed.

'Oh, I don't know,' retorted Harriet. 'It's not as bad as seventy.'

He nodded agreeably. 'Or eighty. Or ninety.' From amongst the unfamiliar objects lying at his feet he picked out a strangely convoluted plastic straw. Fascinated, Harriet watched with him the yellow liquid twist and turn, dip and circle, as it rose towards his mouth. 'Happy birthday,' he said. 'Come to that,' he continued helpfully, 'it's not as bad as a hundred either.'

'Now, that *is* getting on,' conceded Harriet, adding brightly, before he could say it wasn't as bad as a hundred and ten, 'You're my first visitor. The first person I've met in this village, and the only one in the world who knows it's my birthday, so that is quite an occasion. Who are *you*?'

'Thomas,' said Thomas, looking at her unwaveringly. She looked back. At his big round head with its short pale hair. His round pink face with round blue eyes behind round tin spectacles mended with fuse-wire. At his clothes. Not for Thomas the jersey and jeans she might have expected, but a historic pair of grey flannel bags, a knitted tie, a pullover, a shapeless, many pocketed jacket, and gym shoes.

'You'll meet 'em all soon I expect,' he told her, when she had nearly forgotten what she had said. 'Now you're in. They're all talking about you and wondering what you're like. Batty, I say. What's the use? The only one what's actually met you is me. It's only sense. But will they ask me? The one what knows? No. They'll go on asking each other.'

'People can be very foolish.'

'But I've seen you. I know what you're like.'

Harriet couldn't resist it. 'What?'

'*Bit* too fat,' decided the honest Thomas. 'But all right.'

Harriet was definitely flattered. 'Will I like them?'

'Yes.' Thomas skilfully drew up the last drop through the peculiar straw, studying it from beginning to end of its tortuous journey. 'Not but what some of 'em aren't a bit worse underneath than what they are on top,' he amended at last. 'But nobody's rude. Nobody's dirty, or throws things, or hits you or anything like that. Mind you they could, some of them, you can see it in their faces sometimes, but they don't. At least not yet they haven't. Not like school.'

Harriet glanced at him with experienced compassion; she guessed her new friend might not find life too easy at school. 'Well, I'm glad you told me about that,' she said lightly, 'I can come to you for any information I need.'

'Yes, you do that and I'll give it you. I write things down in my book but I don't tell most people. What's the good? They wouldn't believe me if I told them what God said.'

'I certainly will ask you,' Harriet assured him, taking this offer for the compliment it was. 'It sounds very interesting.' Emboldened, she added, 'I wonder what they'll think of me.'

'They'll like you,' said Thomas kindly, after taking rather a long moment to consider it. 'They'll be glad of someone new. Someone safe. Of course,' he admitted frankly, 'they may think you a bit dull at first,' Harriet nodded sympathetically, 'but they'll like you all right.'

He stowed his possessions carefully away in his many pockets and took his leave. 'You can keep the matches. You may need 'em again.'

3

Little Farthings

Harriet woke early the next morning and lay in bed for a while digesting the fact that she was in a white bedroom with old beams.

Where was the traffic? How strange it all was, but how lovely. The sun shone. Outside Harriet's window private birds murmured in her own special, magic, mysterious garden.

Reluctant to break the spell, Harriet remained motionless for another five minutes, allowing her cottage to enter her soul.

Then her eyes snapped open and energy flooded her limbs. Up! To work! For she didn't choose to dream the golden autumn hours away. She would unpack, explore, hang things on hooks, put things on shelves. ...

The ha-ha separating Bassington Hall from the commonland beyond changed abruptly when it reached the end of Harriet's garden, from a meticulously maintained sunken wall to an unkempt ditch, where nettles and brambles wormed their way under a rusty and disintegrating fence. Very different to her neighbour's on the left, with its taut and shining barbs. Harriet decided to grow a wild rose hedge on her portion. Standing by the window in her nightgown she could see the river, across former ornamental parkland where bridle-paths now cut through the encroaching heather and bracken. Some of the original trees remained. The centre of an ancient group of pines had been felled, leaving a rough circle of strange and angular shapes. The scent from these reached her now, and a birch grove beyond her own boundary added to her view.

This land, with its fishing rights, had been donated to the village by an earlier squire. Once it, and hundreds of acres round, including her own cottage, had all belonged to Bassington Hall. By craning her neck to the right Harriet could see most of the few which remained; a rolling lawn, a hammock slung between two trees, part of a tennis court, a Georgian outbuilding of which her own garden wall formed a part, herbaceous borders, the corner of a swimming pool, a glimpse of orchard.

Amongst this orderly charm dwelt the charismatic Kilmarnocks.

*   *

A thick privet hedge divided Harriet's garden from that of Little Farthings next door, and as she walked out that first morning there came from behind it a low grunt of pain.

She stopped, a Londoner, at a loss. Could it be some animal, perhaps, caught in a trap? She peered fearfully through the leaves straight into a pair of cold grey eyes.

'I – I'm sorry,' she stammered, taking a step back. 'I thought I heard a cry.'

'My dear lady, it was me, groaning,' corrected the Poona colonel, for such Harriet rightly guessed him to be. He now stood upright in full view and introduced himself. He was lean and tanned, the top of his head freckled. Although his remaining hair was white his bearing was youthful. A good-looking labrador sat behind him upon the smoothest of lawns.

'I'm apt to groan when I straighten up from a bending position, though I shall endeavour not to, now that you're there.'

Walter Rillington's moustache twitched, revealing pointed, wolfish teeth. His own, thought Harriet.

She looked over his shoulder. 'What an example for me.'

'It passes the time. Where would we retired men be without our gardens! Come in, do.'

Harriet joined him with alacrity and exclaimed politely as her neighbour pointed out his treasures, though all was not entirely to her taste. The colonel's flowers were staked to attention, with measured distances of well-fed earth between. The weeds had been chemically vanquished and all the rest was sprayed, powdered and scientifically manured with the correct amount of the correct substance. Goldfish, each one in excellent health, glided sleekly within a scum-free ornamental pool, amongst flourishing aquatic plants, which together maintained a natural balance.

All this the colonel explained, and to all this Harriet listened, and conscientiously tried to remember.

'It's so kind of you to show it to me. I've already met another of my neighbours; a boy called Thomas.'

Rillington laughed. 'Anybody's liable to meet Thomas at any moment! Your wild garden is a favourite haunt of his, but he's quite likely to pop up behind my delphiniums. He's harmless enough. Wanders about taking notes. Looks at you like an elderly eye surgeon. I suppose he really ought to be in some sort of home. Speaking of which, how are you doing with yours?'

'There are some things I need. I shall go to the local sales.'

'You won't lack help and advice if you're interested in sales,' the colonel assured her. 'Even Fiona goes to those. That's your neighbour on the other side, Fiona Kilmarnock. Jolly clever. Pays next to nothing and polishes them up, and they all turn out to be three hundred years old with special linenfold carving or whatnot all over them. Not that she needs bargains, of course. Then she gets bits of old stuff and makes lamp-shades and so on. Clever at everything.'

'Is that *the* Fiona Kilmarnock?'

'She writes poetry if that's what you mean. Clever at that too I suppose. Gets it published anyhow. Can't make head or tail of it myself, but still, I'm not surprised because as I said, that girl can turn her hand to anything.'

'She sounds rather daunting!'

'Oh, but she isn't, she's perfectly natural,' Rillington looked curiously boyish. 'I would just simply say that a beautifully dressed, very amusing girl who's a corker to look at, brilliantly clever and frightfully good at everything just about sums her up. Everybody likes her. Every man is probably half in love with her. She's got it all. Born rich. This,' the colonel waved a hand towards the lovely Queen Anne house, mellow in the sunshine. 'Very decent husband. Forgot to tell you she's marvellous with the garden too. Just given her gardener the push. (A miserable devil she's better without; Goggins, what a name!) Cooks like an angel, first-class tennis player. Lovely horsewoman too though she doesn't do much of that now because Bobby's like a sack of potatoes. Looked after her mother in that cottage in their garden till she died. Not easy. Bit of a Tartar, but she was wonderful there too, patient as a saint.'

'Was she very fond of her mother?'

'Fond?' Rillington looked taken aback for a moment. 'Of course. Of course. The perfect daughter.'

But Harriet had wearied of this paragon.

'Look, a woodpecker! What a lovely bird-table.'

'D'you like it? I try to cater for every British bird in this place. Look at those little creatures. Don't care a fig which way up they are. I'll make you a contraption like that if you want … no, it's my pleasure. You might have been one of those cat women.'

The colonel's cool face lit up approvingly as he took another metaphorical step towards her. 'Come inside and I'll give you a cup of coffee. Won't take a minute. I've got a special gadget for that.'

Walter Rillington led the way into his cottage, grumbling in a perfunctory sort of way about dampness, rotting beams and other such disadvantages of an old property, but it was already clear to Harriet that Little Farthings and its garden were her neighbour's pride and joy. All was neat and systematic inside as it had been out. The walls were lined with books, cabinets, silver cups, and faded yellow photographs of bygone dogs, horses and military forebears in mahogany frames. She stood upon a tiger skin and looked at them all.

When the colonel returned from the kitchen he found Harriet examining the books.

'I can see you're an expert on natural history,' she said.

'I've got some local lepidoptera in here,' said Rillington, studying the labels on a set of drawers with narrowed but unspectacled eyes. 'You should see plenty of that. Lots of good caterpillar fodder in your garden.'

'Let us hope they appreciate the nettles,' said Harriet, bending over a display table where small weapons were arranged in circles according to size.

Rillington turned round, drawer in hand. 'Your garden's been untouched for five years,' he said. 'Ah, you've found my knives! Ceremonial, most of them, with some very fine workmanship. The one with the elephants on is the most intricate, I think.'

'Elephants?'

'On the handle of the stiletto. My grandfather was given it by some Persian bigwig. Now, I collected these little fellows a couple of years ago, all within a radius of one mile.'

Harriet looked rather wistfully at the graduated rows of butterflies with pins through them.

'Beautiful, aren't they, though I'm mainly a bird man myself. Funny, isn't it, the way we can spend weeks trampling all over the countryside shooting them,' he said confidentially, touching Harriet with his casual assumption that her life was the same as his own. 'And then spend hours watching the little beggars on the bird-table. I know them all.'

'One would.'

'This is the place for you ...' began Walter Rillington, but he was interrupted by a shrill whistle. In a moment he had emerged from a scrupulously clean kitchen, tray in hand, and shepherded Harriet out to the newly painted table and chairs which stood on dead flat crazy paving. They sat down beside the goldfish.

'You have a wonderful view of the village.'

'It's nice living on the green.'

'It makes me feel *in* things already. Now,' said Harriet firmly, 'You've told me about Fiona Kilmarnock. What about the others?'

'Well, there's her husband Bobby for a start. My godson, never had any of my own. Used to visit him at school. Bobby's no athlete but he's a sportsman if you know what I mean. Always ready to have a go. Got up his own cricket eleven at school. Rabbits, they called themselves, and then another school produced the Duffers and they played each other.'

Walter Rillington sipped his coffee and looked out over the green. 'Caroline Metcalfe's a cousin of Fiona's but *she* hasn't a bean. Her husband went into a tree to avoid a child that ran out in front of his car. Child escaped but he smashed himself up. The insurance company said it was his fault or some rubbish like that. He'd had a drink or two I suppose. Hugo never was a fighter; too much of a gentleman. He just died. Typical really, but damn bad luck I call it. Caroline was left on her uppers and Bobby, as an old friend of the family, was awfully good to her. Came to her rescue and leased her the Old Rectory for a peppercorn rent.

'Well, that's her. Nice girl. Then there's ... well, speak of the devil! Or rather, listen to her!'

A bright mauve mini had appeared which, despite its dashing appearance, was trundling along very slowly in the gutter. Finally the engine, which had been noisy and spasmodic, stopped altogether and it slid silently to a halt outside the colonel's gate.

4

Beatrice Cotman (40)

'Be quiet, Rex!' Colonel Rillington rose to his feet. 'It's only Cotty.'

'Bloody Mabel!' exclaimed the large, forceful-looking woman who was emerging from the tiny car like a genie from a bottle, and giving the gaudy bonnet a sharp slap. 'Gone again hasn't she.'

'She has the right sporting spirit, bringing you to my door,' responded the colonel gallantly. 'I'll have a dekko at her innards.'

'Thanks, Wally, but I understand the old girl. If I let her cool down she'll cook up the strength to run me home. Actually I should have taken her in before, too economical.' She lowered what had been ringing tones by one degree. 'Is that our new encumbent?'

Cotty's handsome hazel eyes stared with such lively curiosity over the front hedge that Colonel Rillington hastened to invite her in. 'Miss Harriet Charles. Miss Beatrice Cotman.'

'Cotty, please!'

'Known to all and sundry as Cotty,' he added obediently. 'And very useful she is too, because whatever you want Cotty'll do it. Cubs, Meals on Wheels, OAPs, concerts and get-togethers, Cotty wakes them all up and puts some stuffing into them. Lame dogs, poor things, the halt and the maimed, all specialities of Cotty's.'

Harriet smiled and shook her head rather absently. Where had she met this Cotty before? The wide, full mouth, the strong nose whose outward thrust seemed to push the eyes round to the sides of her head. Large, dancing eyes, so full of life and yet somehow linked in Harriet's mind with pain and illness, darkness and tears. What connection had this so essentially ordinary tweedy woman, so cheerily sensible, so broad-beamedly sitting in so sunny a garden?

As she uttered the usual pleasantries, Harriet racked her brains. A definite, memorable face. Had Cotty been a Maplehurst girl? The firm chin was heavy, the thick hair touched with grey. Much younger than she was, certainly. But not, surely, young enough?

Not as young as Elizabeth Dallington or Leonie Ford-Dixon. Harriet suddenly recalled two stoic faces in early adolescence. Children of old-fashioned, county upbringing, trained from infancy not to complain. Elizabeth's mastoid, Leonie's appendix. Distraught parents, telephone calls, night alarms, hurrying feet along darkened corridors, shattering that usual calm and sheltered atmosphere. ...

'It's Beatrice, isn't it!' cried out Harriet, cutting across the conversation. 'From Greengates School. Without the white coat!'

'Miss Charles; history, Latin and Greek! I'd almost forgotten that dump! Lawks, what a rotten one, but what a handsome games master!' Cotty rolled her eyes reminiscently.

'Greengates, do you mean? We went through some dramas there, didn't we! It must be twenty years ago.'

'Not as long as that surely,' said Cotty rather distantly.

'Perhaps not,' amended Harriet. 'I've really forgotten. I left not long afterwards, for Maplehurst.'

'The headship.'

22

'Yes.'

It was out, but her companions reacted amiably, even admiringly. That's one hurdle over, thought Harriet. Neither of them said 'How terrifying!'

'As a matter of fact,' she confessed, 'I meant to keep it quiet, in case nobody would speak to me.'

'Good God!' cried Cotty heartily. 'It would take a hundred positive *dragons* to stop anybody speaking in this place! Honestly though, it is a friendly village, Walter, isn't it.'

'Hotbed of gossip is what Cotty means.'

'All the old tabbies in general, and Rosemary and Biddy in particular. Rosemary's sensible and Biddy's silly. Pretty as a peach but looks like a pig.'

'Yes, she does, a nice clean one; but nothing could be less like a pig-sty than her cottage,' said the colonel, evidently as big a gossip as anybody. 'Frills with everything.'

'That's Biddy's taste of course. Not Ann's.'

'Than whom nothing could be less frilly.'

The two laughed heartily.

'Who's Ann?'

'Old friend of Biddy's,' explained Rillington. 'They live together and run the Copper Kettle tearooms with a half-witted waitress. Lunches and sponges, you know the sort of thing. They were both on the stage. Can't imagine Ann in the chorus.'

'Ibsen more likely. They're as different as chalk from cheese,' agreed Cotty. 'Ann Markham does the accounts and cooking, while Biddy chats up the customers and flogs the cakes.'

'Nice women,' said Rillington. 'You'll find everybody very easy here. It's rather inter-connected, with cousins and godfathers and so on. I'm Bobby's godfather because I knew his father in the Army. James Ashford is Thomas's godfather because he knew his grandfather as a student.'

'A student of what?'

'Medicine. James is the local doctor. Completely vague.'

'That's all rubbish, Walter. He puts it on because it's reassuring being ga-ga. Remember that new-fangled locum, with his probing questions? We never saw him again, did we now? Not on your life! All the locals prefer James nodding understandingly as he slowly fills his pipe.'

'Nod and fill he may, but all I know is I'd prefer his wife on the other end when I ring up with a long list of alarming symptoms,' said Rillington, looking like Cotty extraordinarily unlikely to do so. 'Knows twice as much as he does. Never at a loss for an answer, Rosemary Ashford.'

Harriet connected her up. 'And she's the *sensible* gossip?'

'That's it. Sharp as a needle and neat as a pin. The attraction of opposites I suppose. Knows the Latin names in the garden, never has a hair out of place, is a top-class bridge player, and remembers the grandchildren's birthdays. James can't remember his own name.'

'Now Caroline Metcalfe is another matter altogether,' said Cotty happily, leaning back in her chair.

'Different to Rosemary, and rather more similar to James,' explained the colonel with methodical courtesy. 'She muddles through, Caroline does. Done something funny to her hair.'

Cotty roared with laughter. Another of Caroline's experiments! Do you remember, Walter, when she tried being self-subsisting and the goat ate the vegetables and a fox killed the hens because it was unkind shutting them up, and the shop with everything priced too low? And mating her dog, what *dozens* of great unsaleable mongrels!'

'And those lodgers, so charming, but so never in a position to pay. Sometimes,' said the colonel, 'I wonder why all Caroline's schemes are such non-starters; she's an intelligent girl.'

'Ah!' said Cotty decidedly. 'That's because she deep down expects them to fail, isn't it. Of course a cousin like Fiona would give anybody an inferiority complex.'

But Cotty had to go, was already late for several frantic commitments. As she got to her feet she said, 'You forgot to tell her about the Clancys, Walter.'

'I always forget about the Clancys,' replied the colonel simply. 'They're just a couple, living in a bungalow.'

'With or without benefit of clergy,' retorted Cotty, folding herself expertly into the purple car. 'There you are, what did I say; back to normal!' as Mabel roared into life. With a triumphant wave and a crash of gears Cotty drove off.

'There does seem to be rather a marked difference in their ages,' admitted the colonel, reverting to the Clancys as he walked Harriet to her gate. He gives me the creeps but she's rather a pathetic little thing.'

5

Drinks at Wood End

Proudly Harriet hung up the swans and the cows. Lovingly she arranged her books in alphabetical order and unpacked all her belongings over the next few days, steadily assisted by Colonel Rillington and spasmodically by Thomas. Proprieties with the front door having been observed he now came round by the garden, where his expressionless face pressed against the window caused Harriet to jump.

But once inside and sitting down, muddy shoes planted squarely on one of the Persian rugs, his calm and ingenuous air of complete at-homeness pleased her. Thomas on her sofa was the Visitor who completed the metamorphosis of Rose Cottage into a real home. A visitor who required no invitation and no entertainment and was even intermittently useful. With sober candour he gave her his opinion on all the new things that had appeared on the scene during his absence; favourable if useful, unfavourable if ornamental, and Harriet accepted him as he had accepted her, unquestioningly and unquestioned, for he vouchsafed no information about himself and she did not ask for any. He might, from his dishevelled appearance, have spent the time away from her hibernating in a heap of leaves at the bottom of her garden.

Thomas's youth cheered Harriet, whose life had once been so abundantly filled with youth. She found his company soothing and instructive, for Thomas, reticent though he might be in some respects, was far from silent. He told Harriet a number of facts, many of which were new to her, as she stood about with her head on one side, wondering where to put what. Facts about electronics, Oliver Cromwell's father, or the interpretation of dreams were patiently explained to her. How to achieve immaculate conception, or build a new sort of snow plough. How to shrink human beings to one tenth their normal size or catch the Loch Ness Monster. If Harriet exclaimed in wonderment Thomas would gravely assure her that it was indeed so, because he had worked it out.

When Harriet's new telephone rang Thomas consulted a Mickey Mouse watch and left as quietly and decisively as he had arrived. She heard Cotty's stentorian tones on the end of the line. Drinks, that very evening.

'Some of your new neighbours will be there,' she said. 'We're supposed to be discussing arrangements for Fiona's fête but one never does what one's come for does one.'

Harriet accepted with gratitude.

'Not at all. They're all frantically interested to meet you. A new phiz down here's worth seeing I can tell you, and you can inspect Cotty's Cot for what it's worth. Not much. Everybody has to take me as they find me here; *that* you'll soon discover!'

Harriet put the receiver down and gave serious consideration to the question of dress. If they were all frantically interested to meet her they must not be disappointed. Nor must she herself be too prejudiced by all that she had heard so far, she told herself severely. Fiona Kilmarnock, for instance, was probably a perfectly nice girl in spite of everybody loving her so much.

As an ex-headmistress Harriet still owned a number of fairly dressy dresses. Even then she had felt it unsuitable for her to wear anything *avant garde*, and now that five more years had gone by they had sunk lower in the fashion stakes. Dubiously, she riffled through her wardrobe. A flowered silk had mysteriously become several inches too short. A yellow two-piece made her look too hot with the jacket on and too fat with it off.

When the time came she settled on a good old stand-by in blue as she had always really known she would, and some smart but uncomfortable shoes. Then she sat down at her dressing-table and looked at her face.

Harriet was not one to remark upon her good points, nor to agonise over the bad. Many years of living with adolescent girls who did both had inoculated her against either. She accepted the spectacles, the fly-away grey hair of sensible cut, the nose that was just this side of beaky and the figure which was just this side of stately, and paid no attention to the strong chin, fine bearing and steady blue eyes. She had decided long ago that if she could look clean and respectable that would do, and now she set to work to achieve that end with lipstick, powder and comb.

*   *

Cotty's Cot, officially called Wood End, was a red brick bungalow built about 1930 with a bay window, a hospitably open door, a porch containing various parcels waiting to be seen to, and a garden whose owner had other interests.

A plump little lady with golden hair, good legs and tiny feet trotted up the path ahead of Harriet, who caught a glimpse of an upturned nose and simple pink face. It was so pretty and yet so undeniably piggy that she felt sure this must be Biddy, the silly but good-natured gossip described by Cotty earlier on.

Harriet slipped unnoticed into the hall and stood for a moment or two on the outside looking in. She saw at once that this living-room had got past the stage of a quick tidy-up. A heterogeneous clutter of letters, combs, tea-cups, post-cards, bulldog clips, lists, programmes and half a dozen unfinished projects had settled on every available flat surface. The only concession Cotty seemed to have made towards her party was to shut the desk to within half an inch, through which a quantity of papers struggled to escape. One or two had succeeded and lay on the floor under a chair amongst the dust. There were photographs rather than pictures, and much neglected mahogany. It was the house of a busy woman.

Within this room a kaleidoscope of those who were soon to become familiar to her moved in ever-changing groups. She had a general impression of pleasant, polite, well-dressed, civilised-looking people, most of whom knew each other very well.

Harriet sat down on a battered chest and changed from her friendly old boots into the new and pinchy shoes. Snatches of conversation came to her ears.

Darling, Biddy hasn't got a drink.
Surely there is a danger that when he reaches puberty ...
An old flame of mine ...
Abandoned ...
Cotty had him in the Cubs for a while ...
... much wrong if you love an animal ...
So public-spirited. Fiona says ...
Bobby won't mind.
Oh, won't he!
Destitute. I wish I could say I'd do the same.
Olly and Polly. Don't they sound dinky!

Now Harriet hesitated in the doorway. Cotty had her back to her. Colonel Rillington looked cool and distinguished in a grey suit. Silhouetted against the window on the far side of the room a tall, friendly-looking man in early middle life caught her attention. He stood deep in earnest conversation with a slim, red-haired woman. As she watched the man bent his head with sudden grace to catch his companion's words. A lock of straight dark hair fell across his brow.

Desire. *Bring me my ar-rows of de-sire.* Suddenly Harriet felt a stab of nostalgia for the old familiar world of school, and the last hymn of the last day of the last term. *Among those dark Satan-ic mills.*

Serried rows of girls in the school chapel, grave-faced in their dark navy blue travelling suits and clean white blouses. Clear high voices, and Blake's immortal words of hope and longing.

Young voices singing the beautiful words, and young ears listening to the early arrivals in the quadrangle outside; to the crunch of tyres on gravel which heralded not the end of term but the beginning of the holidays. Listening to the distant, matter-of-fact remarks and instructions which wafted in through the open window on the summer air. Whose fathers? Whose brothers? Strapping on whose school trunks?

Bring me my bow of burning gold! her girls had innocently sung, *Bring me my ar-rows of de-sire!*

An old-fashioned word. What did they say nowadays? They fancied somebody. Surely by no stretch of the imagination, mused Harriet, could it mean the same thing? Or could it?

The tall, elegant man was listening to the red-haired woman with interest. When she came to the end of her story he threw back his head and laughed.

Harriet stepped forward.

'Oh, sorry!' A pale, gangling youth jabbed her in the stomach with a laden tray and immediately turned bright red. For a moment bottles and glasses wobbled alarmingly.

'Let me take something.'

'C-could you? It is rather heavy. I'm taking another drink over to M-Maureen Clancy. I got the last lot down her dress thank goodness. I mean thank goodness it wasn't Rosemary.' He gave her a harassed look. 'I-I'm sure I ought to be introducing you or something. Myself at any rate. I'm Andrew.'

'I'm Harriet. Harriet Charles.'

He smiled anxiously and jerked his head towards a red and

bony wrist protruding from too short a sleeve. 'Can't shake hands I'm afraid.'

Harriet followed him through the room, with water and ice. Maureen and John Clancy stood silently together. Both looked small and nondescript and, as the Colonel had said, easy to forget. Andrew was struck dumb and Harriet had to introduce herself. John Clancy nodded a square bald head up and down, once only, and fixed her with a ferocious glare, before muttering his own name as if it was the last word he was prepared to allow past his lips. Maureen Clancy looked up at her through a cloud of dark, undisciplined hair. She had rather vacant eyes of Irish blue. 'I haven't seen you before,' she said flatly.

'Just a sec; I haven't put the water in yet.'

Maureen held her empty glass out and Andrew and Harriet filled it from bottle and jug. She raised it to her lips. 'Lovely!'

'That's enough!' said John Clancy sharply.

Andrew grinned. 'Yes, make the most of it. It's the last one you'll get from me. I-I've got to go and do some work.'

But Maureen had got hold of the bottle and pertly topped up her glass. Uncertainly the boy grinned again, rather foolishly, and turned away.

Maureen gave her husband a look that was both nervous and sly and then said confidentially, 'He's very clever. He's writing a book. It's very important, he's been at it for years.'

'How interesting. What is it about?' Harriet asked a pair of small, angry eyes.

But Mr Clancy preferred to play his cards close to his chest. 'It's on a specialist subject which wouldn't be likely to interest you,' he said without appearing to move a muscle of his face. It was greyish, and lined. There must be thirty years between them, thought Harriet, feeling paradoxically interested in his specialist subject, now that she was not allowed to know what it was. Something excessively manly perhaps, like Victorian railway engines, or unsuitable for her in a sexy sort of way? He was the sort of man who might do that sort of thing, just because he looked so unlike that sort of man. …

However, somebody ought to say something. Dutifully she opened her mouth, but her hostess now bore down on her with many apologies. 'Just like me!' Dexterously Cotty relieved Harriet of her burdens and drew her towards the window. 'Let's break those two up.'

'... not quite fixed but Fiona's arranging it all next week when she's got time, after the fête. She says the children seem docile. I only hope our new neighbour won't object.'

'Here *is* your new neighbour. Caroline Metcalfe. Bobby Kilmarnock.'

The couple turned smilingly towards them; the woman healthy and candid, the man genial and debonair, saying 'How nice to meet you!' in unison, the man adding hopefully, 'Oh good. You don't *look* as if you object to much.'

Caroline Metcalfe had attractively crooked white teeth, eager brown eyes with thick pale lashes, gardener's hands, and numerous precarious-looking scarves, brooches, bracelets and different sorts of chains. Efforts had been made, thought Harriet sympathetically, but also mistakes. Even Caroline's freckles were untidy ones, being uneven in size and unevenly distributed, and at close quarters she could see that the red hair was mingled with an insistent shade of purple.

Bobby followed her eyes. His own were a bright and laughing blue, their quizzical look emphasised by one crooked eyebrow. 'Don't look at Caroline's hair, I beg you. Cotty's car is such a baleful influence. Known as Mabel and nothing could be purpler.'

'A gentleman would never have drawn attention to it.' Caroline turned to Harriet. 'It's called Autumn Magic. Cheap, I admit, but supposed, according to the packet, to have an electrifying effect on such as Bobby.'

'It has had an electrifying effect.'

'It's such a disadvantage, always believing the printed word.'

She looks as if she always believes everything. Her children would never lie to her, thought Harriet.

'I was planning to avoid the pepper and salt stage I'm actually at before emerging,' Caroline's eyes flicked tactfully to Harriet's hair, 'into the full beauty of proper grey.'

The two speakers addressed all their remarks to Harriet. Looking from one to the other she felt herself caught up in a gossamer web of joy. 'I would have tried Autumn Magic myself,' she confessed, 'but whoever heard of any self-respecting headmistress having *that* sort of electrifying effect!'

'Oh, were you a headmistress?' cried both her listeners together.

'How terrifying!' said Bobby.

'You've said the wrong thing,' said Harriet.

'I can see you'd be a jolly good one and not terrifying a bit,' put in Caroline at once. 'I wish you had been mine.'

'Would you have liked to be Caroline's headmistress?'

'Yes, I would.'

'Oh, so would I. But I'm afraid I was very emotional and tiresome, so really I'm glad you won't have to be. And a fearful show-off in the school plays. *Not* very attractive. I was a prefect though, in the end.'

'Strong personalities often make good prefects.'

'I was a strong personality,' remarked Bobby, tired of being left out of the conversation.

'Were you?'

'Caroline, you know I was! I might remind you, and inform Miss Charles, since I think she ought to know, that while you were bulging out of an inky gymslip, hitting some unfortunate child who hadn't fed her guineapig, I was acting in my own revue in the OUDS, and what's more I was, and still am, greatly in demand as an after-dinner speaker. In fact my fame is such that I am travelling up to London tomorrow to address those self-same Oxford friends at a reunion dinner.'

'Oh Bobby, I know you're wonderful.' Caroline was immediately contrite. 'Are you going to stay in your flat and is Fiona going with you?'

'Yes I am and good lord no. (a) She'd hate it, (b) she hasn't been invited and (c) it's all men.'

'Where is Fiona, by the way?' asked Cotty, who had circled the room and now rejoined them.

Bobby swung round at the sound of her voice and seized her round the waist. 'Sorry, Cotty darling. Late as usual I'm afraid. I never wait for her nowadays. I'm always ready in time, all brushed and shining. Can't help it, and I'm so rotten at hanging about that I have to just come along all by myself. It's pathetic.'

'Now, I approve of hanging about,' said a rumpled, snub-nosed man who had ambled up to meet the new arrival. 'And I must say, being the local quack round here comes pretty close to my ideal. There's no danger of anything happening whatever, apart from some nice old octogenarian quietly passing away once every ten years. I do hope you won't be bored. Have you met Fiona? Oh well, you'll like her when you do, she's the great thing round here,' he explained vaguely.

'I've heard all about her. She sounds a most attractive person,' said Harriet conscientiously.

On second thoughts, Dr Ashford was not exactly rumpled. His clothes were well-cared for, but he kept running his hands through his grey hair. Some of it was standing straight upwards. 'Oh, she is, she is! Great friend of my wife Rosemary. She and Rosemary and Cotty run this place between them. They'll rope you in for Fiona's fête I expect. People come from all over the place for those. Caroline's very useful there, a real artist. And Rillington's a practical man. And Biddy and Ann are very kind souls too though of course they've got their tea-rooms to run. Mm.' He glanced over to the corner with a rather more penetrating look than she had expected. 'I see that couple Clancy here tonight. They usually keep themselves to themselves, locked up in Botswana.'

'That's their castellated bungalow, not the African state,' said Bobby, in reply to Harriet's startled look. 'I'm sure I've seen them in the papers, or on television,' he added mischievously to the little lady with golden hair.

'For something too terrible to mention!' she gasped.

'Don't worry, Biddy. They probably won the pools and want to keep it dark. Begging letters.'

This last came from an attractive, incisive woman whose name Harriet filed neatly away amongst the others. Rosemary Ashford, married to the local doctor. Now talking to Biddy something, once on stage and now running the Copper Kettle tea-rooms. Her academic career had provided an excellent training for cocktail parties.

'If you ask me, she's petrified of him,' continued Rosemary in such a loud clear voice that Harriet glanced round anxiously. 'It's all right, they've gone. I don't think they enjoyed themselves much. Have you ever met anybody more difficult to talk to than that man!'

Cotty put in a word for her departed guest. 'John Clancy's actually very intelligent when you know him.'

'Oh Cotty, he's dreadful! So stuffy and pompous,' insisted Rosemary.

'How do you know, you've never given the poor man a chance!' responded Cotty with spirit. She was evidently a match for them all.

'It's all very well for you, Cotty. You don't have to live next door to him.'

'Oh don't be so hysterical, Biddy, we've all got to live next door to somebody,' said Cotty firmly, 'and Maureen can talk nineteen to the dozen if you get her on her own. She's quite lively with Andrew.'

'They're more of an age, aren't they,' said Doctor Ashford amiably.

Everybody was now talking at once.

'That's putting it mildly!'

'She's pure victim material. Sexy simpletons always are,' explained Rosemary. 'Asking for exploitation.'

'Talking of cruelty, *there's* somebody who pulled wings off flies when he was a child, if anyone did.'

'I wasn't very alluring myself at the age of four. Had to have my puppy taken away from me.'

'Even gentle Caroline was a basher-upper. She's just said so.'

But now they all claimed that they had been beasts as children. 'We've still got a brutal streak left, from our animal past,' summed up James Ashford. 'The physical part has to go, so we just say things.'

'Jolly boring if we didn't,' said Caroline. 'Look at the lovely gossip we're having now!'

'Yes, yes, yes. I'm just pointing out as an evolutionary fact, for interest.'

'It's not interesting; it's a platitude,' retorted his wife.

'The sex war. Listen to us, we're all so aggressive!' Bobby's blue eyes challenged the party.

Harriet laughed. 'I disagree! I had only come to come out of my door to be befriended by Colonel Rillington.'

Bobby raised his eyebrows.

'Uncle Walter? Now there's a case in point. Dear old boy. You'd think he wouldn't hurt a fly, wouldn't you! Spends all his spare time spoonfeeding bluetits. In actual fact he can be absolutely murderous and is well known in Army circles for conking eleven Germans on the head, one after the other.'

'And I have personal experience of you being pretty murderous yourself, dear boy,' said Rillington mildly, who had joined them at the mention of his own name. 'When necessary. Thank God I thought at the time. Still do.'

Harriet looked with new eyes at the white scar that slashed Bobby's eyebrow, causing one half to settle a little above the other. Now she could see a faint continuation of it on the cheekbone. That bright eye had been lucky, she thought. The nose had been broken too; rather attractively flattened at the bridge.

Bobby was saying, 'So you don't believe it, Miss Charles, or may I call you Harriet? I may, mayn't I. Scratch the surface of any of this lot and you'll find just one horrible subconscious after another.'

'I'm not scratching any of you. I like what I can see.'

'Talking of which,' said Rillington, 'There's a sight for sore eyes.'

Fiona Kilmarnock stood in the doorway.

Bobby looked round. 'I hope you're going to be frightfully amusing now that you're so dreadully late,' he said affably. When he made the introduction he added, 'Harriet's an awfully nice Headmistress.'

'How terrifying!'

Harriet looked up into faintly amused, green-blue eyes, dark fringed, set aslant in a lightly tanned, oval face.

She blinked, For Fiona Kilmarnock was dazzling. There was no other word for it. Harriet was quite literally dazzled by the beauty of her new neighbour, who she now perceived to be the possessor of superb modern jewellery, and to be dressed in simple cream-coloured silk which promptly eclipsed every other woman in the room.

Fiona was tall, and slenderly assured, with fine bones, delicate skin and short dark shining hair that bounced back into place as she moved her head. Lazy, sensual mouth. Straight nose. Perfect teeth. Her manner was easy, amusing and, very slightly, 'social'.

With the arrival of this lovely creature a subtle change came over Cotty's little party, as if it had been quietly joined by Royalty. It became less silly and gossipy and more sophisticated and informed. The women talked less and the men more. The guests stood a little straighter and went into sharper focus. Each was obviously on intimate terms with Fiona and yet at the same time, casually, charmingly, she accepted their homage. Each became more like themselves and also less natural, like actors. Cotty was more hearty and assiduous, Rillington more lean and gallant, Dr Ashford more tousled and lovable, Rosemary brighter and harder, Biddy squeakier and fluffier, and Harriet found herself agreeing with alacrity to help with the preparations for the fête.

Only Bobby and Caroline seemed a fraction less vivid.

6

Mrs Caroline Metcalfe (37)

'That was a lovely party,' said Harriet half an hour later, as she shook hands with her new friend, and she repeated the remark to Caroline as they strolled towards the green together.

'Yes, Cotty is a dear, and a tower of strength,' agreed Caroline warmly. 'I don't know what we should do without her. She's had the most interesting life. An amateur jockey, believe it or not – I suppose they're allowed to be bigger – and helped to discover a lost city in South America. Got lost in a swamp and goodness knows what. She's had all sorts of adventures; I can imagine her quelling the crocodiles with one of her looks! I believe she was in all the papers and quite famous for a bit, but she laughs it all off now; quite content to settle down to the modest life! She knows everybody's troubles round here and is a great success with the young. Nothing to you of course; you're a professional. I don't understand them one bit. People think that being a mother helps. Affection, certainly.' She stopped. 'Understanding?' She shook her head.

They had reached the gate of the old vicarage, only a few minutes walk from her own. It was long and white, with a peaceful old garden.

Caroline's house had a warm and casual atmosphere that seemed to make the offer of pot-luck supper with the children inevitable.

Harriet stepped onto a polished oak floor. 'What a lovely place!'

'I'm very lucky. Everybody was so kind when I came to live here after my husband died.'

'I should imagine Bassington would be good like that.'

'Yes it was. They all got together and lugged me to the surface,

35

where I drifted about like a jellyfish. No guts, as Cotty would say, and she'd be dead right! With young children and no money I ought to have got a job, done something,' the large brown eyes looked at her, aghast, 'but I couldn't think what to do. Oh dear, it's rather untidy I'm afraid.'

The first thing Harriet saw in Caroline's pleasant green sittingroom was Andrew. He lay sprawling on the hearthrug gnawing a pencil and surrounded by *Hamlet* in book form, digest form, and note form.

The second thing was a large, indeterminate-looking dog with ragged hair and an unmistakable air of having been rescued. It took up the whole of the shabby sofa, greying jowls resting on one arm and balding tail, lazily thumping, hanging over the other.

Caroline spoke sharply to this dog, which opened one eye in pained surprise. Harriet guessed that any ruse to lift Andrew to his feet without actually asking him to was doomed to failure, and hastily selected a seat for herself. He nodded to her in a friendly fashion.

'What a lovely cushion!' Harriet picked it up. 'Too good to sit on!'

'*She* made it,' said Andrew, rolling over onto his back, 'but it doesn't usually get such reverent treatment.'

'It ought to be framed.' Harriet studied the beautifully designed Arcadian scene. Wild boar, hare, fox and eagle gambolled heraldically in an English paradise. She looked round the room and echoed James Ashford's words; 'You're a real artist!'

A great vase at one end of the room was filled with such an inspired arrangement that Harriet half expected it to include a bird's nest full of eggs, or a few butterflies.

'I'm fated to enjoy doing things which aren't the slightest use. Look at that!' Caroline indicated a basket of mending which overflowed onto the floor beside her chair.

'Ya. I bet you've forgotten about supper tonight.'

'Not at all. It's in the oven Andrew. As it always is,' Caroline could not help adding. 'But I did think you'd do all right at Cotty's.'

'Ya,' said Andrew again, causing his mother's expression to set slightly. 'Good old Cotty. Big thick wedges with the crusts on. Not like Fiona with her t-tiny silver dishes of almonds. How could I get anything though,' he went on aggrievedly, 'when I was supposed to be d-doing the drinks? John Clancy could have helped. He just stood there, draggy old stick, never said a word. He might have lugged a few b-bottles round. It's all the bits. They all want ice, or lemon, or peel, or olives. It's bloody difficult.'

'Don't swear, you're too young.'

There was much that was young in this house. An Enid Blyton girl's school book lay spreadeagled on the floor, and distributed about the room were a half-finished Disney jigsaw, records, comics, lego, dinky cars, and four very small teddy bears sitting round a pile of birdseed on a Marmite jar.

'How many children do you have?'

'Only two, but they seem rather much in evidence! My other boy is thirteen.'

Harriet tried to mask her surprise; she had imagined a younger child.

But Caroline too was observant. 'In some ways,' she explained carefully, 'Thomas is rather young for his age.'

Andrew stretched out a long arm and looked at the title of the book. 'He's not the sort of kid who minds which sex he is either.'

'Andrew!'

'Girl's stuff,' said Andrew, unabashed.

Harriet knew by now that this must be her Thomas. 'I'm so glad to meet his family. He's been *most* helpful and kind.'

Caroline's vulnerable face lit up with a touching radiance. 'Oh, has he really been useful? I'm so glad! How splendid! Andrew, go and fetch him. Say we've got a friend of his here!'

But before Andrew could either obey or disobey his mother there was a sudden clatter on the stairs and a rush of panic feet along the passage outside, ending abruptly in silence. Caroline started up anxiously as the door opened slowly and dramatically to reveal Thomas Metcalfe, standing as stock still as he had when Harriet had first met him. This time his eyes were tight shut and he held one hand out stiffly in front of him, palm down, with all the fingers extended. The round face was very red.

'It's all right,' said Andrew quickly. He scrambled to his feet. 'You've hardly broken the skin. It's all right,' he repeated.

'It's bleeding!' whispered Thomas.

'Oh, honestly!' snapped Caroline, reacting to the unnecessary fright, 'I thought something terrible had happened.'

Lips trembling, Thomas turned his face away.

Andrew struck an attitude. 'Unwillingly I go,' he declaimed, 'For sticking plaster bound. Tho' 'tis but small and humble start

37

to medical career!' He put his hand on his brother's shoulder and turned him gently round. 'To horse!' he cried rousingly. 'To bathroom, yea, where all the unguents are, for friend and foe alike, whose fingers warrant It!'

Harriet watched them go, with amusement. 'What a kind elder brother!' she said. 'You must be proud of him.'

Caroline's head swung round, her brown eyes wide and searching. 'Oh, do you think so? Do you really think so?' She flushed slightly, and then laughed. 'His accent! Why must they say yew when everyone else is saying yoo?'

'I can't imagine,' replied Harriet truthfully. It was lovely being able to talk like this, instead of always having to be the expert. 'It grates, I know, if you happen to be their mother. But I don't think it matters really.'

'Perhaps. As long as nobody thinks it does,' said Caroline. She bent forward and poked the fire. 'Even his Grammar school's going comprehensive,' she added lightly.

Some train of thought drew Harriet's eyes to the pictures on the panelled walls. Two single figures in sombre black and grey with ruffs faced each other contentedly across a Queen Anne desk; husband and wife of long ago. A large rural scene hung above the fireplace. A groom stood at the head of a horse in an assured and peaceful world of parkland, with a spotted dog at his feet and in the distance, a pillared house.

The door opened and Andrew came in.

'Thank you, darling.'

'He's washing his face. Is there anything to eat yet?'

'Nearly. Harriet, did you speak to the Clancys?'

'Not very much. I couldn't think what to say.'

'Oh, I do understand, he's so silencing. That poor little wife looks terrified out of her wits sometimes. If she ever had any.'

'Maureen's not so thick,' said Andrew stoutly. *He's* some sort of B-Bluebeard. Nobody's been inside Botswana. He hasn't any friends.'

'He has. He's got four,' offered Thomas, who had now joined them, 'Marjorie, Oliver, Mary and Patrick.'

They all stared.

'*Who*?'

'I've just told you,' said Thomas patiently.

'But we don't know who they are!'

'I know you don't, no more'n I do. But they must be friends of his because he's dedicated his book to them.'

'*Thomas!*'

'Well, the window was open, so I just stepped in and had a look at it.'

Caroline's curiosity got the better of her. 'Anyway, now you've done it, but don't do it again, what's this famous book called?'

Thomas wrinkled his brow. 'Well, I couldn't quite read it all. It was difficult words. I could of if I'd had longer. It was a study about a person or something – a person *something*, and there was another bit underneath which I couldn't say but I could probably write it, but then I heard the front door so I went.'

'I should hope so too,' said Caroline feebly, but she and Thomas both knew she had lost this particular chance to be the compleat mother.

'They've got horrible pictures, the Clancys have,' he added brightly, receiving a 'What like?' from all three. 'Oh, naked ladies and black people and clergymen, with their mouths open and that. Teeth. But all funny. Not looking like what they really do at all.'

Silently, they all tried to imagine the Clancys' pictures, and then Harriet asked, 'Is Botswana very dark and forbidding?'

'Only the garden,' said Caroline. 'Botswana itself is ultra modern. In fact it hardly looks like a bungalow at all.'

'All the more sinister, I think,' put in Andrew. 'A horrible person with horrible pictures in a horrible house.'

Harriet laughed. 'He'll probably just turn out to be paralytically shy, like most of these peculiar men!'

'Nice people,' said Caroline, 'always think horrible people are probably paralytically shy!'

'I don't,' replied Harriet seriously, 'I know very well that there are a good many really horrible people about.'

*   *

Caroline's kitchen was warm and homely. The candles on the old pine table glowed on oranges and apples.

'It all looks like the sort of home Peter Pan never had,' said Harriet.

Caroline's expressive face again showed her pleasure. 'What a lovely compliment! But I'm afraid you only thought of Peter Pan because you can hear Tinkerbell!'

'So I can!' Harriet had in fact been hearing the high-pitched jangling for some time, from various directions, and now through the open door a black Persian kitten stalked in, with a bell attached to its collar.

Caroline was dishing up. 'Meet Pusskin,' she said, 'Thomas's friend. We put the bell on because of the birds.'

'You did, you mean. Pusskin wouldn't hurt them,' said Thomas mechanically. It was evidently a well-worn subject.

Thomas, clumsy and concentrated, slowly drew a ball of wool across the floor, with a string. Pusskin, a tiny marvel of muscular co-ordination, pounced and curvetted. Harriet watched and smiled.

'Come and sit down, Thomas,' said Caroline, removing the lid from a steaming bowl and adding anxiously, 'I do hope it's all right!'

So did Harriet. For some reason the atmosphere in the old room, which should have been so fragrant, was not entirely so. She looked doubtfully at the dog, which had followed them in, but Caroline knew better.

'Andrew. What have you got in those bottles?'

No answer. Amongst the home-made wine bottles on the wide window-ledge there were others.

'Andrew!'

'Oh, ya. Sorry, I was thinking of something else. The one with the rat in has g-gone off a bit. I-I didn't think you'd notice ... well, I was trying to economise.'

'Take it out this minute and bury it, as far away from the house as you can!'

'But ...'

'This minute! What can Miss Charles think!'

'How can you expect to be proud of your distinguished son when you discourage him so cruelly?'

'Early struggles are good for the soul.'

'All successful men say "If it hadn't been for my m-mother's unfailing help and understanding I never would have reached the position I hold today.' "

'Well, fail then,' said Caroline heartlessly, 'But take it away before we're all sick.'

'*I* don't feel sick,' said Thomas loyally.

'Andrew!'

Grumbling to the last Andrew finally took himself and rat outside and the others picked up their knives and forks. Caroline watched him go with a mixture of expressions. 'I could curse James Ashford for giving him a microscope,' she said, only half joking. 'Andrew gets paler and thinner every minute, stooping about inhaling poisonous chemicals when he should be in the fresh air. Fiona begs us to use her tennis court. It's only a few *yards*, but he won't, or cricket, or any of the things that other boys do. He doesn't ride, not that we could afford it, and he won't go to parties, not that there are any. He doesn't play football, he doesn't swim, and he doesn't walk a step more than he has to.' Caroline gave a despairing sigh. 'Now Thomas is always out. I never know where he is.'

Pusskin purred on his knee while Thomas ate stolidly on, taking no notice of what was evidently a familiar complaint.

Harriet helped herself to delicious home-grown vegetables. She glanced at her hostess and murmured, 'On the other hand, at least one of your children has the courage of his own tastes and convictions. All too rare nowadays! And as for Andrew, he is charming, and perhaps something of a knight errant.'

She watched him coming up the path outside the window. 'A delightful characteristic, but sometimes dangerous in the young.'

7

Albert Goggins (51)

After supper Harriet walked back across the green to Rose Cottage, after nearly falling over the friendly Pusskin in the hall. The air was balmy, and the garden not quite in darkness.

She looked over the gate at Little Farthings, to where Rex kept watch at the window as usual, forepaws on the sill. He no longer barked at Harriet and she saw his body quiver as he wagged an invisible tail in greeting. Then she strolled contentedly down her future lawn. What a view she had; miles of it! She drew a deep breath of meadow-scented air. Down near the river came the hoot of an owl.

As Harriet stood there, admiring the peaceful scene, a solid object sailed through the air a few inches from her eyes, and shattered amongst her bushes.

Somebody was attacking her from the Hall. The Hall! Gingerly she poked about. Lying squalidly in the undergrowth was the remains of a bottle of Gordon's gin amongst, on further investigation, much broken glass from a good variety of whisky, brandy, vodka, sherry and port. Harriet collected it all up for the dustbin.

Well, whoever it was who was used to doing this sort of thing would now have to stop, there was no question about that. Apart from the danger to life and limb Rose Cottage was now a private residence and no longer to be considered a dumping ground. Armed with a torch Harriet hurried over to the little gate which divided the two gardens, determined to make this clear once and for all.

Silence. Harriet hesitated. On the other side was a cobbled courtyard, two sides of which were taken up with her wall and the next door shed, once a summer house, perhaps, since it was so pretty. It was covered in creepers and had a dusty window, behind which a candle flickered.

Harriet pulled the little gate open, against the tufty grass, and entered the courtyard. The old building had certainly seen better days. There was somebody inside; somebody who needed a sharp reprimand.

All the same, angry as she was, and determined as she was, and forewarned as she was, Harriet was startled when a soft voice spoke from the doorway: 'And what moight you think you're up to then, on other paple's property, eh?'

A thin man sprang out and fastened fingers like talons onto her shoulders. He bent a pallid face to hers and Harriet reeled back. 'Ah'm sick o' being disturbed, it's like bluddy railway station. Ah doan know who you bluddy well are or what the bluddy 'ell you think you're doing but joost you bluddy well kape out of here. Unnerstan'?' He shook her, as a terrier shakes a rat.

'Take your hands off me ...' began Harriet breathlessly. For an instant the man obeyed her but before she could escape she felt them again, palm down on the sides of her head, gripping it clammily about the ears, a thumb in each corner of her mouth.

Very slightly, warningly, he jerked the thumbs outwards. Disgusted, Harriet tasted gritty soil, and sweat, and felt the pain which could lie ahead. His hands were shaking.

'T'aint no use making no noise; no-one'll 'ear yer,' gasped her persecutor, increasing the pressure. 'Joost you kape off.'

Harriet now brought her knee up. It hardly touched him, but to her surprise the man staggered away against the wall of the shed and bent his head, open-mouthed, fighting for breath. Harriet, finding the torch still clutched in her hand, shone it full on her adversary. He shielded his eyes from the glare, a pathetic sight, emaciated, trembling, and hardly able to stand upright.

'You'd better get home,' she said witheringly, 'and sleep it off. If I catch you throwing anything whatever into my garden again I shall report you to your employers. If you molest me I shall call the police.'

'So you're a friend o' thiern,' muttered the man bitterly, 'I mighta known it.' He looked at her like a beaten dog and unsteadily made off. Harriet looked after him with pity and repulsion before she went to extinguish the candle which stood on a rickety table. The interior of the little shed was uncared-for. Garden tools were ranged haphazardly round the walls. There were deck chairs, petrol containers, an old chaise longue, a croquet set, a slatted table, lengths of rope and other assorted clutter, and whisky and gin bottles behind an archery target. Full ones, this time.

She blew out the candle and stood in the doorway, staring unseeingly at the dimly romantic view. Then she went and looked up at the Hall with its lighted windows and air of opulent security. Should she go and tell the Kilmarnocks?

As she hesitated she heard the clang of the old wrought iron gates. So the man was off the premises. A violent but pitiful sight. She guessed him to be the hapless gardener, Goggins, already under notice. She did not particularly want to start her new life by complaining to the neighbours. He was hardly a threat as far as they were concerned. They looked well able to cope with such a wreck.

Harriet went to bed late that night. She switched on the electric blanket that was a new luxury and sat by the window brushing her hair, a soothing and sleep-invoking ritual which her mother had begun, long ago, when the thick grey waves had been soft gold curls.

Not that she was thinking about her hair as she gazed out into the moonlit muddle that was her garden so far. She was busy planning a positive rival to Little Farthings. Swish, swish, swish, swish. How quiet it was in the country.

The rhythmic strokes continued, with their usual hypnotic effect. Absent-mindedly she tried to turn that scratch, scrape, scratch, scrape, into the sound of her own hair-brush.

Harriet held her brush suspended in the air while the sound continued. Somebody was sawing something up in her garden.

But it all looked as empty and peaceful as ever, in its long shadows. She leaned out of the window and listened carefully, shivering a little in her thin nightgown. Outside it was dark and mysterious. Inside the lamp was lit, the bed warm.

The sawing came from the shed next door.

Harriet sighed audibly with relief. Goggins was incapable of such firm, strong strokes. Had only just been able to stumble uncertainly out of the garden and would now, she was sure, be stertorously asleep in ditch or bed. She got into her own, so warm and welcoming, and drew the covers up to her chin.

Silence. Faintly, a door closed. The rightful owner of the Hall, no doubt. Bobby Kilmarnock now going to bed. Having done some sawing in his own shed.

Why not, anyway? Harriet's eyes slid to her bedside clock. Half-past twelve. Firmly she shut her eyes.

Late, for sawing.

8

The Copper Kettle Tea-Rooms

By the following morning the midnight activities next door were almost forgotten. Let the Kilmarnocks look after their own toolshed and all that went on therein. Rose Cottage, radiant in the autumn sunshine, filled Harriet's mind. Slowly, lovingly, totally absorbed, she set to work on the finishing touches.

And now, at noon, here was Harriet, alone in her sitting-room, dusty and triumphant, with all she owned, just as she wanted it.

A mixture of curiosity and celebration now took her off to the Copper Kettle for lunch.

It was quiet and refined. A vase stood in the centre of Harriet's small gate-legged table containing two ferns and three chrysanthemums, exactly similar to that on all the others.

She looked round at her fellow customers. Were these the week-enders that Harriet had heard Walter Rillington speak of, but which she had not yet met? The ones who mowed their lawns at eight o'clock on Sunday mornings, or the ones with the yapping dog, or the ghastly friends, or the pop music played at full volume, or the zig-zag curtains, or who took up all the room in the village shop trying to decide what they wanted, or who never darkened the doors of the village shop at all, but brought all their food with them? Whoever they were, these people in the Copper Kettle Tea-rooms looked innocuous enough.

The muted conversation was shared between four young men with rucksacks, who spoke spasmodically about the route for that afternoon, and an old couple who complained about a guest house that had come under new and evidently inferior management, the local bus service, lack of consideration shown by motorists nowadays and the exorbitant prices that were demanded for post-cards, especially when you considered the stamps. A glass counter displayed madeira, ginger and chocolate cakes on silver doilies, and a brass lady in a crinoline waited to be rung for service.

There was no sign of either Biddy or Ann Markham, and Harriet now propped her newspaper against the chrysanthemums and applied herself to the shepherd's pie and cabbage that was served to her by an adenoidal girl.

She was deep in a home-making article when an elderly, very nearly cultivated voice asked if she would share her table.

'Of course,' she replied absently, before she looked up from the page before her and noted other vacant tables.

So she had a companion who was going to talk, and not a very prepossessing looking one. However, a new life is a new life, and wasn't Harriet interested in all that Bassington had to offer? She smiled agreeably. The old man across the table did not return it, but sat back giving her a knowing look that somehow disconcerted her. A combination of shabbiness and boldness, a smoker's soup-strainer moustache and trembling, thick-nailed hands all added to her unease.

Rather distantly, Harriet now reached for her paper and turned the page, but the newcomer had no intention of allowing this sort of behaviour. He leaned forward confidentially, bringing with him a heady blend of beer, smoke and whisky, and announced in a sepulchral voice, 'My name's Dizzard.'

Harriet was mystified. 'Dizzard,' repeated the man impressively, watching her face with close attention, 'Or, if you'd prefer it another way, Dizzy for short.'

'How do you do?' responded Harriet inadequately. She should know the name of Dizzy at least, if not of Dizzard. Was, in fact, perilously near to gravely offending him. Dizzy? Nothing stirred. She hastened into speech.

'What a charming village this is!'

'Very pretty,' agreed the old man promptly, falling voraciously on a dry roll which lay in the middle of a blue paper napkin. He tucked that into his stained neck-band. 'Quite delightful in the sunshine. A period gem set on its ancient green in this, our sceptred isle.'

Skilfully, Dizzy speared a curl of butter from Harriet's dish, champing meanwhile with all the energy required when one tooth has to do the work of three. 'I think that about describes it,' he said modestly. 'How do I do, though, you are kind enough to enquire. Now, that's a question, that is,' he replied with a mouth so full that Harriet averted her eyes. He turned his head for a moment towards the waitress who hovered behind him. 'The usual, ducky, please.'

Gooseberry eyes swivelled back. 'I could do worse,' he continued. 'Could do worse, in spite of some that I could name. Some persons of machievellian pettiness and spite. Of seething unsatisfied spinsterhood and dark and violent passions churning beneath expensive shirts and suits from Savile Row. Filled with grievances harboured and nurtured like orchids in a bloody greenhouse.'

Harriet looked at her companion in some alarm, fearing that he might actually be unhinged. 'Yes, I could name them all right,' he repeated. 'But I won't. I'll name you instead. Let's see.'

Mr Dizzard pulled a long upper lip still further over the lonely teeth, and thick black eyebrows over pale and crafty eyes, and pretended to study her psychically.

'Harry?' he asked softly, as though calling up the spirits. He

opened the eyes very fully and then squeezed them tightly shut.
'Harry … Harry … Harriet! Got it?' He shot her a piercing look.

'Got it,' repeated Harriet faintly.

'Now. Wait for it.' Dizzy looked at the ceiling and Harriet looked at the yellowing moustache which invaded his nostrils. 'Charlie? Charlie … Charlie …Charles! *Harriet Charles!* Exactly so. No other name will do. Right?'

'Right,' agreed Harriet, astounded.

'That's just a little trick to show you how we all know each other's business in this village. Ev-er-y bit of business there is, we know it.' He wagged a purple finger at her and went on, sounding like a dreadful edition of her friend Thomas, 'But you ask them, they won't tell you. Got it? You ask Fiona Kilmarnock what she does in that shed down by your garden. Do you think she'll tell you who she meets in that little love-nest? Not a hope. All prim and proper and roast beef on Sundays. Talking of which, what's happened to that dratted girl, ruddy place is going to the dogs. Ah, that's better.'

Mr Dizzard bent his head over the plate that had just arrived and carried on without pause, in muffled voice. 'Come to that, ask that husband of hers what he gets up to in London. In that swagger flat of his with no expense spared? All good works and gumdrops is what you'll get out of him.

'Now, if you asked me I could tell you differently. Very differently. Not that I will, not at present, but I'm just saying that I could if I'd a mind to. And that goes for the rest of bloody Bassington. Mind you, I don't know it all,' he shook his head modestly, 'I admit it. I'm not infallible. I don't know who Thomas's father happened to be; some escaped lunatic I imagine but I don't know. I don't know what Clancy's on the run from. I'm not pretending I couldn't give you a damn good guess, but I don't *know*. That is, not to be certain. Now *his* wife's no better than she should be, and that's putting it mildly. Can't get enough of it.'

There was a pause. 'That's rich,' he chuckled suddenly. 'Married to Clancy. What a misfortune! Even babes and sucklings can do better than that!'

Mr Dizzard guffawed loudly at this point, causing Harriet to recoil, and the woman from the unpleasing guest house to lay down her fork and look round. He lowered his voice.

'Nasty piece of work,' he confided. 'But don't tell them I said

47

so. Doesn't do in a country place like this to wash your dirty linen in public. Got to keep a good face on things. Got to be a good wife if you're dependent on hubby. And vicky verser. Got to be the perfect gent if your past history leaves a little something to be desired. Or likewise, perfect lady. Got to be a lovable old buffer if you're ... well, let's call it unconventional,' he suggested. 'Let's be charitable. I mean to say, in a village like this people talk. Let's just say the man does his best for his patients and leave it at that. None of our business what he makes on the side.'

He raised his eyebrows very high but did not wait for an answer. Harriet, who had opened her mouth several times, now settled down, half mesmerised, to listen.

'Very well then, he's unconventional, for want of a better word. Or a worse one. And unconventional brings us unerringly ...' He wiped his mouth with the back of his hand and started on the prunes and custard, '... to Rillington.

'Queer cove, that,' he observed. 'Dangerous when roused. Good God I've roused him myself and I keep my distance now. Like a madman, he is, interfering in a purely domestic matter, a private marital dispute. But then of course, to be absolutely frank with you, he is a madman. Lots of these soldiers go round the bend when they retire, you know. Trained to kill and not much up top. I mean to say, look at the house! The place is stiff with knives and guns and I wouldn't like to guess what he's got hidden away. Cat o' nine tails most likely, behind the lav.'

He gave Harriet a ponderous wink, and if he had been within arm's length would undoubtedly have dug her in the ribs. 'But that,' he added, 'is not suitable for a lady!'

His face darkened still further with suppressed amusement, and Harriet glanced round nervously. 'Of course there are some things,' continued Mr Dizzard with the innocent air of one who reaches a fair conclusion in the face of difficult odds, 'that are suitable for ladies. *Other ladies*, for instance!'

He leaned towards Harriet, who shrank back in her chair. 'Other ladies!' he whispered hoarsely, 'Not a hundred miles from here. If you call them ladies. There are other words.'

But this was too much for Mr Dizzard altogether, who gave himself up so wholeheartedly to enjoying the joke that all other conversation now stopped as the entire clientele of the Copper Kettle turned round in their wheelback chairs. Biddy's face looked anxiously out from the curtains behind the counter, to be replaced by a slim, dark young woman who slipped between them and walked towards Harriet's table with an air of intelligent authority. Mr Dizzard followed this progress as he hurriedly emptied his bowl.

'Oh yes,' he finished lamely, 'I could tell you what you'd never credit. I could tell you ... all sorts ...'

The young woman now stood over him, crisp and implacable in a flowered overall, while the rest of the customers goggled with interest and Dizzy gulped his coffee and glared up at her, bulging-eyed, with a curious expression of cringing rebellion. She made a slight movement, which set the old man to gathering up his paper carrier and shabby overcoat. 'All right, I'm going, I'm going!'

When he was safely in the doorway he turned, jaunty as ever, poked his head forward and laid a grubby finger along his nose. 'Doesn't do,' he said conspiratorially, 'to offend the management!'

Ann Markham stared after him. 'There is such a thing as slander, you know,' she said coolly, as the door banged. She turned to Harriet. 'I'm sorry if he embarrassed you.'

'Oh, that's quite all right. There are always people who ...'

'Yes. One can't always choose one's customers. Old Dizzy drifts in now and again and sometimes makes a nuisance of himself I'm afraid. I hope he didn't spoil your lunch.'

'No, no. It was delicious.'

Ann Markham stacked up the plates with a brisk, efficient clatter. 'You mustn't believe a word he says.'

Biddy's face was older on closer inspection. Much older. In fact, in the daylight the parting in the fluffy yellow hair showed dead white. But it was still a pretty, cheerful, sexy little face that smiled at Harriet across the table marked 'Cashier'.

They chatted in a friendly way until Harriet exclaimed, 'Oh, I must go! I promised to help at the Hall.'

'I have to work here today but we'll meet at the fête if not before. It's quite an occasion.'

'I'm looking forward to it.'

'Ooh it's lovely; it really is! There are a lot of artistic people round here who take ever such a lot of trouble. Collector's pieces I call them, I'm sorry you had that little spot of bother.' The last words came in a breathless rush, and Biddy's face took on a hunted look. 'He only − occasionally comes. Ann's better with him than ... but he's not usually quite as − bad as that.'

'I didn't mind at all,' Harriet said quickly. 'But I'm sorry if he is a nuisance for you.'

Biddy nodded sadly. 'He is, dear, he is. But we all have our cross to bear.'

9

Before the Fête

Bassington Hall, with its jumble of roofs and chimneys, which protected the gun-room, butler's pantry, pigeon loft, nursery wing, and other such charming anachronisms, dominated the village of Bassington Green. Subtly urban, it might have been transported, brick by peach-coloured brick, from Chiswick. Just right for the Kilmarnocks, decided Harriet.

Fiona Kilmarnock answered her knock, with a welcoming smile. She made a delightful picture standing in the doorway, fresh, cool and clean as ever, in printed cotton, her dog beside her.

'Harriet! How lovely to see you. I can't believe you've actually come!' she cried absurdly, extending two delicate hands with perfectly manicured silvery nails, reputed to be unbelievably good at gardening. 'Down, Krysta! Don't take the faintest notice of her!' The Alsation dog instantly dropped to the ground. 'I'm so grateful to you for coming to my rescue when you must be absolutely up to your eyes. We're all so delighted you've got that gorgeous cottage.'

The beautiful eyes shone with their secret laughter. 'It's a godsend having you, Harriet. Today of all days. What with Bobby leaving at the crack of dawn and all these proofs come in, I shall simply have to opt out.'

As Fiona talked she shepherded Harriet into her long drawing-room, now in disarray under heaps of papers, shavings, ribbons, lists, balloons, raffia, paints, brushes, cardboard, and other aids to fête preparation, and crowded, like a Harvest Festival with home-made and home-grown produce. Harriet gasped at the abundance and quality of these.

'You haven't seen half of it,' called Caroline from across the room. 'We haven't got it all yet!'

'Jams and cakes and biscuits,' said Rosemary.

'Fudge,' said Maureen.

Cotty waved cheerily from a Chippendale table in the corner, where she was working out the treasure hunt. 'I'll show Harriet what to do, Fiona,' she called. 'You go out in the garden and get on with those proofs.'

'Cotty my sweet! Can you really manage without me? I've simply got to catch the first post with these tomorrow. Being poetry, they have to be read so terribly carefully. The Americans always send them in a wild rush.'

'Child's play, my dear girl. You've got us all so beautifully organised already.'

And indeed, the place was a hive of ordered activity. Outside on the terrace Colonel Rillington stood on a stepladder hammering wooden frameworks for the stalls. Inside Maureen Clancy received directions from the masterful Rosemary. She was given the bran tub presents to wrap, and told to be careful of the bran.

Harriet labelled and priced – as highly as she dared, as a reward for loving workmanship, and keeping a stealthy eye open for what she longed to acquire for herself. That patchwork cushion and that gros-point fieldmouse, for instance. She must be there on time.

'Fiona is wonderful. Catch *me* letting people loose with bran tubs on a carpet like this one!'

'What shall I do with this sort of lady? Is it a doll, do you think? Or does she do something?'

'Bung it in the bran tub. That's what bran tubs are for.'

'Well, she may not be beautiful, but she's certainly a bargain at 5p. Shut up, Krysta, you're not helping.'

Fiona, who had been conferring with Walter Rillington outside, put her head in at the french window for one last assurance.

'Are you *really* sure you're quite happy? Don't hesitate to interrupt me. It's a purely routine job. Ask me anything you like. Promise, won't you?'

At renewed assurances from her friends, Fiona crossed the lawn to a hammock slung between two apple trees and settled herself gracefully amongst the cushions with her papers.

'She's such a wonderful organiser.'

'She certainly is, but trust Fiona to organise herself right out of it,' grumbled Rosemary Ashford. 'Trust Fiona to get herself into a hammock like *that*, instead of a netted porpoise like an ordinary human being. Trust Fiona to be in the sun and us in the shade!'

But this more or less affectionate remark was treated with the indignation it deserved. Wasn't Fiona a poet? The wonderfulness remained intact.

Gradually the fête took shape. The stalls were set up and Colonel Rillington, after a word with Fiona, left. The ladies chatted amiably, each at her appointed task.

'Caroline, you've over-reached yourself this year!'

'Look at this; isn't it sweet?'

'I wish we could just buy them all ourselves right now, and call the whole thing off.'

'What is it in aid of?'

'Oh, village things. Keeping up the green. The children's playground and sports. You know. The Old People's Outing. That's tomorrow, by the way.'

'I'm fed up to the teeth,' lamented Cotty. 'Not coming to that. I enjoy the oldies.'

'Not *coming*?'

'No, I told you, Rosemary. I'm going to the Spurs' weekend conference tonight.'

Rosemary gaped. 'Oh Lord, I'd forgotten.'

'I'm sorry to miss the old dears, really I am,' Cotty told Harriet. 'But this great chum of mine is giving the first lecture tomorrow morning and I promised him I'd go. It's a question of one or the other and I finally gave in. Then there's another do tonight they're relying on me for. I'll have to go.'

'Of course, it's quite all right,' Rosemary said at once. 'We can manage perfectly well.'

'Kind Caroline's taking me to the station.'

'What's happened to Mabel?'

'Need you ask!'

'It's the blind leading the blind,' warned Caroline. 'My car just totters from one MOT to the next. Better than my bike though; chain's gone again.'

'Oh, money, money, money! Why can't we divide the proceeds of this amongst ourselves? After all, we deserve it.'

'If only we could.'

The conversation turned to the possibilities of making money, cutting down, or doing without altogether.

Maureen Clancy, Harriet noticed, sat a little apart from the others. Quiet and very slow, she got on with the simplest jobs. Every now and again one or other of them visited the hammock, to ask for advice or further instructions. Across the still air Fiona's clear, unquestioned decisions came wafting back. Of course the only place for the white elephants was behind the tennis court, the children's games just here, the teas there. ...

In between, calm and omnipotent, Fiona worked on. The pile of papers on her right increased and those on her left slowly sank. The weather was set fair.

'She'll never keep awake. Nobody could work for long on a day like this. In a hammock, for goodness sake. Not even a superwoman like her.'

'It's sultry, isn't it. Like summer. Not a breath of wind.'

'She's half asleep already.'

'Oh, is she? I'd better catch her before she goes right off then. I've forgotten where she said she wanted the Old Gypsy Fortune Teller's tent; it was either by the rockery or the shrubbery and as it's me in that old wigwam thing of Thomas's I ought to know.'

Caroline ran lightly across the grass to the hammock. How could such a woman have produced a son like Thomas, wondered Harriet, as she watched the lithe, athletic figure speeding away from her over the velvet lawn.

'She's wide awake, working hard, and simultaneously remembering about my fetching the netball posts for the children's obstacle!' Caroline reported on her return. 'What a marvel!'

Cotty sighed. 'Nerves of steel, what I wouldn't give for her ability to switch off.'

'Oh yes!' breathed Caroline with feeling. 'And all those marvellous dinner parties; most people think she has a cook. After all, a house like that does look as if it's got more than three chars doesn't it! Preparing a cordon bleu meal for a dozen distinguished strangers means nothing to her. A mere half-hour out of her life. You're a bit like that too of course, Rosemary.'

'You could do it, Caroline. You're actually a very capable person.'

'Thank you, Rosemary, but no. The very words "dozen distinguished strangers" felt like toads falling from my lips.'

'Ugh!'

'They did, exactly like the fairy story! And then this poetry which she must write in one second flat and never suffer from writer's block with or anything like that,' persisted Caroline. 'Analysed and sought after all over the place. If she has a spare minute she gives an interview which has them swooning over their TV sets. I need hardly add that she's bound to be the world's most successful mother when she is one.'

'Perhaps she won't be,' suggested Harriet. 'Perhaps they'll all be completely out of hand.'

Rosemary Ashford tapped her on the shoulder. 'She will be and they won't be but cheer up. We're all in the same boat. Fiona's in a class of her own, like the Queen.'

'Or God,' suggested Maureen devoutly.

'She has this incredible ability to relax. She told me that she can drop off for five minutes at any time during a busy day and awake refreshed. It's a gift, like Napoleon. I'll just pop out and show her this final lay-out of mine for the treasure-hunt and take her a cup of that tea since we've just made it. It's going to be a damned good show, though I says it myself.'

'Listen,' said Caroline. Echoing smiles appeared on their faces as Cotty's loud and infectious laughter reverberated across the lawn. 'It must be exacting, correcting proofs for poetry, mustn't it, but she's got time to be funny, too!'

Cotty heard the last words as she walked in with a grin. 'Nobody can tell a story like Fiona,' she said.

The beautiful drawing-room gradually returned to view as the items for sale were identified, sorted, packaged, labelled, priced, collected and removed. A background of delicate green and gold set off the gleaming furniture, the needlework chairs and even the needlework sofa, which the miraculous Fiona had found the time to do, pictures of ancestors and their possessions, Bobby's grandfather's sword, flowers, silver, glass, and a wallful of leather-covered books, each containing, Harriet felt sure, bookplate with Coat of Arms, and Author's Signature. And through the tall windows the garden, and beyond that the view.

'How I love this room,' Caroline was stroking Krysta's noble head. 'It's so ... tranquil.'

'It's rather like your room.'

'Harriet! May God forgive you! How I wish that those kind words were true.' Caroline raised a flushed face, crowned with unruly purple and ginger and with a streak of gold paint on the chin. 'I'm totally untranquil.' She looked at her watch. 'What about your train, Cotty. Hadn't we better go?'

'God, yes, thanks for reminding me. Mustn't cut it fine when it's the only one. I must just finish this.'

'I'm all ready. I'll just go and say goodbye to Fiona.'

'Say goodbye from me too.'

'I won't be a sec.'

Caroline looked down on Fiona in the hammock, who lay in the sunlight with her usual grace. Long dark lashes lay on lightly freckled cheeks. Bright pink lipstick provided a dash of colour. Smooth brown arms. Smooth brown legs. Bees buzzed amongst the flowers beside her. Caroline picked up her empty tea-cup and brought it in and gave it to Rosemary. 'She's asleep,' she told her. 'I thought she would be. Looking just as languid and elegant and beautiful as ever!'

'Trust her not to have her mouth hanging open and her skirt ruckled up round her waist.' Rosemary was always sharper than the others. 'Look at that, even her lipstick doesn't come off!'

The three women cleared up after Caroline's battered station-wagon had borne Cotty away. The sun sank. The floor was swept, and overflowing waste paper baskets tipped by Harriet into dustbins. One paper, covered in capital letters, caught her eye as it fluttered down. She picked it out, glanced at it idly, and then put it in her pocket.

'There. Finished. As much as we can do today. We seem to have been at it for weeks.'

'It's the heat. Extraordinary for the time of year. I'll tell Fiona we're going.'

But Harriet did not need to go far to see that Fiona was still asleep. 'Had I better wake her, do you think? If the proofs were so important?'

Rosemary hesitated. 'No, I wouldn't bother her if her way of doing things is the occasional cat-nap. I'm off, got things to do at home. Maureen dear, could you very kindly wash up the cups in the kitchen? And bang the front door behind you?'

As the obedient Maureen left the room Rosemary seized Harriet by the arm. 'Come on!' she hissed through her teeth. 'Keep me company. I know you only live next door but a little toddle up the road will do you good after all that sitting about. She and I live in the same direction; Botswana's about half a mile further on along our road, and it looks so pointed, sloping off on my own. But she's such a bore, poor girl. Isn't it funny how one always speaks to her as if she's one's grandmother's parlourmaid.'

10

Mrs Rosemary Ashford, SRN (64)

'... don't stand any nonsense, I always say.'

The sky was clouding over as the two women started off up the road towards Red House which stood four-square on the outskirts of the village. The diminutive Rosemary Ashford had a fast, decisive walk and a brightly continuous flow of chat. Astonishing lungs, thought Harriet, as she struggled to keep up with her. Also astonishingly pretty when you looked at her, like a Dresden shepherdess.

'... so kind of you, Harriet, but now I wonder if we should have left her. Maureen, I mean.'

'What could she do wrong?'

'Oh I don't know, leave the door open or something. Muddle the merchandise. Poor little thing. Normally I should say that girl wanted marrying but I can't, can I, in this case! Well, one can't always be right I suppose,' she said, in the breezy tones of one who always was. 'She is so slow, legs as well as head, and I've got some people coming for dinner and bridge. The local parson and his wife. He doesn't live here. We have to share him! That's how Caroline got the house.'

Harriet had involuntarily glanced at her watch. 'Oh, it's all organised,' said the indomitable Rosemary. 'The whole thing came out of the freezer this morning and James will have laid the table for me.'

She proceeded to give Harriet a great deal of expert advice about freezers. Harriet planned her garden. Perhaps Thomas would help her. And Ted Baxter of course. Kind Colonel

Rillington might suggest rather too martial a lay-out.

But Rosemary had become personal again. '... doesn't like missing his golf but honestly Harriet you'd never believe the number of patients who get better all by themselves if they're left for an hour or two. I remember once when James had gone off with an accident victim in the ambulance and Caroline Metcalfe rang up in such a tizzy. Andrew had lost about half his sight, just like that! Detached retina I thought or some such thing. Of course you get these dramatic cases referred to a big London hospital, I sometimes think that as a training for ordinary life they give you the wrong ideas. Anyway, I left a message with the girl for James and dashed round myself. We laid Andrew out on the sofa and told him not to move an inch. That peculiar little Thomas was about six then I suppose and just sat there like a log as usual amidst all the agitation – I mean most six year olds are never still for a minute are they! – staring at his brother, you know, like he does, and then he says, "His head's not hurting this time." '

'Whatever did he mean?'

'Exactly what he said, Harriet, and he was perfectly right! Andrew suffered from migraine, you see, and this time he had the vision disturbance and not the headache; growing out of it I suppose really, like they do. Before James arrived Andrew was as lively as a cricket with eyes like a hawk! He never had another migraine after that, one thing less for his mother to worry about. Poor girl, she does make heavy weather of those children of hers. "Caroline," I tell her, "Relax. Children go through umpteen stages and it doesn't amount to a row of beans in nine cases out of ten." Of course I'm lucky in my boys – tough as nuts and none of those tiresome problems. Loved school, good at games, good companions, good wives and good jobs. Of course they always had loads of friends. If you don't go away to school this can be rather a one-eyed place for a young person and Caroline could never afford anything like that. Hugo Metcalfe was the most delightful man, generous to a fault and great fun to be with but not what you'd call a saver, not the careful type. I think Andrew feels the responsibility now he's gone especially as Thomas is so, well you know how Thomas is. Of course he's got an accent but what can you expect in a little local school, miles from anywhere?' demanded Rosemary crisply. 'And good heavens, as I tell her, accents are nothing nowadays. Everybody seems to have them even the wireless. Not that I don't think they're hideous, mind, and I'm only too thankful that my young speak the Queen's English, but it's no use *worrying* about them!'

Harriet sighed. 'I know. The trouble is, with one's own children, it's much more difficult to see the wood for the trees.'

Rosemary looked vague. 'Yes,' she said. 'Do you play bridge? It's atrocious round here. Not that I can talk. My poor James is getting very absent-minded though he used to be quite a reliable player. Honestly though, Harriet, I sometimes wonder how that man survives when I'm away! When I got back from our latest grandchild I found all the stuff I'd prepared for him still in the fridge, covered in mould. I sometimes wonder if he can actually *see*. Mercifully people do invite him out.'

Rosemary Ashford smiled, and sighed, and touched her neat hair with a small, be-ringed hand. 'He was always just the same. Such a good-looking young doctor. I remember the first time I met him, five minutes late as usual, hurrying along the corridor pulling on his white coat. I was his cover-up girl. There's always one for a man like James, have you noticed? "Excuse me," I'd say, "Wouldn't that be mcg, not mg surely? I can't quite read your writing!" "Oh, good grief, Rosie," he'd say, tearing his hair (he does it still, can't think how he's got any left), "saved by the bell again! I don't know what I'd do without you." "I'll have to marry you, I suppose," I said, "to keep you out of trouble." "Do you know, Rosemary," he said, "I think you'd better had."

'And really, Harriet, I don't know where he'd be if he hadn't. Killed off half the county, I tell him, his mind's always half on something else. But seriously, country life suits him. He does a bit of shooting with the colonel, potters about, gossips with the patients, plays his awful Bridge, does a little bird-watching. Always got plenty of time. Very good with the village people, James is, they know they can trust him. It's a good thing he's like he is in a place like this.'

Harriet regarded Rosemary Ashford's firm little profile, her shapely legs and her sensible shoes, her discreetly dashing tweeds, and imagined how she must have been in her nurse's uniform.

'And you?' she asked. 'Has country life suited you?'

Rosemary Ashford turned her large china blue eyes on Harriet in some surprise. She paused to consider the question. 'Me? Oh yes. Funny you asking that because I've never really thought about it. But yes, of course it does. If it suits James it suits me.'

11

Up on the Melchester Road

Maureen Clancy was not sorry to find herself alone in Bassington Hall. Keeping an eye on the hammock in the garden she put her bag by the front door, ready for a quick get-away.

It was not until thirty minutes later that she set off for Botswana, still half-bemused. Harriet, walking back from the Ashfords' house, was just entering her own gate. She gave the girl a friendly smile and was mildly disappointed to encounter the furtive confusion of one of her pupils caught out in a misdemeanour.

Andrew, cycling back along the Melchester Road, with his long hair in his eyes and a heavy load of books wobbling precariously on the carrier, nearly collided with Maureen in the dusk.

'Oops sorry! Brakes need adjusting. They always need adjusting. T-trouble is, I don't know how to adjust them.'

Maureen Clancy's pale eyes gazed up into his face with a limpid blankness. So might Joan of Arc have looked when she heard the heavenly voices, thought Andrew romantically, but she seemed to take longer than most people to react to what was said to her on this earth. Used to his brother Thomas, Andrew waited patiently.

'You're late from school, aren't you?' she said at last.

'Ya. Stayed on in the bio lab. We're allowed to in the Sixth. I can get on better alone. I-I think I've got the answer to ...'

Andrew checked himself as he caught the total lack of interest on the girl's face. Maureen was evidently no biologist. 'Ooh, you are clever,' she said vaguely.

Lacking a boon companion, this would have to do. Until such time as Sir Andrew Metcalfe, OM, FRCP should be bombarded with compliments Andrew was prepared to accept this one gratefully. Maureen looked pathetic and the road was a lonely one. Chivalrously, he turned his bicycle round. 'I'll walk back with you.'

'Oh do, Andy! It's ever so spooky out here at this time of day.

It's all lonely, and I don't like the trees. I wish we lived in the village like you lot. I get fancies.'

'Poor old Maureen.' I suppose she must be at least twenty, thought Andrew, but I feel older than she is. 'You're not very far away really, you know. The road curves round. We're only a few fields away; I could probably hear you if you screamed.'

'Don't say those things, Andy. They scare me.'

'Don't worry, you just scream, I'll come,' promised Andrew lightly. 'If strictly necessary. I'm not a very courageous bloke.'

Maureen slipped her arm through his. 'You're a great comfort to me,' she said confidingly. 'You really are.'

Andrew looked down at her thin, peaky little face and for a moment did feel quite a courageous bloke. 'I don't think it's really very dangerous round here,' he smiled.

'You don't know,' muttered Maureen darkly. 'You don't know the half of it. Nobody does.'

To his surprise her voice shook. She gripped him tighter and they walked on in silence, hip to hip. Rather painfully, Andrew's young body responded.

The Clancys' bungalow, whose concrete, steel and stained glass made an unexpected impact with the gentle countryside, was ablaze with light. A large black Daimler stood outside.

Boy and girl stopped in the darkness of the hedge. 'You've got visitors.'

'Oh, her.'

Maureen's childish voice was dismissive. Then it changed its tone. 'That's not visitors,' she said dreamily. 'That's only old Beakyface.' She turned towards him and suddenly giggled.

It was more than hips. It was warm expertise. It was nailbitten hands which had turned soft and knowing, burrowing under his jacket, against his back. The cold red fingers crept beneath his shirt like frogs. It was breasts, surprisingly full on so small a frame, lolling unconfined and not very clean.

Hopelessly entangled with his bicycle, Andrew gave in as she pressed her lips to his. Hell, he thought, shamefaced, bloody hell, not what I meant. Not ever.

'Naughty boy!' said Maureen throatily. She pulled away and looked over her shoulder. It was she that looked the naughty one; the rather drab little creature was transformed. Her eyes flashed as Botswana's porch lantern caught them, laughing, insolent, triumphant, anything but frightened now.

Jangled, red-eyed, ridiculous, unsatisfied, Andrew watched her from the shadows as she walked up the brightly lit concrete path.

At the door Maureen paused, put her hands to her hot cheeks, composed her expression, attempted to smooth the curly hair. Her eyes, she knew, were bright and bold. On to everything he was, didn't miss a trick, jealous as a kid. Well, chances were he might be a while yet. She'd have time for a cool sponge. She turned, confident that Andrew had not moved, as indeed he had not. She put her fingers to her lips. 'See ya,' she murmured.

'See ya,' he replied.

*   *

Biddy turned the notice on the door round to CLOSED.

'I've got an hour's more work to do,' said Ann, who was sitting at the table in the little back room.

'Right-ho, dear. I'll have supper ready.'

And I'll have a bath too, and a glass of sherry, and put my feet up, thought Biddy, as she let herself out of the Copper Kettle and started on the walk home. She was proud of her small feet and ankles but they gave her trouble on busy days in weather like this. They puffed up over the smart shoes she insisted on wearing. They were too delicate to support without rebelling the extra stone or two, or three, she had put on over the years.

Through the village, up the hill, and along the Melchester Road she toiled. A depressing, lonely stretch of nothing, Biddy thought, as she covered this last half-mile. Why did one always feel obliged to hurry through it? The blue sky had clouded over. She never liked this time of day, when she was feeling tired and dishevelled. Grey and gloomy she called it, just before the twilight began. She wished she and Ann could have lived in the village proper, instead of in the back of beyond.

Of course Pine View was a dear little cottage, once you reached it, real olde-worlde, but pines were about all you *could* see, and she would have appreciated some neighbours. Not another house in sight, except for that eye-sore, Botswana, that was a blot on the landscape, and she could have done without the Clancys, thank you very much. Grey and gloomy just about described him too, and Maureen wasn't exactly a barrel of fun.

Dutifully, Biddy said 'cheese' to herself, to pull her face up so that she wouldn't get bad lines. They'd taught them to do that when she first went into the chorus, but usually she didn't need to remember it. She was a happy mortal even if she did say it herself.

But today had been a shocker. Lord knows she was patient but there were limits. Here he was again, talk about bad pennies. She had seen him through the kitchen door at lunch-time, sitting with Harriet Charles. Seen him and kept well out of the way though the Lord himself only knew what he had been saying about her. There was nothing he wouldn't stop at. Now she'd have to set to work to undo all the harm Dizzy would have done with his lies and innuendoes. Yes, there was no doubt about it, she was down in the dumps today.

Funny to look at him now and remember that he hadn't been all that bad once, when he had been on the up and up. Hard to imagine, really. Of course he'd always been a good bit older than she was. Soured him, she supposed, that he'd never really made it, but then neither had she, and she was cheerful enough. She believed in enjoying life.

Biddy paused when she came to her gate. In the gloaming the cottage looked empty enough, innocent enough, but past experience warned her that Dizzy seldom let her off so lightly. Warily she turned the key and heard a distant, muffled yapping instead of the usual welcoming skedaddle across the hall. Stiff-armed, Biddy pushed open the door and then jumped back, teetering on her high heels. Just in time. Something flew past her nose and crashed into smithereens on the doormat.

Nothing kept a cunning old fool like Dizzy out of anywhere he wanted to get into. Up to every trick in the bag that one. Practically a common criminal. Biddy, her pink face flushed deeper with distress, bent to inspect the damage.

The remains of the booby-trap, a rose covered china bowl, lay just inside the door. It might have hit her on the head of course. But her precious bowl with the roses on, that was the really upsetting part. Memento of that last weekend in Brighton with Joe. Not that Dizzy would have minded; he never minded that sort of thing. Give him that. You might say it never entered his life much, that sort of thing. Not what you might call a real man. The little bowl had been so pretty. Her eyes filled with tears.

As she stooped on the threshold a hand appeared from round the corner and roughly shoved her from behind. Awkwardly Biddy fell forward onto the coconut mat. Aggrievedly she sat amongst the ruins, sucking a cut finger, eye-black running, glowering up into her husband's contorted face.

'Oh, ho ho ho ho! If only you could see yourself; I've never seen anything so funny in my life!' The old man danced before her, hugged himself with joy, coughed and cackled, staggered and twitched, stamped and guffawed. His rheumy eyes overflowed onto loose cheeks flouncing with laughter. His face was purple with merriment.

Biddy remained where she was, a tide of black rage rising up inside her until it seemed as if she must suffocate. The usually placid blue eyes glittered like ice in the powdery little face. Quietly, rhythmically, she sucked her finger, and watched him.

'Now, now, Bid,' said the old man at last, wiping his eyes on a filthy handkerchief and taking a step backward. He held up a blue-veined hand placatingly. Biddy looked up at it in deep distaste. 'Now then, Biddy! Watch it, girl!' His voice began to whine. Can't you take a joke?'

Biddy got slowly and with dignity to her feet. 'Get out!' she whispered. Then her voice rose. Tweaky Poo, shut in the kitchen, whimpered and scratched at the door, impotently barked. 'Get out and stay out, you disgusting old sod! *I've had enough*!'

Dizzy backed away, mottled with alarm. 'All right, lass. No need to make such a fuss; it's all in fun. I'm going. I'm going.'

He turned and shuffled off down the path, pursued by Biddy's shouts. When he considered that he was at a safe distance he stopped and gave a jaundiced glance over his shoulder. 'Stupid bitch,' he muttered. 'All these years, she never had a sense of humour.'

The light of a bicycle wavered as it breasted the rise in the road. It stopped outside the gate and with considerable agility Dizzy sprang back into the rose-bushes behind him. Silently he withdrew still further as the rider dismounted, paused for a moment, and then walked up the path.

Not that he had anything to be ashamed of. A man had the right by law to do what he bloody well liked with his own wife. A little joke never hurt anybody. On the other hand there was no point in courting trouble.

Anyway, he might as well relieve himself now he was here. Serve her right with her damned prissy garden.

Biddy shut the front door, and released the pekinese dog from the kitchen. She buried her face in his soft orange ruff and gave a deep shuddering sigh. She felt shaky and old.

She was startled when the doorbell rang. Andrew stood outside, round-eyed, looking very young. 'Oh ... are you? ... you look rather ... I-I mean, are you all right, Biddy? I-I thought I ... heard something.'

Biddy's plump little hand flew to her tear-stained face and disordered hair. 'Oh ... Andrew! How − how nice of you, dear. How kind. No, it's perfectly all right. Nothing really. Only a little bit of trouble with You-know-who. It's all over now. Come in, dear, do, and have a glass of sherry with me; it would be an act of kindness. If you don't mind it sweet?'

Andrew sat down on the edge of his chair and regarded her anxiously. Biddy smiled. 'I was just a little fluttered, but I'm quite all right now. Biddy and Dizzy; sounds silly doesn't it, and silly it was, I can tell you; whatever induced me to marry that man I can't imagine. Still, what's done's done I suppose, but I don't see why I should have to go on paying for it till Doomsday, do you, really? Just you learn a lesson from me to be careful who you marry, dear.'

'I will.'

Biddy nodded. 'Once you've married a wrong'un you're never done with it though you can divorce them till you're black in the face. I never tied the knot again, dear, though it wasn't for lack of asking. No more wedded bliss for me. Dizzy really turned me off, though we had some good times when he was in the money. But look at him now!'

'Still, don't you listen to me. You're young, you'll make something of your life. Marriage and all. It can be good, you see,' she insisted rather pathetically. 'It can be good. With the right partner.' She took a deep breath. 'There! Seeing you has made me feel much, much better and Ann'll be back soon.'

'Well, if you're sure you're all right. I-I'll be getting on home. All these A-levels. Having no father to make me do 'em I suppose I'd better do 'em,' explained Andrew eliptically, with his rare, and crookedly appealing, smile.

Biddy nodded wisely. 'Oh yes, dear, you do that. I never did what mine told me. A shame really isn't it, when you think. I'm sure you'll get them very well too, and be a credit to your mother. Ann and I were just saying the other night what a good doctor you'll make. See, you've cheered me up and that's what doctors are supposed to do, isn't it! We all agree in this village, you're just the type.'

Andrew swung himself up onto his bicycle and set off down the road into a cool evening breeze.

12

Departures of Cotty and Bobby

Cotty leaned out of her empty carriage and waved to Caroline as the Rampton Train drew out of Loxley. She could relax. There were none of those tiresome changes that usually dogged these cross-country journeys; the first stop was hers.

She slung her battered grip vigorously onto the luggage rack. It contained little more than a long cotton skirt and blouse for the evenings and a pair of plimsolls for folk dancing. The Spurs were an informal group and Cotty, as usual, had packed in a hurry. Anyway, she believed in travelling light. She took no hot water bottle, though the Spurs invariably met in spartan surroundings, and no book to read. Cotty was always warm, always had plenty to say, and always slept like a log.

She lay back, closed her eyes, and conscientiously relaxed; Yoga had been on the agenda last time. A slight change of personality was necessary to suit the company she would be joining in a few hours. Cotty prided herself on being all things to all men, of having a circle of friends that was wider and more varied than most. The variations required certain adjustments.

The Spurs were her friends. The Bassingtonians were her friends. But just how would the Spurs fare in Bassington Green? Pretty hopelessly, she guessed. Impossible to imagine the juxtaposition! Rillington, Fiona, Bobby, the Ashfords, even the easy-going Caroline. No, polite avoidance would have been the fate of the Spurs in Bassington, no doubt of that. Except possibly with the Clancys.

But now here was Cotty, preparing deftly to leap the gap. By dint of a subtle leftward swing politically and socially, a broader manner of speaking, a more direct approach to things generally, she was about to turn into a typical Spur. More than that, a super-Spur was more like it. Heroine to all of them, with their chequered histories, insolvency, eagerness, oddities, loneliness and foredoomed love-affairs, and friend of a chosen few. Yes, friend and confidante to the Spurs, but also friend and confidante to her respectable neighbours.

Cotty was a good trencherwoman. It was a long time since her small and hurried lunch, but she did not look forward to the meal ahead of her with any great enthusiasm. The gastronomic standard was not high at Spurs Conferences but then, to be fair, neither were the fees. Had she remembered to slip in that packet of biscuits and the circular leather case with the twin half-circular bottles inside? Cotty stood up on the seat and investigated. Her eyes brightened; she had.

Cotty lived, with gusto, in the present, and although all her friends knew that her leather case of whisky was of great sentimental value the truth was that by now Cotty herself had, strictly speaking, forgotten exactly who had given it to her. Was it the young John Grant, killed so tragically? Or Duncan Maynard, so touchingly devoted? Or Ivan the handsome? Sometimes she thought it was one and sometimes another. These days she could imagine it from any, when it was so long ago and life was so crowded. All she knew for certain was that it had been a gift of love. She poured out one tot into a silver-plated top, and then another tot, which she drank rather slower. A gift of love.

Spurs or swains, coronets or common herd, the dog-collared and the lame dogs, human beings all, with their frailties and their secrets, all had common factors, reflected Cotty, pulling off her mother's half-hoop of diamonds and rummaging in an untidy bag for a purse to put it in. The ring was too Bassingtonian and not sufficiently Spur-like. Even Fiona, when you came right down to it, was just as human as the rest of them.

*   *

Bobby Kilmarnock drove his Bristol into St James's at half-past nine and parked it in his usual place. There was no sign of life in the building. The other tenants were out for the evening or away for the weekend. Preoccupied, he let himself in and climbed one flight of thickly carpeted stairs, looking straight ahead of him.

Whereas Bassington Hall was charming and feminine, and full of carefully tended objects, valuable to any collector, Bobby's London flat was homely and masculine, and full of shabby objects, valuable to him alone. The view from the window was again beautiful, but impersonal this time. A huge leather armchair of great antiquity and comfort awaited him, the table beside it bearing decanter, a heavy glass engraved with a little device and the words *Who dares Wins*, an ash-tray, and dark-shaded lamp. A white bear skin, left over from nursery days, lay mangily in front of an elderly but powerful gas-fire. Relics, trophies, boyhood treasures, an oar emblazoned with signatures, a toothy photograph of 'The Rabbits', his father's citation, all the things that Fiona had indignantly banished when she had married him, all had come crowding happily back to roost in here, loved and cherished. The ravaged copies of Jules Verne, the thirty-two William books and the complete run of *Punch* from 1913 to 1930 waited patiently in St James's, ready for the child that Bobby and Fiona intended to have next year.

Usually these surroundings soothed and cheered Bobby. Much as he loved his country life he enjoyed these occasional lone sorties into the world of clubs and pied-à-terres like this one, and the company of lifelong, utterly predictable and trustworthy old friends, either of his or of his father. These last were sometimes, he had to admit, running slightly to seed, becoming so gallante and sprightly in Fiona's company and unfortunately boring her to death. He could see her point of view of course, but on his own he looked forward to seeing them. The very tedium was effortless and familiar in an enjoyable way.

But tonight Bobby's face had lost its usual cheerful expression. It was pale and tired. Half an eyebrow settled heavily down over one blue eye. Abstractedly he poured himself out three fingers of whisky and a splash of soda and sat down wearily in the old armchair, lifting his feet as usual onto the trusty head, whose glassy eyes had watched his infant games and which had ever been his companion.

The softly popping gas-fire, the polar-bear, the lamp-light, all were the same as they always had been, but Bobby stared sombrely at the trees in Green Park, dimly tranquil between the undrawn curtains. Tonight the magic did not work.

13

Pusskin

MY DEAR MRS KILMARNOCK,

I FEEL IT MY DUTY TO DRAW YOUR ATTENTION TO THE FACT THAT
THE FAMILY YOU INTEND TO 'ADOPT' IS EXTREMELY UNDESIRABLE IN
EVERY WAY AND WILL CAUSE YOU NOT ONLY EMBARRASSMENT BUT
ACTUAL HARM. YOU WOULD BE WISE TO RECONSIDER YOUR DECISION
AND INDEED IT IS ESSENTIAL THAT YOU SHOULD DO SO.

YOU WILL UNDERSTAND THAT THE LAWS OF LIBEL IN THIS COUNTRY
OBLIGE ME TO SIGN MYSELF NO MORE SPECIFICALLY THAN

YOUR WELL-WISHER

Harriet studied this letter that she had retrieved from the dust-
bin at Bassington Hall with some interest. It bore yesterday's date
and was written on cheap lined paper. Fiona had evidently dealt
with it as it deserved but Harriet, on reflection, decided to keep it.
Suppose it was actually *true*? Anonymous letters were always
supposed not to be, of course, but if by any chance her new next-
door neighbours, unknown to all, *should* cause not only
embarrassment but actual harm perhaps this slender piece of
evidence should be preserved. She put it in her desk.

Otherwise she spent a tranquil evening.

It was Krystra's distant and muffled bark that first disturbed her
in the night. Only one or two, but enough to momentarily rouse
her in her alerted state of mind. Later she was woken again.
There was the bang of her gate and then somebody running across
her garden. She saw a flicker of light reflected on the ceiling.

Really, thought Harriet grumpily, as she stubbed her toe trying
to find her slippers, the night life in this garden was a good deal
livelier than it had ever been in Kensington. Goodness only knew
what the time was, and it was chilly too! She pulled on her thick
dressing gown with the hood and crept silently downstairs where
she felt for and found the poker. Spinsterly it might be, but it was
solid and reassuring.

Thus armed she boldly sallied forth into the moonlit garden. She was not going to slink about amongst the shadows. Let, if absolutely necessary, battle commence; Harriet Charles was ready. From now on her territory was not to be used as a passageway to any goings-on next door, nor as a rubbish dump, nor anything else that was bothersome and a nuisance for her, the rightful owner.

She stood there, straining eyes and ears for an intruder, and deciding that one week was far too long to live in the country without a dog. She had not considered anything more formidable than a cocker spaniel but even he, aged six weeks or so, might have been useful at that moment.

There was a very very faint rustling, as if footsteps were stealthily retreating. Beyond the shrubbery a light flickered and went out.

Harriet sped towards it over the bumpy grass, leaving a long line of dewy footprints.

Once the dark, mysterious bushes surrounded her the bravado faltered. Each one seemed to shelter a marauder or two, all eyeing her, thought Harriet, as she now picked her way more cautiously through the blackness.

Ah, the gate. She let out her pent-up breath in a sigh of relief. The flickering had come from next door. Would you believe it, Goggins again, in his shed. At this time of night! Her courage returned. Harriet had become inoculated against the wretched gardener. She felt only anger and outrage at thus being annoyed by him a second time, and quite prepared to wave the poker about, if not to use it.

She opened the little gate between the two gardens and passed through. But the cobbled yard and garden shed were both in darkness. Nothing seemed to be happening there tonight.

She tiptoed on into the garden proper. Now Harriet could see the hammock that Fiona had lain in that afternoon, swaying gently in the night breeze. A cloud passed across the moon's white face for a moment. That must have been it, thought Harriet, as the fairy light dimmed and renewed. Flickered — well, near enough, flickered. And the rustles and so on, the pattering footsteps, had also, no doubt, been enlarged by her imagination into human terms. Harriet smiled to herself and allowed her clutch on the handle of the poker to relax. She was aware, for the first time, of the wet seeping up through her slippers, of the heavy sweet scent of the honeysuckle, of her heart beating, and of the tingling in her hands as the adrenalin went to waste.

For a little longer Harriet remained in the garden of Bassington Hall. Now that she had ceased to be nervous all was as silent as the grave. The dark house stood above her, graciously forbidding, rightly accusing her of trespass. Within those mellow walls Harriet imagined Fiona asleep in the master bedroom, inviolate and beautiful.

She turned and made her way back through her own garden and had nearly reached the back door when there was a movement amongst the lilacs, very close to her. All her doubts returned in a rush and turned into certainties.

Within a few yards of each other two human beings froze in unison. Then at last Harriet heard her own name, waveringly spoken.

She spun round: 'Who's that?'

'Me.'

'Thomas; whatever are you doing here?' Harriet's voice was louder and sharper than she intended. 'I don't know what time it is but ...'

'It's Pusskin. He's gone.'

The boy followed her into the kitchen, blinking behind his thick lenses when she switched on the light and shivering with cold. His striped pyjamas were soaking wet below the knee.

'I hope I didn't disturb you,' he said hopefully. 'I didn't recognise you at first in that dressing-gown thing. I thought you might be the cat burglar, and seeing you were armed I was following you. I thought you might of got a lot and hid them somewhere. If you'd been him of course.'

'The cat burglar?'

'Well, I woke up, you see, and I heard something going on downstairs and I thought at first it was just an ordinary burglar and then I thought: suppose *Pusskin's* being stole. There are cat burglars you know. His basket's at the bottom of the stairs because he's not allowed in with me with his tray, dunno why. So I got up.'

'But cat burglars behave like cats, climbing through windows or up drain-pipes. They don't steal cats. It would be your mother's silver, or one of her lovely old pictures, or something like that. Not Pusskin.'

Harriet kicked off her slippers (there was blood on one of the

70

soles – ugh! she must have trodden on a frog!) and pulled on the Wellington boots which stood inside the door. 'Come along, we're going straight back to your house, right now. You're absolutely freezing. I'll come along with you and get you a hot water bottle and some clean pyjamas and we'll try not to wake anybody up.'

Harriet put her coat round his shoulders and marched him back across the green, Thomas talking long and earnestly, at the top of his voice.

'Well, I suppose he might of behaved like a cat then, being one, and got out of a window or down a drainpipe but anyway, he's *gone.* I heard something outside but my room's at the back so I came out and stood on the grass and listened *really hard* and I thought I heard his bell coming from up this way. He could of come to see you.'

'Hush! You'll wake up the whole village! Why should he?'

'Well, you liked him. You played with him,' said Thomas plaintively, 'and your garden's all wild and jungly like what he'd like. I looked in your bushes. I thought he might be stuck in one.'

'I'm sure he's not in my garden now. One of us would have heard his bell, wouldn't we, while we were out there. Don't worry; if he climbed out he can climb back.'

'But perhaps he's lost, or up a tree, or freezing to death. ...'

The young voice thickened.

'Cats can always find their way home.'

Thomas's stricken face relaxed a little as he looked up at her reassuring smile, as so many had before him. Harriet went on. 'It's Saturday tomorrow. No school. If he's not back you'll have plenty of time to look for him. I'll help you.'

'Will you?'

As they neared The Old Rectory they saw that the porch light was on and Caroline standing there awaiting them. She scanned him anxiously and said, frowning, 'Thomas, what have you been doing!'

Harriet handed him over with a brief explanation. Thomas's vociferous attempts to justify his excursions were received with a good deal of agitated scolding, rubbings down with a towel, pyjama finding, hot water bottle filling and warm milk producing.

'Poor Harriet, what can she think, having you wandering about in her garden at all hours of the night? I can't think what possessed you.'

'I did look in at Fiona's too,' said Thomas, pacifically. He gave her a sidelong look, but Caroline was just as indignant with this red herring.

'Well, I only hope to goodness you didn't wake her up too. She might not be so patient with you.'

'No I didn't. She's still asleep.'

Caroline turned on him, bottle in one hand and kettle in the other. 'How do you know? You can't mean you went right into the house and walked upstairs? It's – it's practically breaking and entering!'

'I didn't. I don't, hardly ever. Gardens are gardens, for people to go in. That's what they're for. It's only when windows are open and that. You were jolly interested in Mr Clancy's book and you never would have known about it if I hadn't gone in then, just a little way. You know you were. And it's jolly interesting now too. I'll tell you ...'

'Tomorrow, Thomas. You've done enough talking for tonight. It's bed for you, and bed for poor unfortunate Harriet.'

'Oh, all grown-ups are bonkers,' concluded Thomas wearily. 'At least I sleep in my own bed, but nobody ever listens to *me*.'

'We'll all listen tomorrow,' said Caroline rashly.

'And if Pusskin's not back tomorrow morning I'll have a good look for him, first thing,' promised Harriet.

Thomas's face brightened a little. 'We could of got up a proper search-party, only Bobby's away in London, and Cotty's at that lecture thing of hers, and Biddy'nann'll be at the Copper Kettle and Dr Ashford will be on his rounds and Mrs Ashford's always too busy and the Clancys wouldn't bother. But Colonel Rillington might.'

'Don't bother Colonel Rillington, darling,' said Caroline automatically as she shoo-ed Thomas upstairs.

'... he likes dogs and he likes birds and he likes horses,' Harriet heard him say. 'The question is, what does he think of cats?'

When Caroline thanked her she added, 'It's awfully kind of you. I'll let you know if Pusskin turns up.'

Harriet trudged back to her own home, sleepy, wet and cold. She gave a cursory look at the garden, shut the back door, turned off the kitchen light, went upstairs, switched on her bedside lamp and climbed thankfully into a bed which she seemed to have left many hours ago.

It was that uncertain, greyish time of dawn when it is hardly worth going to sleep again and yet still rather too early for the earliest of birds to actually get up. Harriet took the middle course of sinking into a medley of uneasy, half-waking dreams, where she neither quite lost track of her surroundings nor quite kept a grip on reality.

That sharp, anxious voice. *Thomas, oh Thomas, where have you been?*

I've been up to London to look at the Queen.

Harriet shrugged her shoulders and turned over in bed, trying to get warm. Of course Thomas had said nothing of the kind. ... What had been said, exactly? Harriet's mind drifted uncomfortably off again, too tired to think properly because she, and Thomas, and somebody else, were skipping round the bushes playing catch-as-catch-can and it made them breathless. Round and round the mulberry bush, three little teddy bears dancing in a moonlit world of crackles and snappings and foot-steps and sharp intakes of breath, before they all went indoors for their birdseed. Where nobody knew quite who was doing what, or where, or why, or to whom.

14

The shed at Bassington Hall

True to her promise, and having heard nothing to the contrary, Harriet put on her galoshes as soon as she had washed up her breakfast and prepared to have a look for Pusskin.

Poor Thomas, she knew how he felt. Really, sometimes it seemed hardly worth while letting children keep pets when one considered the awful likelihood of disaster. Even simple old age was traumatic enough. Like the dreadful time when Toby, her faithful friend from babyhood, had had to go for his last visit to the vet, despite all her begging and pleading. 'He's nearly blind, darling, it's kinder. He won't know anything, I won't leave him, I promise'. ...

And what about Binkie the guineapig? Much more attractive, the very young Harriet had felt, than this brother Simon; she had definitely loved him best. She relived again the agony of discovering the disordered cage, the twisted wire netting, the nightmare traces of blood and fur, and the realisation that it was the precious Binkie that had been taken by a stoat in the night.

Extraordinary the clarity of one's childhood days, thought Harriet to herself, as she stumped dutifully through the long grass, and peered into the overgrown flower-beds and bushes. All those other claims on her memory, all those important people that she had met and forgotten about in the meantime, and yet in her mind's eye the two brown and white animals were still clearly etched, after fifty years.

'Pusskin?' she called hopefully. 'Pusskin?'

'Miaow!' came a facetious voice from behind the shared hedge. Colonel Rillington's face appeared, smiling wolfishly, fingers like ears.

'Oh! You startled me! You are up early! I'm looking for Thomas's kitten. He's lost it.'

'Oh dear! Alarm and despondency! Action stations!' he exclaimed in mock horror, throwing up his hands. 'Fetch the fire brigade!'

'I suppose you wouldn't understand how children can feel about animals,' said Harriet severely, ignoring the faithful Rex. 'You were probably too busy shooting them.'

Her neighbour's irritating expression immediately changed to one of compunction. Really, thought Harriet, he wasn't nearly so stiff as he appeared at first. And what right had she, the newest of acquaintances and the recipient of so much kindness, to speak to him like that? 'I'm sorry,' she said, remembering the cowed look on Maureen's face outside the Hall, 'I'm afraid I still play the headmistress.'

'Nonsense,' declared the colonel handsomely, 'I play the fool.'

Harriet got back to the business in hand.

'Do you think he might be in your garden, with all those birds of yours?'

'I doubt it. Everything in my garden is known to me, down to the smallest slug. Besides which, Rex is not good with cats. Has Thomas already been round to see you then?'

Harriet retailed her night's adventures, ending up, 'So you see, he really *is* worried about it.'

'Well, maybe he is,' allowed the colonel, 'and maybe he isn't because, believe me, that boy's quite capable of making up the whole story just to explain his presence in your garden. Some of the places he gets into need some explaining. Mad as a hatter. I found him reading my letters once, nearly gave him a walloping, and then I thought, poor little beggar.'

Harriet nodded.

'Come in and look round if it would make you happier.'

Harriet examined his garden with interest though not much hope as far as Pusskin was concerned. He must be the only man she knew, she thought enviously, with bean-sticks really long enough, and strong enough, and enough of them, and who finished his lettuces just as the next ones were nearly ready. Now *his* toolshed, noted Harriet, was neat to distraction, with its stacks of seedboxes and flower-pots ranged according to size. Not that she approved of all those fertilizers and insecticides but if they had to be they were certainly all to hand in the most convenient way. So was everything else, hanging on thoroughly adequate hooks.

That was how a proper toolshed should look. Spick and span. How Fiona would like hers to look. How infuriated she must have been with the sluttish Goggins all this time, when she herself was so tidy and clean in every way. No wonder she had given him the sack.

Thus mused Harriet, as she returned to her own garden. A nasty piece of work, Albert Goggins, not above taking a nip or two from his employer's cellar in that little shed of his.

And not above sawing things up in it in the middle of the night. Awkwardly, by the light of a torch.

Having walked all the way from his cottage at the other end of the village to do so.

She stood still amongst the long grass. But why should he? Any gardener, however awful, is by his very nature king of the toolshed, and free to do his sawing in the daytime. Anyway she had already decided that he was too drunk and that it must have been Bobby Kilmarnock, the dedicated carpenter. Had gone back to bed again on the strength of it.

A dedicated carpenter? Bobby? So keen on carpentry that he went on doing it, by candle-light, into the small hours?

Harriet remained standing still for a moment longer, trying to picture this in her mind, before walking pensively down her sloping garden. She had meant to cross the nettle-filled ditch at the bottom and search the common land beyond, but now the next-door shed had impinged itself on her mind. Perhaps Pusskin had been attracted by its warmth and shelter, its floor soft with sawdust and musty with decay, its sacks and day-bed and garden cushions. Could the door perhaps have swung to, trapping him inside?

Harriet hastened across to the little connecting gate and then stopped dead. Through the bars she saw on the cobblestones, across the yard, as she had done in the old Binkie days, a splash of blood.

Her heart sank. Perhaps the kitten had also fallen victim to some predator.

Hesitantly she opened the gate and glanced up at the house, palely glowing in the morning sun. There was no sign of life. Fiona the efficient might be an early riser. On the other hand Fiona the glamorous might sleep late, and of course she had no help at week-ends. Harriet's imagination raced ahead. She must go in. Perhaps poor little Pusskin had been only *half* eaten, and she must search for, and bury, the awful remains so that Thomas. ...

The tumbledown door stood ajar. It revealed a soft leather Italian sandal, on a foot, attached to an ankle, which was attached to something else lying within.

Harriet stood stock still, her face devoid of expression. If she remained standing thus for ever, if she was turned to stone, if some rift in the earth's surface appeared beneath her feet, or a hurricane swept through that clear blue sky and whirled her away to a distant country, then she would never need to see more than that sandal, that foot, and that ankle.

She would never have to enter that shed.

But none of those things happened. Slowly Harriet walked the few steps necessary and looked, appalled, through the merciful gloom at the chaos and confusion within.

Fiona lay spreadeagled on her back amongst a litter of sharp and heavy objects. She had been struck heavily on the upper part of the body. Her head was knocked to one side, but Harriet, stooping over her, now saw with horror that the left eye had gone, leaving the socket brown-encrusted. The delicate nose was nearly destroyed, and the lovely front teeth broken.

And everywhere, in hideous and scarlet profusion, there was blood.

For a moment Harriet remained, transfixed and hardly breathing, in the doorway, then she stumbled back to her cottage.

There she rang up James Ashford.

15

James Ashford, MD (69)

Rosemary put her head round the door of her husband's waiting-room and was not surprised to see that poor sot Goggins just coming out of the surgery. It was no secret in Bassington that Goggins was for the chop; you only had to look at him to see that. He had everything in the book wrong with him, all brought about by himself, she considered. Nothing much that James could do there.

He jerked his head morosely to the only other patient as a signal for him to go in. Clancy, equally glum, rose and went through the open door as the telephone started to ring.

Rosemary glanced at her watch as she left Red House. Only one patient left at 9.15! It was a sad reflection on human nature that so few people visited their doctors on a Saturday, when there was no work to miss, and other things that they wanted to do. It was a pity they couldn't space themselves out; Monday morning invariably found the little room packed with customers. And week-day evenings, when they could call in at the Dog and Duck on the way home.

She wondered fleetingly what had brought John Clancy to the surgery; it was the first time she had seen him there. Anyway, now he could have a whole half hour of James's time to himself; he never left on his rounds before 9.45 on Saturdays when there was no girl to mind the telephone. Rosemary smiled as she hurried up the road to the village shop. Half an hour; that should be enough for the taciturn Clancy.

She was later than usual this morning. Both her daughters-in-law were marathon telephoners. They looked to Rosemary for womanly advice and she was never niggardly in giving it. Half these women who complained about their sons' wives just didn't give enough time to it all, didn't listen or understand. It was as simple as that.

Well, she'd be back as soon as she could, twenty minutes perhaps. James always had plenty of paper-work to do.

James Ashford picked up the receiver as John Clancy entered the room, and motioned him smilingly into a comfortable chair. The surgery was cheerful and well cared-for. Silver and brass shone. A bowl of fresh flowers caught the sunlight amongst the scattered papers on his desk. As well as the tools of his trade there was a stack of classical records.

The doctor was standing by the window and for a moment he didn't recognise Harriet's voice as he stared out at his roses. They hadn't done so well this year. 'Oh yes, of course,' he said easily into the telephone. He would have to feed the soil.

John Clancy eyed him with sour attention. Ashford's height, his relaxed air, his casual clothes and his domestic set-up all combined to irritate him, but presumably he was as good as the next man at removing wax from the ears. He had better be; the next man was eleven miles away.

Dr Ashford's bland, good-humoured face suddenly hardened. 'Fiona!' he exclaimed.

A woman's voice murmured inaudibly on the other end of the line, despite Clancy's straining to hear it. 'Dead?' said Dr Ashford in a soft voice, almost pleadingly. He sank down into his swivel chair and listened attentively for some minutes, his face gradually paling. 'Are you quite sure?' Then he said 'I'll come at once,' and jumped to his feet, blindly facing his last patient.

'It's all right,' said Clancy, rising also. 'No hurry. It's an emergency, isn't it.'

'Oh, thank you,' said James Ashford absently. 'Yes, I must go.' He turned and strode out. John Clancy, left in the empty house, heard him start up his car and drive away. For a moment or two the little man remained where he was and then he also set off, not

78

up the road towards Botswana but down, in the direction of the green.

*   *

Rosemary was a little surprised to find the house empty on her return. She did not glance at her watch to verify the time; after a lifetime of unremitting punctuality she had no need to. She was well within her half-hour. If she had been unavoidably held up, which she had not, James would normally have waited for her. Though not the most organised of men he was particular about leaving the telephone unmanned.

As it happened it remained silent until nearly 10.15. Rosemary listened kindly to little Mrs Yaxley over at Lovat's Farm, worried about her Pam. Rosemary's experienced ears extracted the grain of the symptoms from the chaff of the apologies for bothering the doctor, the dampness of the house and the fact that Mrs Yaxley's mother had been nervous as a girl, and decided that they did not give rise to much concern. But on the other hand Mrs Yaxley was an anxious young thing with a first baby living in a lonely place, and she was undoubtedly right in saying – or implying, since she was far too timid to state it as a fact – that a very slight temperature might conceivably be the start of practically anything, and that it was arguably more prudent, though also a lot more time-consuming, to be safe than sorry. Running her eye over the list of calls in James's appointments diary Rosemary saw that the first one, a Mr Singleton, was not far from Lovat's, so that her husband would not be much inconvenienced. She promised to ask him to look at Pam before lunch.

However, Mr Singleton had not yet seen the doctor. Neither had any of the next three patients on the list.

By half past ten Rosemary had still failed to locate her husband. She rang Mrs Yaxley and told her that the doctor would ring her when he returned for lunch. Mrs Yaxley replied that little Pamela seemed ever so much brighter and she thought it was a tooth coming through. She remembered now, it had been exactly the same last time, but thanked Mrs Ashford for her trouble. Rosemary asked her to ring again if the improvement was not maintained, and put the incident out of her mind.

Rosemary was not yet disconcerted that James had not seen any of his morning patients. He had been known to stop at a roadside accident and travel with the victim to hospital in the ambulance. Most of his calls, she knew, were old chronics, the Saturday morning specials. None were, as far as she knew, urgent. He could always pop along to see them this afternoon, though it would mean missing his golf. Rosemary looked out at the beautiful day and smiled to herself. No, the chances were that he would ring them up after lunch, hoping that a brief chat could suffice.

And honestly, thought Rosemary, the chances were that it would. There was a lot of friendly common-sense in James's easy running of his practice, as well as a dash or two of hedonism. It was surprising how many patients got better all by themselves if they were left for an hour or two. Making the telephone call seemed to heal them up, all by itself.

*   *

Harriet was waiting for James Ashford at her gate. Together they knocked and vainly rang at the door of Bassington Hall.

'This is only a matter of form,' said the doctor, as they stood listening to the echoes die away, and Krysta's eager whining. 'Bobby's in London and neither the cleaning ladies nor Goggins come at the weekend. There was just the chance that she might have had a friend staying with her.'

When it was obvious that the house was empty they went down to the shed, in silence.

James's professional demeanour faltered as he knelt amongst the wreckage. He applied a stethoscope, picked up Fiona's slim wrist with its stiff hand, touched an eyelid, cleared his throat. A few flies were already buzzing in the shed. Harriet stood quietly by, hearing, as from another world, birds singing outside.

Now that she was no longer alone, Harriet felt able to look more closely at the body, with its cherry covered dress, once so crisp and clean, now crumpled and torn over the firm breast, where the scarlet fruit on its green leaf, once so bright and pretty, was now a rusty, uneven stain. At the short black hair, once so soft and bouncy, now lifeless and solid, with a little patch of other short black hairs indented bloodily on the sawdust alongside.

A lump rose in Harriet's throat and she blinked back the tears. James, miserable though he was, had a job to do. She could only stand there, silent and helpless.

80

She averted her eyes to the surroundings. Above her head a wooden shelf hung askew in two halves. Beneath it, all over the floor, lay shears, secateurs, wrenches, an axe, metal boxes and tins, a drum of oil, and other lethal looking tools, while the head of a motor-mower lay half across the body itself. The table lay on its side against a wall. All was defiled.

What havoc the broken shelf had caused, thought Harriet. The whole place looked as though a holocaust had hit it. Even the old garden blanket, huddled right at the back, had brownish streaks on it, and as she had already seen, a drop or two of blood had reached to the cobblestones outside. But doubtless the police would be able to reconstruct the accident, would know exactly what had hit her, and when.

'Killed instantly,' said James in a gruff voice, getting to his feet. He took a clean handkerchief from his pocket and spread it gently over Fiona's face. 'Been dead for some time. All night, certainly.'

'I felt she — must have been,' said Harriet shakily, 'but I thought I'd better ring you. ....'

'Of course. You did absolutely the right thing. She must have come out here yesterday evening and reached for the mower and had the whole shelf come down on her.'

'Thomas and I might easily have discovered her very early this morning.'

'Thomas?'

'Yes, I found him in my garden, looking for his kitten.'

Ashford smiled faintly and looked hard at Harriet's pale face for the first time. 'This must have all been a great shock for you. Would you like to — to go and get a cup of tea or something?'

'No, I'm all right. I just realised how — near we came to finding her and — so glad we didn't.'

'Did you hear anything unusual last night?'

'No, it was quite peaceful, though as a matter of fact I was half expecting some sort of disturbance. ....' She explained about her trouble with Goggins.

'A nasty experience for you, but I don't think that old fellow could hurt a fly.'

'I know. I realised that as soon as I caught sight of him. It was only that I was unprepared for such an attack! I seriously considered bringing my torch down on his head.'

'It would have finished him off if you had I should think. Well, we shall probably never know exactly what happened here.

Several of these tools could have done the damage. I think the lawn mower was probably the culprit as it was lying across her chest. The whole set-up was ridiculously careless and dangerous.'

He kicked the skirting of the old building savagely, dislodging a cloud of mouldy dust. Harriet recognised anger used to blanket grief and remembered someone telling her that every man in the village was half in love with Fiona.

'I shall have to treat it as an accident,' James Ashford went on, leading her out into the sunshine and up the garden towards the Hall. His face was drawn and white. 'Because that's what it technically is, though I would like to prove criminal negligence against that old soak. She would still be alive if Goggins had kept his shed properly. Any reasonable man keeps heavy stuff like that on the floor. I must get hold of Bobby at once of course, poor fellow.'

'He said something about a reunion dinner. Would you like to ring him from my house?'

'Thank you, but I've got his London number at home. In fact, I can do all the necessary ringing from there. I wonder what his plans for today are. It's just possible that he has already started for somewhere else.'

'There's sure to be a diary by the telephone,' said Harriet. There was, just inside the french window, beside a pile of proofs. *The* proofs, she supposed.

James pushed open the door. 'All right, Krysta, give over, I know you're pleased to see me.' But the handsome black leather volume, gold embossed, neatly filled up in Fiona's large, dramatic writing, revealed only a brisk and businesslike 'Bobby to London a.m.' for Friday and 'Bobby back p.m.' for Saturday.

'I was afraid of that,' said James. 'All the details will be in Bobby's pocket diary, with him. He's very methodical, it always has everything in it, down to 'I owe Rosemary 10p' when he came to play bridge with us and forgot to change the pockets in his suit. Gave it to her too, the next day, poor boy.'

In the pause which followed Harriet handed over the anonymous letter, which she had brought with her. 'Perhaps you ought to see this,' she said, explaining where she had found it.

The doctor read it with bewildered eyes. 'Odd,' he said. 'Quite an educated hand but it sounds like a veiled threat.'

'It only came yesterday,' said Harriet. 'She lost no time in throwing it away.'

'She wouldn't,' said James, stuffing it into his pocket. 'You couldn't intimidate someone like Fiona. I'll give it to Bobby sometime. He ought to see it I suppose, though I hardly like to bother him with ridiculous stuff like that just now.'

'Is there anything more I can do? Shall I ring the police?'

'No, I'll take care of all that and – the body and everything. You've been marvellous. It's routine arrangements now. I can see to that. It's all quite straightforward.'

James Ashford went over to his car as though to drive away. Then he changed his mind and walked back past Rose Cottage. As he stood with his hand on the gate of Little Farthings he heard a hurried trot behind him. A pudgy hand caught at his arm and he turned rather coldly, as the sallow face of John Clancy, shining with exertion, looked up into his. A strangely excited face, thought James with some repugnance.

'Forgive me, Dr Ashford, but I couldn't help overhearing something of what you said on the telephone. What a very dreadful thing. And I – well, I was taking my morning walk down this way, my constitutional, and I wondered if I could be of some assistance.'

James Ashford gazed down at him for a few moments without affection. The man's strange eyes were almost popping out of his head. 'It's not very pleasant, I'm afraid.'

'Oh no, I assure you,' Clancy's thin, rather academic voice insisted, 'I'm perfectly well used to the sight of blood.'

'Very well,' the doctor surveyed him thoughtfully. 'Since you know all about it, and if you have time to spare, I think we might be glad of your help.'

*   *

Maureen Clancy heard the sound of her husband's key in the door of Botswana and ran into the hall to meet him. 'Ooh, you are late.' She looked into his face and noticed the heavy pink flush. 'Whatever happened?' she added apprehensively.

'The even tenor of life in Bassington has been somewhat disturbed.'

'Even what?'

'Never mind. Trot along and get us a drink and I'll tell you all about it while you're getting on with a few little jobs I've got for you. There's plenty to do.'

16

Baxter on the scene

Harriet stood uncertainly in her front porch. Then she went into her sitting-room and, looking out of her window, saw the roof of the next door shed, just visible over her wall. She felt restless and jumpy, with John Clancy's high-pitched voice still ringing unpleasantly in her ears. If only Dr Ashford could have found her something to do as well.

All was silent. She pined for some familiar, trusted face, longed to be out and away. On an impulse, she fetched her new bicycle and wheeled it out over the bumpy grass.

'Hullo, Thomas! Oh dear, what is the matter?'

The boy stood red-eyed and disconsolate outside her gate, holding a narrow circlet of green leather; the little bell tinkled.

'You said he'd run off but somebody's stole him, they must of.'

'Oh Thomas, I'm sure ... where did you find that?'

'Just here, in the grass.' Thomas's look was tragic. 'Could you ...?'

Harriet hesitated. 'I'm afraid I can't just now. There's something important that I've got to do. Pusskin's not in my garden, or Little Farthings, I'm sure of that. I've just – had a very good look, so don't come in here. What about one of the hay barns at the farm? Is Andrew at home this morning?'

Thomas nodded.

'Ask him. He'll help you.'

'We won't be able to hear him now,' said Thomas sadly, 'Not without his bell.'

Harriet looked regretfully after the forlorn figure stumping slowly back across the green, and then bowled off down the road towards Loxley, faintly surprised to see James Ashford's car still standing outside the Hall.

Ted Baxter was already working in his front garden when Harriet arrived.

'Miss Charles!' He flung away his spade and hurried over to

meet her. 'This is a real pleasure!' He ushered her into a spotless little room in a new, detached house. 'I was going to ring you but I wanted to give you a chance to get your bearings first. You'll have a cup of tea, won't you? Excuse the mess.'

Harriet suddenly realised that tea was what she yearned for.

He whisked the *Daily Telegraph* off one of the chairs; the only object, as far as Harriet could see, that could conceivably be tidied any further. 'The kettle's on,' he assured her. 'I was just about to have one myself. I'll be right back.'

He bustled about, talking through the doorway. 'I've been wondering how you were getting on. In that cottage.'

A moment later he was back, bearing a tray complete with tray-cloth saying MARGARET on it, in the cross-stich of a seven-year-old. He put it on the small table between them. 'Well, how is it?'

He leaned forward, hands on knees, and scrutinised her, as he had on the train. 'What's the matter? Something gone wrong?'

'Yes,' said Harriet, looking gratefully into the honest square face as at a very old friend. She spooned in plenty of sugar and took a deep gulp of the hot tea. 'It certainly has.'

But she wanted to lead up to it gradually. Could not bear to look it in the face yet. Or to think about faces at all.

'It was lovely at first,' she said. 'Everybody has been most kind and welcoming and made me feel at home right away. I went to a cocktail party and helped prepare for a fête and I feel as if I have lived there for a year.'

Baxter nodded. 'That doesn't surprise me,' he said. 'Everybody always liked you and – well, it doesn't sound too complimentary, but you're *ordinary*, there's nothing peculiar about you. You're not stand-offish nor a ferret neither. You've got the right face. People trust that sort of face.' He gazed at her. 'But now something's happened to shock and upset you.'

'Oh Ted, it was awful.' Harriet took another gulp to sustain her before telling him in a low voice the worst part of the story.

Ted Baxter's eyes widened. 'Not Mrs Kilmarnock? Why? What was the matter with her?'

'Nothing, but a shelf had come down on top of her and I'm not surprised, considering what was on it. A lot of heavy stuff had hit her, the head of a motor mower amongst other things. It was all in a terrible mess. Like a – a whirlwind. Blood, you know.'

'Poor Harriet.' The catastrophe had brought out the christian names. 'What did the doctor say?'

'He came right away and examined her and said it was an accident that had happened last night.'

'It must have been a nasty shock for him too.'

'Oh yes, he was very much upset.'

'And then?'

'Then I didn't quite know what to do next.'

'The police have been informed, I take it?'

'Dr Ashford said he was going to do all that.'

'And you went back to your cottage.'

'Yes. I just stood there in the sitting-room, thinking. It makes it all so much worse when you remember how – how pretty she was.'

Ted Baxter nodded gravely. 'Yes, she certainly was that. Look, I've got nothing on today. Would you like to drive round and look at the countryside? Have some lunch? A picnic perhaps? Take your mind off it all?'

'How very, very kind of you! I would love to do all that in a – a way, but I did just wonder if I could possibly ask you to come and have a look at it – her – yourself. While there's nobody there. Doctor Ashford was going home to do all that ringing up. Bobby too. Oh dear, he's such a nice man. He was only going to be away one night. It was such an unfortunate coincidence. I mean ...'

'You mean unless it wasn't a coincidence at all,' suggested Ted Baxter in level tones.

Harriet took a deep breath and met his gaze. 'Everybody knew that a family with three young children might be coming to the cottage quite soon. That is, the one that's actually in their garden, practically part of the house, which would probably mean that Fiona would never have been alone again. While Doctor Ashford was examining the body I looked at it all and it didn't look quite right somehow.' She paused. 'The shed itself was so very chaotic. Not so much as if Fiona had had an accident, more as if she had fought for her life. I started wondering if the tools could have been used as *weapons*.' Her voice trailed away. 'Of course Doctor Ashford saw all that too.'

'But Doctor Ashford has probably never come across a single case of murder in his whole career.'

The word had been spoken. It lingered in the air between them.

'I know,' said Harriet. 'That did occur to me too.'

Under careful questioning from Tex Baxter, Harriet now told him much of what had happened during the last twenty-four hours. Then she described the shed in detail. He listened intently. 'And what conclusions did you reach?'

'It was questions, rather than conclusions. What was she doing in there at all? It must have been annoying for her to drop off to sleep when she was so pressed for time, with the fête on her hands as well. Why start bothering with the garden at a time like that? Why was there some of her hair on the floor beside her and none on the tools that fell on her head? Why was she lying on her back with her feet towards the door? And the blood seemed wrong. It was so scattered that it was almost as if — as if some maniac had somehow swung her whole body round in a circle. And that shelf had already been sawn nearly through; it would have been all jagged otherwise, wouldn't it. Anyway I think I heard that sawing the day before yesterday, or rather the night. *Some* sawing, anyway. Oh, lots of things, like I told you. But above all ...'

'Yes?' said Ted Baxter. Harriet looked at him very earnestly.

'It seemed so absolutely unlike Fiona.'

Ted Baxter leaned back in his chair and regarded her indulgently. 'Well now, there you are in the witness box. There's no telling what the lady of the house went to her own shed for but it could have been almost anything, to fetch a nail for instance or a piece of string. It's quite possible to find traces of hair where the impact occurred and none on the lethal instrument. It's more likely she would have fallen away from the shelf if she was looking up at it but not impossible for her to fall the other way. A moment's staggering could account for that and also for the state of her clothes and the distribution of the blood and the furniture. The shelf may be a rough and ready affair, originally made from two pieces of wood. The sound you heard may have been something else. You have met Mrs Kilmarnock twice. Scarcely enough to form an accurate judgement as to her character and efficiency.'

'Perhaps I would be wasting your time.'

Ted Baxter gave her one of his rare grins.

'You know quite well how interested I'd be and what my time's worth! No, I think you may have something there. I was just pointing out that you haven't said anything to bring a gleam into a Coroner's eye exactly. But my own eye gleams easier.'

Harriet had already observed this gleam. It had a professional quality that gave her a good deal of comfort.

'It's just up my street, this affair,' said Ted. 'I should like to visit the scene and sum it up. Keep my hand in. The local lads will be giving it the once-over but there's no harm in you and me having a look, too, in our strictly unofficial capacity. There should be no difficulty there; you've been there already and they know me well enough. And we're free agents. *We* don't have to have solid evidence!'

He jumped to his feet. 'Come along. We'll go in my car if you don't mind. We can fetch your bike later.'

He led the way out to his garage. '*Being* unofficial we might as well cut a few corners and presume the worst.'

'Whatever the cause,' said Harriet, as they drove out of the gate, 'we can give a definite time to Fiona's death; between about five o'clock when I left the Hall with Rosemary Ashford, and about five thirty when I returned home. That would be possible according to Dr Ashford. You see, there must have been a tremendous crash and I never heard a thing, when I was really half expecting some disturbance having had them before. Later on I was actually woken from sleep by quite a small sound.'

'What time was that?'

'About four o'clock in the morning. Hours after she died, according to James. I went out to investigate but I only found young Thomas Metcalfe, wandering about my garden in his pyjamas, looking for his kitten.'

A moment or two later an ambulance passed them in the narrow road and Ted Baxter swerved to avoid it. 'Sorry,' he said. 'I'm not usually that kind of driver. Rum kid, Thomas. Quite a well-known local character.'

'If there really was a murderer whoever it was must have acted on the spur of the moment,' said Harriet. 'How could anybody know beforehand that I was going to be out of the way for that half-hour, walking home with Rosemary Ashford?'

'Why did you, by the way?'

'She asked me to. We chatted for a while at her gate but I didn't go in. She had asked some people in for an early supper.'

'Did she mention who?'

'As a matter of fact she did. It was the local Vicar and his wife. I remember her telling me what a good bridge player he was.'

'Oh well, that's easily checked on.'

The Superintendent drew up outside Rose Cottage and reached behind him for a small dispatch case. There was no sign of any police car, which pleased him. 'Looks as if we're first on the scene. Well, it's facts we need now, and that's what we'll look for. I'll tell you all about it as soon as I've seen that shed.' He closed the car door with a confident click. 'I've got a nose for such things.'

'One thing against the murder theory,' mused Harriet, 'is lack of motive. Everybody loved Fiona.'

Ted Baxter stopped dead on the path and looked back at her in mild astonishment. 'Now that,' he said, 'is the most convincing argument *for* the murder theory you've given me so far. In my job we never take love for granted, however much it's talked about. *Especially* if it's talked about.'

'But she was so kind, so popular, so charming,' insisted Harriet. 'Why should anyone have wanted to kill her?'

'How long did you say you'd lived here? One week?'

'But honestly, of all people ...'

Ted Baxter said drily, 'When you've been in the force as long as I have I'm afraid you get cynical about motives. Why, I can give you a dozen motives from what you've told me so far. Great black ugly motives growing up amongst all those buttercups and daisies.'

Harriet glanced up at this unsuspected streak of poetry but Ted nodded at her, back again on solid earth. 'There's money there. Mrs Kilmarnock was a very rich woman in her own right, with no children as yet. There's jealousy. In a little place like this you can't go away for a single night, with however good a reason, without somebody thinking something's amiss. There's fear, for yourself, or for others, fear of the future, fear of the past. There's hatred, there's love, there's drink and drugs which can unhinge the mind. And there's mild eccentricity which can conceal plain downright pottiness.'

Harriet led her friend down through the long grass to the little gate. 'Now, I've found plain downright pottiness,' he went on cheerfully, 'in thoroughly decent, law-abiding, God-fearing men of probity and self-respect. Once the facade has gone, hey presto! plain downright pottiness. There's a lot goes on at the station after the arrest has been made. I could hardly credit it when I was a young man but I'd believe anything now.'

Ted Baxter stopped with his hand on the latch. Harriet realised he had been talking in a pleasant, regular voice to soothe her. 'No need for you to come any further,' he said in a different tone. 'I won't be long.'

'No, that's quite all right. I ...' Harriet stopped short. 'It must have been just about here that I got some blood on my slippers last night.'

'I had better have a look at that.'

'I'm afraid I washed it off.'

Ted Baxter had pushed in front of her protectively and now his big frame filled the doorway, brushing the creeper on each side. 'Which was the shed, exactly?'

'That one.' What could he mean?

'What's wrong with it?'

Harriet had expected any reaction but this. 'What's *wrong*?' She followed him in and stood staring in disbelief.

Never, during all his time at Bassington Hall, could Goggins's shed have been so clean and tidy. The floor was slightly damp and smelled of antiseptic, with not a scrap of wood shavings or saw-dust left upon it. The shelf, which had hung so menacingly above Fiona's crumpled body, was back again in position, apparently in one piece, neatly stacked with the various small objects for which it was designed. The garden tools, including the mower, immaculate and shining, stood in rows against the wall attached to their handles and ready for use. Day-bed, deck-chairs, slatted table, all were in their places. The transformation was complete. Even the secret hoard of bottles had been retrieved from their hiding-place and now stood grouped together in the middle of the floor for all to see, dusted and unashamed.

'Albert Goggins seems to be a model gardener.' Baxter's voice was sardonic. 'I wonder why he got the sack.'

17

Fiona's poetry

'Now it's just you and the doctor and whoever's done all that,' said Baxter. 'You're the only witnesses.'

'It's nice of you to believe me.'

'Of course I do!' said the Superintendent stoutly. 'There are always fools about who mess everything up, given half a chance. It's the speed that staggers me; we can't have been gone as much as an hour.'

'If only I'd rung you up and asked you to come to me. None of this would have happened then.'

'Of course you wanted to get away from the whole scene. How were you to know Dr Ashford would be so officious? He seems to have done everything possible to hinder the police.'

'And I had the impression that he was rather a slow, relaxed sort of person!'

'Nobody could have done it alone. He must have had some pretty quick and efficient helpers. Well, at least we've got the body. We almost certainly passed it in that ambulance. May I use your telephone? I'll ring the boys at the station and find out what's happening.'

He walked up the garden path with jaunty step and Harriet followed him in, remembering the high voice outside her gate. 'I think,' she said, 'that John Clancy helped him.'

Ted raised his eyebrows, but before he could reply there was a knock at the door.

Harriet opened it to find Walter Rillington in a blue and white apron, Krysta at his heel. 'A horrible business,' he said sombrely. 'I came over to tell you that we've cleared it all up so you needn't feel that she's still – lying there, or anything like that. I looked for you before, but you were out.'

'Oh, Walter, but why did you do it?' The words came out before she had time to censor them. Harriet met the cool grey eyes, which held hers in easy authority.

'We thought it best.' What did he mean, exactly? His pleasant expression gave nothing away beyond a natural gravity. What was he feeling?

She walked down towards the gate with her neighbour, as though she were on her way out. 'I've just seen it,' she said. 'You've made the most – the most amazing job of it. And it was – horrible – thinking of it like that. You've been terribly quick, it was only an hour ago when I ... but Walter – shouldn't the police have seen it as it was – as it was? First?'

'The police? Oh no, I don't think so. I mean, it was an obvious accident wasn't it. James says so and he should know. I suppose

91

strictly speaking we ought to have notified them but that takes time. Don't worry, we'll soon fix them. No, it's Bobby we were thinking of. I mean nobody knew exactly when he was expected home and we naturally couldn't risk him seeing it like that. The police will understand. Do you know, Harriet, that fellow Clancy was a human dynamo. Good in a crisis like so many of these neurotics. I'd always looked on him as an inert sort of beggar but you never know. I'm beginning to feel I've misjudged him.'

'Walter,' said Harriet earnestly. 'Are you absolutely sure that it *was* an accident?'

The grey eyes rounded. 'My dear girl, whatever put that into your head? James will sign the certificate to say so. Don't you worry about anything more. You'd better go and have a rest or something. Nasty shock. There's nothing more to do now. I'll just take Krysta back. Thought she ought to have a little outing.'

A commanding man, thought Harriet as she retraced her steps, and efficient, even remembering the dog.

Baxter was on his feet in her sitting-room. 'Marvellous parade-ground voice that chap's got! So that's that. Body will be in the mortuary by now, labelled DOA. The hospital will be awaiting instructions.'

'The police have been informed, haven't they? By you.'

'Actually not, no,' Ted Baxter's honest square face managed to look almost shifty. 'The doctor's bound to be just about to do so, if he hasn't done so already. They'd only waste time talking to us. He can tell them all that we can and more.' His face brightened. 'The post mortem won't be until tomorrow at the earliest, more likely the next day, tomorrow being Sunday. We might as well go down to the shed again and see if there's *anything* left.'

'But ...'

'I shall depend a lot,' said Baxter, 'on your feminine intuition.'

Harriet felt a surge of detective zeal, proud to be his partner. After all, somebody or other must have told the police by this time, and it was good to see Baxter's retirement melt away. Now he was back in harness, his bulk turned to strength, his efficiency to mastery. She admired him as he surveyed the immaculate shed with practised eye.

'Better not touch anything I suppose, ridiculous though it sounds by this time, but we can use our eyes. Here's something those busybodies missed!'

One of the deck-chairs had a few short black hairs caught in the angle of the wood. 'Must have been moved with the chair when they were cleaning up the floor.'

Harriet looked at it carefully. 'It's very soft,' she said. 'Just like the hairs I saw beside her, where she fell. Fiona did have lovely healthy, soft hair. She really was such a very attractive-looking girl ... oh dear.'

'Look at this,' said Ted Baxter tactfully. He stood in the doorway to let her pass. There was a scattering of earth on each side of the path.

'Might mean nothing,' said Baxter. 'Might mean something. So might those broken flowers. But all that could have been done by those clumsy oafs this morning.' He sighed, 'They haven't left much, have they!'

'Clumsy and oafish maybe, but they certainly were thorough,' said Harriet, as she looked round. 'They've even washed that old garden blanket; it's dripping wet. I call that exceeding the line of duty.'

'We could do with those three in the force,' said Baxter bitterly. 'They're wasted here.' He stared with unseeing eyes through the groups of trees and over the heather and bracken towards the distant winding gleam of the river. 'We shall just have to think, that's all. Think, and remember, and pool our resources.'

Harriet was in the gateway. 'Here's where I stood last night. Perhaps Thomas too. Anyone who passes through must tread on this spot.'

Her companion carefully examined the trodden down grass. 'Yes,' he said. 'Looks like blood. Just discernible traces. They missed that, not surprisingly. Clever of you.'

They went into the garden and stood on the lawn beside the hammock where Fiona had lain with her proofs the day before. Baxter looked up at the house. 'Nice place.'

'Oh look, there's a page of Fiona's poetry in the flower-bed!' Harriet looked at it curiously. 'I must put it inside with the rest of the proofs before it gets lost.'

'What's it like?'

'It's the end of a sonnet.' Harriet read the lines aloud. There was something about them that discomforted her:

> *Behold this plump intruder on our land,*
> *Encumbered by genetic hairsbreadth fault.*
> *Snatched from soft night by cruel devoted hand*

And pitchforked into daylight's harsh assault.
Condemned to everlasting monotone.
A crippled dog that couples with a stone.

'Nasty idea,' said the Superintendent dispassionately, 'Not too keen on the wonky.'

'Of course she was so physically and mentally gifted herself,' Harriet replied. 'She and her husband made a very attractive couple.'

They walked up towards the Hall. 'An A1 Combination, perhaps? The perfect he and she?' His tone was dry. 'I daresay. That is, if he didn't murder her.'

'Bobby isn't the murdering sort, he's much too kind,' said Harriet confidently. She pointed out the empty cottage that formed an L-shape with the house itself. 'Pretty kind letting an unknown family with three young children have that! Imagine them screaming and quarrelling just outside his french windows! Somebody was very anxious for them not to come.'

She told him about the anonymous letter; she was practically word-perfect.

'I'm glad you remembered that,' Ted Baxter shook his head. 'I expect it lies forgotten in Dr Ashford's pocket among the charred pipes and bits of fluff.'

They peered in through the elegant panes. There, beside the telephone was the diary, open where James had consulted it, and Fiona's pile of proofs. Krysta, ears pricked expectantly, looked out.

Harriet opened the glass door a crack and gave her a tentative smile. 'Don't you remember me?' she asked.

But Krysta would not admit to remembering Harriet. She bared her teeth. Harriet hastily slipped the remaining page onto the pile and withdrew her hand, just in time.

'Let us,' said Ted Baxter, 'go back to your house.'

'Well now,' he said, sitting down in Harriet's smallest chintz armchair and causing it to look excessively fragile and feminine. 'Let us imagine the events last night.'

'I suppose someone must have been hiding in the garden, waiting for the last of us to leave.'

'Someone who knew of the household plans and was very well acquainted with the dog.'

94

'Then this person made some sort of commotion in the shed and woke Fiona up. But before going to investigate she took her precious proofs inside.'

'After carelessly allowing a page to blow into the flower-bed,' added Baxter. 'And foolishly leaving the dog shut up in the house before investigating the shed, though carelessness and foolishness were not typical of Mrs Kilmarnock. The intruder could have seen you start off with Mrs Ashford, but you might have only walked a very short way.

Harriet smiled. 'No. Anybody who knew Rosemary Ashford could be reasonably certain that I wouldn't be back in my cottage under half an hour. Rosemary is a great talker. She might also, if she hadn't got a supper party to prepare, have asked me in and I might have agreed, especially as she would undoubtedly have been in the middle of a story.'

Baxter pursed his lips. 'Somebody who *knew*. We keep coming back to that. Somebody who knew the dog, who knew where the toolshed was, how it was kept and what it contained, who knew Mr Kilmarnock would be away for that one night, who knew that Mrs Ashford was a non-stop gasbag. Somebody who knew all about this village.' He took out his notebook. 'Right. Let's start with the three men who destroyed all the evidence. The one who suggested it was Dr Ashford; you heard him do so yourself.'

'Dr Ashford? Oh Ted, what nonsense!'

'Right. Or maybe not right. Colonel Rillington falls into more or less the same category. No motive for either of them. Apparently, though we must always bear in mind a possible sexual slant.' Harriet frowned. 'Difficult, isn't it.' There was a pause. 'I also admit,' continued Ted Baxter with dignity, 'that I'm a retired policeman who hasn't seen more action lately than a few caterpillars crawling in his cabbages. Any remarks I made based on pure supposition will be treated accordingly.' He added reluctantly, 'All the same I suppose I ought eventually to make a few.'

'But Ted, if Dr Ashford, in spite of his medical knowledge, had chosen this particularly messy way of killing Fiona, why did he leave it all night before asking two other men to help him clear it up, perfectly openly, out in the road?'

'I know. What do you make of him?'

'Genial and vague. Easy-going and affectionate. Attractive and approachable. I can't imagine him really *disapproving* of anything much. He's the sort of man who loses things and has a wife who finds them for him. Possibly a little woolly and sentimental. Surely far the most suspicious of those three men was John Clancy. He could have heard the necessary information at Cotty's party and the strangest people can have a gift with dogs.'

'I'll find out about him and let you know. It shouldn't be too difficult. The official channels would be easier there.'

18

One cherry

'If the post mortem findings agree with Dr Ashford and nothing further crops up, what happens then?' asked Harriet.

Ted shrugged his shoulders. 'Some polite questioning by the police, mostly about the state of the shed which they were never allowed to see. At the inquest, unless anybody tells an obvious lie, it'll be Death by Misadventure. The coroner may advise Dr Ashford not to do the police's work for them in any future accident, however accidental it may appear. His explanation about saving the husband's feelings will be received with general sympathy and understanding.'

'And will that be the end of it?'

'Some village gossip afterwards, no doubt, knowing what villages are. Centred on Goggins. Could be violent when drunk, under notice etc. Of course he is not an attractive character.'

'He certainly isn't. I forgot to tell you what happened after my supper with Caroline Metcalfe.'

Ted listened sympathetically. 'Very unpleasant for you, and typical of the man. But in my opinion he wouldn't have the strength for this job. Everybody knows that Goggins is in a bad way. As I say, apart from that sort of thing the Coroner's verdict would be the end of it.'

Harriet was thoughtful. 'Everybody knew, you see, that Fiona wasn't at all a silly sort of person, and would find it difficult to imagine her pulling a heavy object off a high shelf onto her own face. It's the kind of thing that Maureen Clancy might do because she was ignorant, or Andrew Metcalfe because he was clumsy, or Caroline because she was flustered and in a hurry, or James Ashford because he was thinking about something else, or Biddy because she *is* a silly sort of person. But not Fiona.'

'Right. Let's go over it once again, starting with your arrival in the village and anything you may have noticed.'

Dutifully Harriet told him every detail she could remember. 'Oh, and there was a horrid old man who sat at my table at the Copper Kettle and took the most gruesome interest in everybody round here.'

'With a purple nose and bushy black eyebrows?'

Harriet laughed. 'Is there nothing you don't know?'

'Old Dizzy is a small-time local pest and we get the occasional complaint. He's been up twice on drunk and disorderly charges and got off with a caution. I doubt he'll be so lucky next time. He descends here at intervals on a cheap day return and hangs about the tea-rooms in the hopes of annoying his wife.'

'His wife?'

'Or ex-wife. Biddy Dizzard. She runs it. He won't let her off the hook. Enjoys having a finger in unsavoury pies. Come to think of it, he might have heard that Fiona was to be alone last night, from the barmaid at the Dog and Duck. She's the only one can really manage Dizzy, I'd say. She hears all the gossip and tells even more. A motherly soul, all bust and brassy hair. It's roughish, the Dog and Duck. I doubt you'll find any of your neighbours you've met so far in there.'

Baxter's lips twitched slightly.

'What are you thinking of?'

'Nothing important. It just occurred to me that little Mrs Clancy'd look a sight more at home behind the bar at the Dog and Duck than she would behind a stall at that fête of yours! With a good wash and a bit more spirit she'd be quite a decent looking girl.'

'I know what you mean. There's a bold touch under the timidity. Funny mixture. It was the Clancys you were talking of in the train, wasn't it?'

'That's right. The village oddities.'

'And where else but a village would you find the lady of the Manor taking an unknown family practically into her own house?'

'Now, what do we know about them?'

97

'Only that Fiona was going to fix it all up soon and that she had heard about them through a friend of a friend on the other side of the county and, being who she was, immediately did something marvellous about them.'

'Was their name mentioned?'

Harriet frowned. 'No. Yes. Three children under four and two of them twins. *They* had names, funny ones. Olly and Polly, and I remember thinking, you know, about how saintly *Bobby* must be! I heard about them at Cotty's party, and about him going away, but anybody could have known that of course. The daily helps at the Hall, for instance.'

Needless to say, Ted Baxter turned out to know about all three. 'There's a Mrs Meeson and her daughter and her niece. The daughter is walking out with one of our boys and the niece runs the Girl Guides. The Meesons have lived here all their lives.'

The impeccable respectability thus invoked silenced Harriet. Ted sucked on his pipe and waited for more information.

'I can't remember who said what when,' she said at last. 'I know we gossiped at the Hall in a friendly sort of way. Fiona looked just as happy and out-going as usual, not pre-occupied like some people might who had just had an anonymous letter. Not upset at all. I don't think she was a nervous person. Cotty talked about her visit to the Spurs, whoever they may be. She seems an energetic, responsible sort of woman with a lot of irons in the fire; friends, committees, and quite a few hangers-on I imagine. Colonel Rillington was working on the terrace outside. He's a practical man and very good at that sort of thing. He was half listening to our conversation and making silly remarks every now and then, you know, like men do when women are talking to each other. I remember him saying he thought the Spurs were a football team and Maureen Clancy explaining proudly that they were *intellectuals*, and me noticing that she was a great admirer of Cotty's. Maureen Clancy just fits the bill for that. Almost slavish really. Caroline and Cotty chatted away. That was when I learned that Fiona had no help between Friday lunch-time and Monday morning because it was one of the things we talked about, the difficulty of getting help in the country.'

'Yes, I can imagine all that,' Baxter smiled. 'Did anybody speak to Mrs Kilmarnock in the garden?'

'We all did, often, because she didn't mind being interrupted. She wasn't temperamental, as you might expect a poet to be. She

98

gave me the impression of being always on top of things, never at a loss.'

'Do you think Mr Kilmarnock appreciated being married to somebody who was always on top of things and never at a loss?'

'Oh yes, I'm sure he did. He adored her. I mean ...'

'What?'

'I can't remember who said it,' Harriet wrinkled her brows. 'It just surprised me because I'd been given such a glowing picture of Fiona's absolute and total perfection and I'd assumed that adoration from her husband automatically went with the rest of it, like one does.'

'What was the remark, exactly?'

'Probably just some vague mutter while we were working at the Hall. Oh!' Harriet's brow cleared. 'Of course, it must have been that awful old Dizzy in the Copper Kettle, who said the most dreadful things about everybody and of course none of it meant a thing; it just shows how easily malicious stories stick in your mind, and how dangerous it is to listen.'

'Yes indeed. Did you all leave together?'

'No. Colonel Rillington went fairly early, as soon as he had finished nailing up the stalls. He went over and said a few words to Fiona and we all stayed on for quite a long time after that, deciding what should go where and so on. Then Caroline took Cotty off to the station to catch the Rampton train for this Spurs conference thing before going on to Thomas's school to fetch some equipment for the fête. We all thought Fiona must doze off, lying in a hammock in the sun after lunch like that, not a very good working position, and she did, even her. When we cleared up I caught sight of that peculiar letter fluttering down into the dust-bin, with its capital letters, so I read it and then put it in my pocket.

'I started off to say goodbye to Fiona but I could see she was still asleep, so I came back and we debated whether we should wake her up and decided not to. Rosemary Ashford sent Maureen off to wash up the tea-cups and then begged me to walk home with her because Maureen lived in the same direction and she wanted to avoid her. The poor little thing does seem rather dull I must say. She's got a very blank look. So Rosemary and I left together. I walked up to her house, chatted for a few minutes at her gate and then strolled back.'

'Can you remember your conversation?'

Harriet relayed it as well as she could.

'Did you come straight home?'

'Yes. I met Maureen just starting off from the Hall as I went in at my gate. I lit my fire, smoothed out that letter and read it again, and put my supper in the oven.'

'You didn't go out again?'

Harriet shook her head. 'No, it was getting rather cold by that time. I wrote some letters and went to bed.'

Ted thought for a moment and then said, 'There is a third explanation. That shelf might have been weakened and overloaded as a practical joke. Possibly in the hope of causing a serious accident. There are such people about, ranging from graffiti to arson. I don't know why they do it, and neither do they.'

'We had a pointless succession of thefts at school once,' said Harriet, 'and the police found ...'

Baxter interrupted her suddenly, his face aglow. 'The police! Why should they be satisfied with this, any more than we are? Lawn-mowers falling on the faces of people whose bodies are removed before they are informed. Mysterious moppings up. By the time they've seen Dr Ashford, especially if he remembers to hand over that letter, they'll be moving in and asking questions. You mark my words − we'd better get going!'

'Get going with what?'

'Stalking an unsuspecting quarry.'

'But Ted, it probably *is* an accident. After all, we know now why they tidied up the shed. It was only an idea of mine.'

'Right. It's only an idea of mine too, so we won't be doing any harm. We can't help them. We don't know any more than the others and probably less. Now's the time to go, don't you see? While it is only an idea. It may be an accident and it may not be an accident. We shan't be obstructing the course of justice. But if we hang about they'll latch onto us. I know it.'

Harriet felt little surprise at what he was going to ask of her, but an uprush of sadness and anxiety. Some doubtful tittle-tattle about the ailing gardener, unpleasant and near to death, seemed preferable to what lay before them now.

Baxter's eyes, perfectly serious now, were on her face. 'You are clever and observant, neither cynical nor easily shocked. You have courage and perseverance and are the type of person that others confide in. You give forth an aura of trustworthiness and sympathy. People might tell you things they would never admit to a policeman.'

'But what people?' cried Harriet in distress. 'People who knew the dog, knew Bobby was away, knew the cottage couldn't be empty much longer, knew we were all at the Hall, knew about Goggins, knew about the shed, even knew about me walking home with Rosemary! Ted, don't you see, it must have been somebody I know, who heard what I heard. *Somebody who came back*. I should feel such a Judas. How could I ask them questions, and tell you their answers? They've all been so kind to me, so open and friendly. Oh, can't we leave it to the police?'

'I understand, but think of it this way. Whatever they may think the police have nothing more to go on than the opinion of a newcomer with no medical knowledge who disagrees with a highly respectable doctor who has lived here all his life. With the best will in the world they can't act on that! If we wait until the official verdict it may be too late. As long as the accident theory is generally believed the second victim is reasonably safe.'

'The *second* victim?'

'After the p.m. he may not be. If you are right. It is only too easy to murder a second time if you think you've got away with the first. The trouble with a village like this is not that everybody knows everything. That's impossible. It's that anybody might know anything. That's certain. Husbands, wives, the street, the school, the waiting-room, the pub, the shop, the casual remark over the garden hedge. Somewhere, someone may know something that they may in all innocence come out with, and that person will be in danger. We have been given this golden opportunity to gather our private, unprofessional information now, while the trail is hot. We mustn't waste it.'

Harriet nodded unhappily. Yes, truth, however unwelcome, must be their goal. From a verdict of Murder by Person or Persons unknown until the final arrest the whole village would be in a state of mutual suspicion; everybody would suffer. And perhaps, because of what they had not done, there would be no final arrest, only danger and unhappiness. She trusted Ted. He trusted her. Against the evidence of his own eyes he had believed what she had said and drawn similar conclusions to her own. She must do what she could to help, for everybody's sake. Except one.

'We'll make a good pair,' said Ted Baxter encouragingly. 'I'm trained not to show my emotions but I know what I look like, and that's a policeman. You have the advantage of not looking like a policeman but you must guard your expression. You had about five on your face just now, one after the other. You must trust nobody now. *Nobody.*'

'All right,' said Harriet.

Ted Baxter relaxed. 'You were just about certain, weren't you. All along.'

'I – I think so. At least, all the little things that puzzled me seem to add up. James Ashford never noticed how she died because he had tears in his eyes. He just saw the general picture. The body and the shed and the cherry pattern on Fiona's dress. But I had nothing to do but stand and look. I could look at *one* cherry. And oh, Ted, I'm already so afraid that ...'

Ted Baxter held up a warning hand.

She followed his glance. Biddy was hurrying past in her little high-heeled shoes. Seeing Harriet through the window she gave a cheerful wave. Harriet smiled back.

'Never say more than you have to,' advised Ted Baxter. 'That's lesson number one.'

'I do see what you mean,' said Harriet in a lowered voice. 'I just wanted to tell you that I think Fiona was stabbed, with a knife that belongs to Colonel Rillington, and has elephants carved on the handle.'

19

Plan of Action

Baxter whistled.

Harriet said wryly, 'I told you headmistresses develop filing-cabinet minds. I noticed that knife was gone because Colonel Rillington was such a methodical man. The sort of man who had a place for everything and kept everything in it; who assured me that he knew every slug in his garden. He told me about that knife while his back was turned and I vaguely wondered where it was. There was no gap; the knives were in their perfect circle, but none of them had elephants. The conversation changed, but I automatically filed away that missing knife because it didn't *fit*. Until I saw the cherry, and then I wondered if it might be connected. It was so easy, you see, not to notice that, with all the other injuries.'

'I agree with you. It is very useful to keep a private file on what you have noticed about people's personal habits. Especially in this case, as it seems likely that the murderer is somebody you already know; in fact it might be just about *any* one of the people you already know. And you have an objective view.'

Harriet opened her mouth, but Baxter swept on relentlessly. 'I know you're fond of them but you can't be as deeply involved yet as the others are.'

He glanced at his watch. 'If we jot down some brief notes about these people, with your impressions and my knowledge of the general, or police view, it may clarify our minds and give us something useful to go on.'

Baxter was right about them making a good team. In a short time they had produced the following:

	Length of residence	*Local opinion and remarks*	*Alibi?*
JOHN CLANCY	1 year	Generally unpopular and regarded with suspicion. Married to …	No
MAUREEN CLANCY	"	Generally pitied.	No
AUGUSTUS ('DIZZY') DIZZARD	None	Generally unpopular. An intermittent visitor who was here yesterday. Police record. Practical joker and hoaxer. Old-time comedian and general music hall all-rounder. Previous husband of …	No
BRIDGET DIZZARD	10 years	Generally popular and considered goodhearted and friendly. Former actress who runs Copper Kettle tea-rooms with her friend …	No

	Length of residence	*Local opinion and remarks*	*Alibi?*
ANN MARKHAM	"	Generally respected. As above but considerably younger and more reserved. Considered strong-minded, with a good business head.	No
BEATRICE COTMAN	4 years	Generally popular and considered adventurous and sporting. Has small private means but takes temporary jobs (companion, children, literary research, etc).	Yes
CAROLINE METCALFE	12 years	Generally popular. Distinguished ancestry. 'Poor relation' cousin of Fiona Kilmarnock. Widow with 2 sons ...	No
ANDREW METCALFE	12 years	Generally popular and considered shy and hard-working. Educated locally, as is his brother ...	No
THOMAS METCALFE	"	Generally indulgently tolerated. A big, powerful boy physically, but opinions differ as to whether he is a little 'light on top'. Godson to ...	No
JAMES ASHFORD MD	Life	Generally popular as his father was before him. Musical. Relaxed and easy-going to point of idleness but local opinion is that 'he suits us'. 2 sons and 6 grandchildren. Married to ...	Probably
ROSEMARY ASHFORD SRN	38 years	Generally respected. Considered to be the brains of the marriage.	Probably
ALBERT GOGGINS	Life	Generally unpopular but a 'tolerated nuisance' in the village. Wife left him 20 yrs ago and has since died. No children. Is in failing health. Kept on as gardener at Bassington Hall for charity but now under notice for drunkenness and dishonesty.	No

	Length of residence	Local opinion and remarks	Alibi?
COL. WALTER RILLINGTON MC	20 years	Generally liked. Widower with no children. Well-known Army family. Sporting interests. Godfather and one-time CO to ...	No
ROBERT KILMARNOCK JP	15 years	Generally loved and respected. Family lives in Scotland but has local connections. Inherited the property from an uncle and owns much of village. Served with the 22nd SAS in Malaya and the new Korean theatre, 1951–1953 (National Service).	Yes
FIONA KILMARNOCK	8 years	Generally popular and admired. An only child of Scottish landowners (dec'd) and knew her husband from childhood. Murdered 12–18 hours ago (est.)	

'So both Bobby and the Colonel were in the SAS?' asked Harriet.

'Yes. Meaning they were both brave, fit and resourceful, and trained in un-armed combat.'

Harriet again ran her eye over the list. 'Most of them sound very respectable and nice. Oh, if only it could be that wretched old Dizzy!' Goggins was really becoming almost too pathetic to be a satisfactory scapegoat.

'Well, it might be yet,' said Ted Baxter. 'With a few more facts he may become quite a reasonable suspect. Our first job is to check the alibis. As usual there aren't many yet but if they run true to form at least half these people will be vouched for by somebody. So far only two were apparently well away from the neighbourhood during the entire time possible for the crime to be committed. That is, Miss Cotman and Mr Kilmarnock.'

'I was with Rosemary Ashford the whole time until I heard her greeted by her husband.'

'Theoretically she could have jumped into her car, done a neat little murder and driven back while she was supposed to be stacking the dishes in the kitchen; she's a determined lady.'

Harriet demurred. 'She looks very trim but she is in her sixties. I imagine there must have been a tremendous struggle and Fiona was a strong, athletic person.'

'But if she was an unsuspecting one there may have been very little struggle if, as seems possible, the knife was inserted directly into the heart.'

'But the holocaust in the shed.'

'Ah. We can be thinking about that shed as we go our separate ways. It's a mercy about that OAP Outing. It puts a large part of the village on ice for half the day.'

'Our *separate* ways?'

'Could you drive my car?'

'I think so, after the one I've been used to.'

'Good. Then I suggest we do the long-distance jobs now and get well out of the way. They may have been trying to get me at home already. They'll be on to you next.'

'But ought we to leave the neighbourhood entirely if they might want to see us?'

'Why not? We're saving them time and trouble. Even the anonymous letter is in Dr Ashford's hands. They can ask the others. All those three men had been in that same shed and could have seen all, or more, than you did. Lots of others have been to the same gatherings as you and could have heard all, or more, than you did.'

'But ...'

'Come on, don't spoil my fun ... fine, that's settled then. Now, one useful part of *my* old job is that I do know what most of these little societies stand for. Those Spurs of Miss Cotman's, for instance, are the "Society for the Protection of Universal Rights". Sound less sympathetic towards the force than, say, the Country Gentleman's Association might be, so you'd better do that one. I'll take on Dizzy who's a bit of a handful, and call in at Mr Kilmarnock's flat while I'm about it.'

'But why waste time on them? The only two firm alibis we've got?'

'Ah, I said *apparently* firm! No alibi is ever firm without the Baxter seal of approval. Both these will cool quickly. Miss Cotman's weekend presumably ends tomorrow and the members disperse to their different homes, as will Mr Kilmarnock's fellow guests. Memory quickly fades. When was who exactly where? You would be surprised at the distinguished witnesses I've seen swearing on the Bible about the wrong dates and times. It's weary work following a cold trail.'

'But the police! Won't they ...?'

'We're not stopping them,' said Baxter patiently. 'We're helping them. We're not answerable to anybody. *We* don't have to have *facts*!'

Harriet looked into his eager face. 'But Cotty knows me perfectly well. What can I say if I meet her face to face?'

'Plenty of time to concoct some story or other,' he said airily. 'Rampton's at least seventy miles away.'

'That's all very fine but ...'

Ted Baxter cut her short by walking purposefully towards the door. 'I'll nip up to London on the 11.03 if you'll drop me at the station on your way.'

Harriet jumped to her feet. 'Good gracious! We'd better go. Won't that take you all day?'

'I hope not. It shouldn't take long once I get there. I shall aim for the 3.28 back though as you say, it's a bit of a rush. I'll take a taxi back and meet you at your cottage as soon as I can, to compare notes. Leave the car outside my house, put the key under the mat, collect your bike and come back here. Petrol should be all right and there's a map in the car.'

Harriet's head spun. 'But ...'

'Meanwhile, good luck.'

'I shall need it,' grumbled Harriet, seizing her coat from a peg in the hall and allowing herself to be bundled into the car. She looked down at her heather-mixture skirt and jumper. She had a red scarf at her throat. 'Luckily she hasn't seen me in this outfit before but all the same ...'

'You'll manage, you always have,' he dropped into the passenger seat and thrust the key callously into her hand. 'Don't dawdle on the way, will you.'

Harriet, on her mettle, grabbed the wheel.

'Remember,' Baxter looked at her doubtful profile as they bowled along towards Loxley, 'Ashford will tell what he saw in that shed to Mrs Ashford, Clancy to Mrs Clancy, Rillington to anybody he happens to meet, and from there the ripples spread, more and more distorted, more and more damaging.'

Harriet nodded. 'Biddy will be sure she isn't left out and she'll tell Ann Markham and all the customers at the Copper Kettle. Everybody tells everything to Caroline and Cotty and even old Dizzy will probably pick up a few fag ends at the Dog and Duck if he's still around. Both schools will be agog ...'

Baxter said, 'In fact there is only one person who will probably never be told exactly what that shed looked like.'

'You mean ...?'

'Yes, Mr Kilmarnock himself. Nobody will tell him and he probably won't ask. After all, as we know to our cost, the great cover-up has already begun. Broadly speaking, "Fiona is dead" is probably about all he will be told until the facts are made public and he is unlikely to ever know the details. A bereaved man is in a state of shock and unlikely to enquire much further.'

Harriet turned into the station with a dashing flick of the wrist, and Baxter was out of the car. Harriet marvelled again at the lightness and quick reactions of so big a man. He put his head in at the window. 'Well done,' he said warmly. 'Ten minutes to spare. Don't forget, if anybody asks you (not that they will if I know human nature, probably too interested in their own affairs), you came because of a personal column advert. There's bound to have been one. Cheerio!'

*   *

Rosemary Ashford was hovering by her front gate when Caroline walked past with Thomas.

'Can I look in your garden for Pusskin?' he asked at once.

'Yes of course, dear,' Rosemary looked absent. There was a pucker of anxiety on her usually smooth brow. She looked at her watch. 'I'll give your mother a cup of coffee.'

Thomas glanced at her neat and brightly polished shoes. No help from her. He preferred Harriet, who was always prepared to wade about in the long grass. And if they were going to have elevenses what about him? He wouldn't have minded a biscuit or something like that. Oh well ... 'Run along, dear,' said Rosemary.

Rather disconsolately Thomas did so, at his usual slow walk. Where, oh where, could Pusskin have got to? Surely not this open, formal garden?

The two women sat in the sunny, shining kitchen, sipping instantly produced and excellent coffee out of dainty rosebud cups. 'You look worried,' said Caroline. 'Can I help?'

'It's nothing really. At least, I wouldn't dream of saying so to anybody but you, but I'm beginning to be a tiny bit anxious about James. Where he's got to I mean. Just vanished off the face of the earth.'

'Well, he can't be far away,' said Caroline comfortably. 'We noticed his car just now, parked on the green. Thomas pointed it out. He always knows such things.'

'I wonder if he came across an accident and went off to hospital with the victim; he does that sometimes and there was nothing very urgent on his list.'

'Ah, that'll be it. We saw an ambulance.' With relief Caroline remembered that Thomas was with her and Andrew safely at home sighing over his physics. 'I do hope nobody's badly hurt. There's such a lot of Melchester traffic coming through the village now.'

'You've taken a weight off my mind,' Rosemary sounded more cheerful. 'Oh, hallo, Thomas, no luck? Of course I could have rung the Cottage Hospital to find out but somebody might have told him and doctors do hate fussy wives don't they. It's having to deal with other people's fussy wives all day I suppose. It would be more than my life's worth to express concern over an earthquake. If he's not back in time I'll just have to get that scatty girl from next door to mind the 'phone. Can't let the OAPs down.'

'Don't you dare! It's bad enough losing Cotty. I can't do the whole outing alone.'

'Don't worry, I won't. Talking about scatty girls, Maureen rang up just now asking me to leave a message for the milkman. He calls on us first. She sounded so breathless and peculiar. All squeaky.'

'She is rather excitable, isn't she; funny little thing. Gosh! I must get back and organise lunch for the boys.'

'Yes, but she was even more than *usually* breathless and so on, if you know what I mean. So I said, "Is anything the matter, dear, you sound upset? *Why* don't you want any milk?" and she said, listen to this, Caroline, "Oh, haven't you heard?" and I said no, what was it, and she said "Oh, in that case I'd better not tell you, he'd half kill me if I did!" I ask you!'

'Whatever could she have meant?'

'That's just what I said to myself. And then I thought, oh well, really it might be anything. She's highly romantic, pig-headed and pretty well bonkers.'

'What a combination!'

'All the same ...'

'She *might* of meant something about Fiona ...' began Thomas slowly.

'Fiona? Why should she, dear?'

'Well ...'

'I can't think why she should have meant anything about Fiona, dear.'

'Come along, Thomas, we *must* go. We shall have to run. Why is it always later than I thought! See you at the bus, Rosemary.'

Mother and son set off down the road. Caroline tried to think of something hopeful to say about Pusskin, and failed. On an impulse she put an arm round the drooping young shoulders beside her, and for once Thomas allowed it to remain.

'Funny the impression people give about their husbands sometimes,' said Caroline dreamily. 'I can't imagine James minding at all if his wife fussed him, can you? He's such a mild sort of man.'

Thomas pursed his lips. 'She may of wanted him to seem a bit wilder than he is, sort of like a mad bull,' he said wisely. 'What I can't understand is why he ever left the house in the first place. He never has before. Someone *must've* took him.'

20

The Spurs

It was not until Harriet was happily speeding along the motorway in Ted Baxter's little Simca that she gave serious thought to her plan of action as far as the Spurs were concerned. Events had moved so fast that there had simply not been time. Never mind, thought Harriet optimistically, she would just have to be as inconspicuous as possible and keep out of Cotty's way. Not too difficult, she hoped, when you remembered that she would be looking out for Cotty, whereas Cotty would not be looking out for her.

Also the fact that she *was* rather happy and excited obtruded itself unwillingly into her consciousness. It was not every day that Harriet helped to catch a murderer. All the same, not a very estimable emotion considering that the quarry might well be somebody who had been civil to her and very likely downright kind.

Unless of course it turned out to be one of those three useful cleaning ladies that she had never met, who were presumably trusted by their mistress, knew the dog, could arrive, leave, or hide in the garden of Bassington Hall any time they chose, and do whatever they wanted in the shed. Such good conscience savers, those cleaning ladies were, so conveniently nameless and faceless.

Those cleaning ladies: one walking out with a policeman, one a respected matron, and one running the Girl Guides. Harriet drove on through the flaming autumn landscape. She frowned.

She considered the people she had met so far. She frowned again. Then she gave her mind to the task ahead.

As she checked up on Cotty's alibi she must necessarily mention Cotty's name and be prepared for these remarks, however unobtrusive, to find their way back to Cotty. To begin with why, exactly, was she, Harriet, travelling seventy miles, today, to join this conference?

It was not reasonable, Harriet decided after due consideration, for Harriet Charles to behave in this way. If she had been interested in the Spurs she would have said so before (and Cotty had previously talked about the Spurs and Harriet had not been especially interested in them), and then Cotty might possibly have asked her to come too and they would naturally have gone down together. To arrive now, one day late and uninvited, was eccentric.

And, reasoned Harriet, she could not afford to be considered eccentric, either with the Spurs or in the village. Eccentrics attract attention, and she did not wish to attract attention.

No, somebody quite different must visit the Spurs today.

About five miles from the village where the conference was being held Harriet turned off into a country lane and drew up on the verge, beside a wood. Here she peered creatively into the car mirror at the friendly, English-looking face peering creatively back. When Harriet plucked away the spectacles it blurred, but the blue eyes sprang into prominence, considerably enlarged.

Harriet was pleased with her new image. Not only had her eyes got bigger with the removal of the spectacles but the lines on her face had miraculously vanished as well. She felt younger and prettier.

Her grey hair was swept back in a simple style that had varied little in twenty years. Now she combed it forward so that it hung wispily into the new big eyes. A few snips from the First Aid box scissors transformed it into a long, artistic fringe. She took the silk scarf from her neck and twisted it round her head in a way that was vaguely reminiscent of a Rumanian gypsy. But a Rumanian gypsy who still retained an authoritive, highly educated expression. Harriet now poked her head forward, peeped from under the fringe, smiled slightly, spoke a few words whilst she smiled, blinked foolishly, diffidently, humbly, eagerly. Suddenly she had it.

A nice little woman, she decided, and not one to be noticed.

She searched the tidy car in vain for further props. It really was a pity, thought Harriet, that she had not given thought to the need for a disguise before she left home. The rush to the station to catch Ted Baxter's train, the learning of the controls in the unfamiliar car, the general air of urgency and hurry had left room in her mind for nothing else.

Still, all things considered, not bad. Harriet left her red coat, folded lining outwards, in the back of the car, and undid the top button of her skirt, tugging it, against all her instincts, downwards on the right hand side. The inconspicuous skirt and jumper were a lucky chance, if she imagined the Spurs correctly, as were the sensible shoes and well-worn handbag.

The little car started up again down the country road, Joan Pliny now at the wheel. Both names were, Harriet considered, easily forgotten in their different ways. She practised her new role in the village shop as she asked where the conference house was. 'New to them, are you?' the post-mistress asked kindly. 'They come here regular every year.' She eyed her shrewdly and Harriet goggled simply, bluely, back at her. The woman nodded. 'Aye, you'll enjoy yourself I'm sure.'

Success, thought Harriet triumphantly, before I've begun!

Half a dozen weekenders stood by the impressive stone gateway. They waved their arms, engrossed in each other, deep in discussion. Harriet drove slowly past them, gratified to note that of the three women two wore tweed skirts, one rather too long and one distinctly short. So far so good, and they were certainly unlikely to notice much about her.

In a few hundred yards Harriet turned off up a rutted track where the undergrowth was thickest, locked up the car and, stooping a little, returned on foot. The drive was deserted. Evidently most of the Spurs were occupied indoors, and indeed as she neared the old grey house she could hear recorded folk music, turned up to full volume, and the rhythmic stamp of many feet.

The front door, once splendid and now shabby, opened at her touch and she found herself standing in a large empty hall, surrounded by doors. A long table was laden with the pamphlets of affiliated societies, and above it a notice board gave news in bold letters of TODAY'S ACTIVITIES, but the list below, typed by a faulty machine on worn ribbon, was a challenge for Joan Pliny.

She had just decided that one of them said 'Sunday ramble' and another 'Quiet time' when an elderly man appeared through one of the doors and asked her where the hell Les was. Harriet poked, smiled and replied in all honesty that she hadn't seen him that morning.

'Bloody nuisance, that man,' said the newcomer irritably. 'Never in the proper place, but then who else would do the job? Too busy having a good time. Jawing away. Jabber jabber jabber, don't know what they find to talk about.' He glared accusingly at Harriet. 'You haven't any name-tags, have you? We've run out. Or drawing-pins? Or glue? Oh well, I'll have to do it all myself as per usual. Always the muggins.'

The idea of always being the muggins seemed to cheer him slightly and he looked Harriet full in the face for the first time. 'Forgotten your name ... Oh, Joan, of course. Well, tell him I've gone down to the village on Shanks's pony will you? Oh, and you might tell Babs that I've put Norman before her tonight because he's down for the tea, not that he'll do it.'

Apologetically, Harriet bent her head and admitted that she hadn't seen Babs either. 'Not to worry,' said the elderly man philosophically. 'She'll take offence one way or the other anyway. That's the female of the species for you, say I, but somebody else can deal with that lady this time. I've had my whack. Not after Loughborough!'

'Oh, Loughborough.'

'Oh well, no rest for the weary.' He sounded quite agreeable now. 'But she is *not* an angel of sweetness and light.'

Three women came in through another door, looking, she was glad to see, like smaller versions of herself. He turned to them. 'Can't see the funny side of things, that's her trouble.'

'She's not easy,' ventured J. Pliny, 'Babs isn't.'

'You can say that again.'

'I remember ...' began a little spindly one who was evidently not to be listened to.

113

'Babs is a typical neurotic. You've only got to read Kraft-Eb ...'

Harriet took a risk. None of the Spurs so far had given her the impression of material success. 'Of course, she's had a hard life.'

'*And* trades on it,' snapped one of the women at once.

This remark produced general murmurs of agreement as the scratchy record in the next room reached its final chord. A number of hot, plimsolled and mainly female Spurs trooped out into the hall and joined enthusiastically in the conversation. Joan Pliny watched them through narrowed eyes, poised for flight should one of them be Cotty. Meanwhile she stood her ground, seemingly accepted by this chatty, friendly, informal sort of society, and remarked upon by none.

'Of course Cotty can deal with her,' announced a tall thin woman with a drooping skirt.

Harriet gave her own a surreptitious tug and said casually, 'Oh, Cotty can deal with anything.'

'She's marvellous.'

'Grand.'

'Wonderful.'

'Mind you, she can be awkward at times,' said one infidel, a small weasley woman with a wig. 'She made ever such a fuss about her room when she arrived; complained about the draught.'

'Well, there was. I'm sharing with her. There is a draught in that room. I can feel it in my neck. My neck always ...'

'At least you've got her. Think of me,' complained the weasley woman bitterly. 'I'm with Babs and she never stops smoking and going on about Herman ...'

Harriet neatly deflected her. 'Cotty's usually so good-natured,' she insisted.

'Yes indeed,' said one of her loyal friends, 'I always say things get going when Cotty arrives. It was really nice when she turned up after all. She's a scream; I always look forward to her letters.'

'Funny, isn't it, how we can perk up! I fell asleep during 'Our Heritage'. Decided to go to bed and then I thought oh well, I'll look in at the dance. I ended up at the moonlight bathe, chirpy as anything.'

'Well, who's interested in National Trust Gardens or whatever, when you live in a bedsitter like me.'

'Exactly. I couldn't care less, so I finished those oranges I started in Doug's painting session, and then I ...'

'It was much livelier this morning. "Is Monogamy Outdated?" Trust old Cotty to ask him if he carried his theories into his own married life! I couldn't have! Everybody turned to look at her!'

'Oh you,' said one of the newcomers, 'You couldn't say boo to a mouse, Doris. You never open your mouth, Cotty'll say anything. Always has done, and I've known her for twenty years.'

'She wasn't too good at breakfast.'

'Not like our Cotty.'

'I felt just the same. It was that mince last night,' said a pale, anxious looking lady with fuzzy white hair. 'It was off. I said so at the time. It's off, I said.'

'Looked funny too. Greyish. Too much onion I thought without my glasses, but I think it was fungus growing on it.'

'I mean it isn't as if we aren't paying for it. I took one of my pills. Tranquillisers really but they seem to do for everything. She said she was just the same.'

'And she's as strong as a horse, but of course I'm very sensitive. Really nasty, I said so at the ...'

'She was quite snappy with Roma.'

'It was that mince hitting us all.'

'No it wasn't,' interjected a little old man. 'She was just the same at the dance. Aggressive. Changing that record in the middle without a by your leave. I told her straight; I'm in charge of those, I said.'

'It was cracked.'

'No it wasn't,' he repeated doggedly. 'It was old-fashioned. Old-fashioned my foot. It was no more old-fashioned than it always has been, or any of our other records come to that. We've always had the same records. She's never complained before.'

'Never mind, we all have our off days,' said the mince lady peaceably. 'And she did get the women asking the men.'

'We're so short of men.'

'That's because the women have the ideals, dear. I said so from the beginning.'

'That's rich, Mavis, coming from you.'

'Just you listen to me, Norman Parkin ...'

Harriet watched and listened as the Spurs chatted and squabbled together with the ease of long acquaintance. Who were they, these friends of Cotty's, who combined a genuine tolerance with a certain engaging naivety and a simple ruthlessness as they interrupted each other and lit up cigarettes for themselves alone?

Many of the women were fellow teachers, Harriet felt sure. The men had a certain pervasive foreignness. ...

It was not long before Cotty was mentioned again.

'Is she running the party tonight?'

'Bound to be. Does she want any of us to sing, do you know?'

A man with a wedge-shaped head shook it firmly. It was poetry she wanted tonight.

'We don't want all poetry, not all the time,' said the musician firmly. 'It's supposed to be a party, with something for everyone. I'll talk to her. After all, she is one of my oldest friends.'

'I think I saw her in the garden with that African girl, right down by the greenhouses.'

'Never mind, I'll have a word with her at lunch.'

As the last word was spoken a gong rang out from the kitchen regions and all was thrown into disorder as the Spurs in the hall were galvanised into action, and others hurried in from all directions. Harriet, willy-nilly, was swept along the passage towards the dining-room and caught a brief glimpse of long tables, with plastic plates on them and jugs of water. Seizing her luck while it held, she melted unobtrusively from the throng and passed alone through the front door, confident in the certainty that she was already forgotten.

That was what it was all like, realised Harriet, as she straightened up with some relief and set off down the deserted drive with her old swinging stride, pursued by clatters and shouts and the scraping back of sixty chairs. School. That was why she had felt so much at home there. Cheerful, lively, ravenously hungry, uninhibited old school!

A school with prefects, teachers, work and play and a well-established pecking order. A school to grow old in, where nobody ever sang their last hymn.

She parked Ted's car in the same leafy lay-by she had used before, removed the scarf, combed back the fringe as well as she could and replaced the spectacles. The golden world about her clicked sharply into focus. She glanced at her watch, made a few notes while the memory was fresh, took a deep breath and started off at a spanking pace for home.

The lemon drops from the glove box provided an inadequate lunch.

21

About Robert Kilmarnock, JP (40)

Ted Baxter stood on the mat outside a door marked 'Caretaker' and pressed the bell. He had decided to make almost a clean breast of it with no mystery about himself, apart from not actually mentioning that he had retired from the force. He preferred it this way.

A quick, experienced glance at the respectable and respectful-looking elderly man who opened the door confirmed him in this decision. George Bateman asked him in with courtesy, gave him the particulars he asked for and sat down opposite him at a small table in a spotless basement flat, with his fingertips together and a grave and sympathetic scrutiny, looking rather like a Harley Street doctor. Baxter wrote in his notebook: 'George Bateman, 72, 11 years Caretaker at 3 St James's Court, SW1.'

He then told him in a few words of Fiona Kilmarnock's death, and said he was making the enquiries necessary after an accident of this kind.

'I'm sorry to hear that, sir, sorrier than I can say.' The polite expression wavered, the mouth trembled. The caretaker appeared genuinely shocked and distressed as he spoke of the grief the family would suffer, of her many friends and good works, qualities and gifts. 'I can hardly believe it. She was – so alive, Mrs Kilmarnock was, if you take my meaning, sir, so gay, so happy, so young.'

'Oh indeed, everybody says that.'

'That's right, everybody would.' The old man's voice was eager. 'It's the first thing you thought of with Mrs Kilmarnock you see, sir. He was a bit older than her but they just seemed like a couple of children to me. I'd see them out of my window there, getting into the car to start out for the evening, laughing and talking nineteen to the dozen like as if they'd just met. He always kept his car in that little yard there. There's just room for one.'

'They were happy, then. Though I daresay they had their differences, like most married couples.'

'Not that I ever heard of, sir. Who wouldn't be happy with Mr

117

Bobby? It's always Mr Bobby to me because I knew him as a boy. Mind you, he could be mischievous!' Mr Bateman smiled. 'He had his fun. Liked the odd practical joke, but never overstepped the mark if you get my meaning. Considerate.'

Ted Baxter nodded. 'So you knew him as a boy.'

'Oh yes, sir. I was butler to his grandfather up in Scotland. Very fond of his grandson he was, and we would all look forward to young Master Bobby's visits in the holidays I can tell you. The old place could do with a bit of brightening up, we'd say. A bit of warming up too. And softening up. Miles of old stone corridors it had.' Mr Bateman looked down at his carpet slippers. 'It was them as gave me the trouble with my feet and it was Mr Bobby found me this job here. Remembers everybody. When they say God knows every sparrow that's just like Mr Bobby, I says to myself. Snug little flat it is as you can see, and right in the centre of things, and a very nice class of gentleman to see to.'

'I'm sure you look after them very well.'

'It's kind of you to say so, sir, but it's not a hard job. I'm very lucky.'

'What time did Mr Kilmarnock arrive yesterday?'

'Well sir, I always know when Mr Bobby's in London because he puts his car as I said, just outside my window. I let him into that little secret − it's only a matter of unhooking a bit of chain really to make room for it but nobody else has cottoned on to it. It looks more private than it really is. Of course it takes the light off my room when there's a car there, but I'm always pleased when I see it because then I know Mr Bobby's back again. It usually stays put. As he says, it's not worth taking it out and finding a place to park. It's very convenient for his clubs and the shops here, and quite a lot of his friends live within walking distance. And he's a very energetic gentleman, Mr Kilmarnock. Very fit.'

'So it was here yesterday afternoon?'

'No, sir. He wasn't here at six, because I went in to see if there was anything wanted doing and there were a few circulars and so on still lying on the mat inside the door and the cushions all plumped up like they are when he's not here. Mr Bobby's not a messy man like some of them here, but you can tell when he's been in. He always opens the window, for instance, first thing, and he usually sits in his big chair and has a whisky after the long drive from his country house. I could tell he hadn't been in.'

'I wonder when he did arrive.'

'I didn't notice him come in at all, but he must have because his car was there early this morning, when I took in the milk. It must have been after 9.30 because I went to put the cat out and his car wasn't there then. Out she goes, at 9.30 on the dot, every day. I turn in early nowadays and I daresay I wouldn't have heard him, I'm a bit hard of hearing.'

'We haven't been able to get hold of him since, you see, to tell him of the tragedy.'

'Must be on the road, on his way home, sir. He knocked on my door about ten this morning just to say "Hullo" as usual. Ah, I remember now, he'd some flowers in his hand, said he was just off to see Mrs Mackenzie and had I any message for her. That would have delayed him of course. She does appreciate it. She was the cook who was there in my time and you know how children always love the cook. She had a stroke and lives in a nursing home somewhere round Muswell Hill I believe, sir. So I sent my regards to her. It's always a pleasure to see him; always got a cheery word and a smile.'

'So he was just the same as usual.'

'I didn't say that, sir.'

Baxter waited a moment and then prompted gently, 'In what way was he different this morning?'

'It's not what he said so much as how he looked. Not quite the usual bounce if you see what I mean, sir. Not quite with us. He didn't look quite himself. A bit down, like as if he was worried about something, and then he mentioned some reunion dinner in Pall Mall and I thought oh well, that's it.'

But the caretaker's expression was faintly puzzled.

Baxter said casually, 'Taking the car?'

'He must have done. I expect he left it a bit late, sir. He usually leaves it here when he's celebrating.'

'Doesn't do for a magistrate to be caught on the breathalyser!' suggested Baxter with a smile.

'No indeed sir. Some of them do, and worse than that. You read about them in the papers but that isn't Mr Bobby's way. He's one of the old school, not a parking ticket has he had. No, you won't see Mr Bobby in the papers, that's one thing you can be sure of.'

'But his manner to you was just the same?'

The old man again hesitated, and then said with dignity, 'I've told you, Inspector, he was always everything that he should be. Everything he should be, remember that. If it's an accident you are investigating I don't really understand why – why you should be asking me all these things. All I can say is that he is a very nice gentleman and I'd stake my life on that.'

'Thank you very much, Mr Bateman. I'm afraid we always have to do routine checking up after an accident. Just as a matter of form.'

'I hope I – I haven't said anything wrong.'

'On the contrary. You've shown me that Mr Kilmarnock has loyal friends. You have been most helpful.'

Ted Baxter then made a short telephone call.

'Did Mr Kilmarnock leave his dispatch case in the club last night by any chance?'

'I don't think Mr Kilmarnock was in the club last night, sir.'

'Oh, really? I must have made a mistake. Perhaps I've got the wrong club,' (for a moment Ted Baxter thought he might have done), 'I thought he was attending a reunion dinner.'

But the porter assured him that there had been a reunion dinner, with a number of Mr Kilmarnock's friends, but Mr Kilmarnock had rung up on Friday morning to say that he would not be able to make it after all.

'Thank you. If he never came he couldn't have left his dispatch case then! I'll try somewhere else.'

'Just a minute, sir.'

In the ensuing pause Ted Baxter leaned against the wall of the telephone booth and studied his notes.

'Are you there, sir? I've just checked with the diningroom staff and Mr Kilmarnock did drop in late last night to see his friends. I rather think he was in time for the speeches, but I wasn't on duty myself at the time. I'm afraid we can't see his dispatch case though. Is there any message?'

'No thank you. I think I know where it must be. I'm sorry to have bothered you.'

22

Augustus ('Dizzy') Dizzard (80)

Out in the street again, Ted Baxter hurried into St James's Street and hailed a taxi, which then had some difficulty locating a dingy backwater near Marloes Road. The houses presented a marked contrast to that which he had just left, though once again he found himself shaking hands with an old man who was perfectly willing to be interviewed.

In fact this time Baxter had no chance to state his business before being overwhelmed with an enthusiastic welcome in the dark and crowded little hall. 'Delighted! Delighted!' Dizzy Dizzard put his face unnervingly close to Baxter's, baring some yellow teeth of differing lengths. 'But a certain degree of Hush is required. For some reason best known to herself the old bitch here frowns on visitors. God knows why unless it's because she frowns on everything on this earth. Landladies,' he wheezed portentously, as he led the way up a narrow and odiferous stairway, carpeted in threadbare crimson and purple and surmounted by the motheaten heads of stags, 'are the bane of my life. Always have been. Every last worrisome whaleboned one of 'em. Fusspots, naggers, nosey-parkers, witches, thieves, pests, blights and bitches. You name it and I'll show you one I've had. Excuse the smell of cabbage; landlady's loathsome lunch. Cabbage this afternoon; landlady's dismal dinner. Doubtless she has it again in the small hours; landlady's nauseous night-time snack.'

All this eloquence, together with the steep climb, induced a fit of coughing which shot the cigarette end from Dizzy's lips. It disappeared into the gloom of a half-landing and the old man stooped in search. 'Waste not, want not,' he explained hoarsely.

Baxter nimbly retrieved the butt and Dizzy inserted it into a convenient gap. 'Ta muchly! We used to say that sort of thing in the old days, you know. Not now. There's a whole new line in patter now. Not that I hold with it. Give me the old days, you know, naughty but nice. We had some fun I can tell you. Some good times.'

Dizzy came to a halt and drew some wheezing breaths preparatory to embarking on the last flight of stairs, now covered in cracked linoleum. Ted Baxter was able to speak for the first time.

'I'm sorry to have brought you down all this way. It's very good of you to see me.'

'It's a pleasure. We thespians can always do with a bit of publicity and frankly, it's not untimely. Oh, I can tell you a few things. Make your hair stand on end. You can't get to the top honestly now. There's a fellow called ...'

'Just a minute,' said Baxter, enlightened, 'I'm not a journalist. I wondered if perhaps you could help us on a police matter.'

Baxter's professional eye discerned that Dizzy's expression did grow a shade less welcoming and a shade more wary, but it was a good performance.

'Something to do with the wife, is it? She lies in her teeth.' He leaned against an attic door and gave it a practised heave with his shoulder. It burst open onto meanness and squalor. 'You can see she doesn't exactly keep me in luxury.'

'Aren't you divorced?'

Dizzy took no notice. 'I hear she's doing well. The ingratitude of women never ceases to amaze me.'

He gazed round pathetically as though to an unseen audience and was confronted by the state of his room. 'Of course if I'd had a bit of notice I could have tidied up for you. To be quite honest I was going to give it a good do out this very day. As it happens, you've caught me on the hop.'

He bent over the narrow bed and gave the sheets and blankets, all of a uniform grey colour, a disheartened tweak with one hand and then pulled the Indian counterpane roughly over the top. As he did so his foot touched the pot beneath. 'Ting ting the welkins ring,' he observed. He indicated a wooden stool. 'There you are. Take a pew. I'll have the chair. I understand it. I cough at it and it creaks at me.'

He lowered himself gingerly into the basket chair and leaned back against the pile of clothes draped over the back, breathing heavily. 'Ciggy? Cuppa?'

'No thank you,' said Baxter. A used tea-cup already stood on the hexagonal bamboo table. There was also a packet of Player's No 6, a glass of water with fluff on the top and a very large pile of very small stubs in a tobacco tin lid. On the floor was a worn

122

brown mat and a very old towel which lay crumpled under the stained wash-basin. 'Cold and cold,' explained Dizzy, following his eyes. 'But a godsend, saves two flights. I've got that,' he indicated an encrusted Baby Belling, 'to make my meals. Not much is it.' His voice turned plummy, 'Of course I'm invited out a lot. I've got my friends.'

Dizzy shakily lit another cigarette from the half-inch he had left of the first. 'I know who are, and who aren't, and that's more than some do. And now, Inspector, what can I do you for?'

'I would be much obliged if I might ask you a few questions in connection with the death of Mrs Kilmarnock, of Bassington Green. It's purely a matter of routine but I understand you were visiting the neighbourhood at the time and as an observant man you might be able to help us.'

Baxter said this in his best official manner, looking the old man expressionlessly in the eye.

Mr Dizzard's eyebrows shot up and a jaundiced rim appeared all round each bleary eye. Tickled pink, thought Baxter.

'Kicked the bucket, eh? Fiona Kilmarnock! That's a turn-up for the books. Fancy that. Well, she was asking for it but if you think there's any connection there with Yours Truly you can think again, old son, because I *happen* to have had nothing whatever to do with it.'

'With what?'

'Her murder.'

'What makes you think it was murder? I didn't say so.'

The jubilant expression did not change. 'Well, wasn't it? Must be my dramatic streak. My stage experience. My lifetime of observing my fellow men. Call it what you will.' Dizzy flung out an arm and cocked his head.

'It's generally believed to be an accident, Mr Dizzard. As far as I know there is no evidence to the contrary, but every accident has to be investigated.'

'What happened to her then?'

'Some heavy equipment fell on her while she was reaching up to a high shelf in a shed, or summer-house.'

Dizzy was unrepentant. 'Heavy equipment my foot. Blunt instrument more like.'

'What reason have you for saying that, Mr Dizzard?'

'Ah! That'd be telling, wouldn't it. But that summer-house has a ve-ery funny reputation. A very very funny reputation indeed.'

Dizzy held Baxter's eye for a moment and then added, 'Apart from which, she'd never do a damnfool thing like that. Not in a month of Sundays. Not a girl like her.'

This fellow's no fool, thought Baxter. Aloud he said, 'Do you know which summer-house I mean?'

'Of course I do. But don't ask me about it, laddie. I don't live there. I may hear things but I don't live there. I should ask the husband if I were you, or some of those poor relations, or the people she snubbed or sniffed at or saved from their own worse selves, or what have you. Don't come trailing up to London wasting your time and our money asking *me*.'

'Perhaps you would be good enough to tell me how you spent yesterday afternoon.'

'Oh, that's it is it? Certainly I will; I've got nothing to hide. I had lunch at the Copper Kettle. My wife saw me there and so did Ann Markham. I sat at a table with the woman who's just come to live at Rose Cottage. Harriet Charles her name is. Didn't half give her a turn when she found out I knew it either!'

'And then?'

'Then I took a bus into Loxley.'

'It's market day there on Fridays isn't it?'

'That's right. Very crowded, it was.'

'What did you buy there?'

'Not a sausage. To be perfectly frank I was a bit short of funds.'

'But you visited the market.'

'I did. To the best of my knowledge we're still allowed to. As yet. I grant you there soon will be shopkeepers leaping out of their shops, forcing us at knife-point to buy what we don't want' (Dizzy suited the actions to the words, with a hideous grimace), 'but just at the moment, by some no doubt temporary oversight, some loophole in the law, they do let us walk about on our own two feet absorbing the bloody atmosphere of some bloody market without some bloody policeman breathing down our necks, until such time as we take a bus back to Bassington Green and walk along the road to our wives' bloody little pink cottages. It's not a capital offence.'

He ran out of breath, allowing Baxter to continue impassively, 'But you aren't short of funds now.'

'Why shouldn't I be? I never said that!'

'What did you do in Loxley if you didn't buy anything?'

'Good grief, man, is this an inquisition or what!' Mr Dizzard gave a spirited attempt at righteous indignation. 'I just wandered about as I said. Took a bus back. Waited for Biddy at home.'

'What time was this?'

'About five I suppose.'

'So you spent several hours in Loxley. You didn't call in at the Hall on the way back? I was thinking your wife might have been there, bringing some cakes, for instance, for the fête on her way home.'

'I did not.'

'Any particular reason?'

'Very upstage, the Kilmarnocks were. I don't believe in pushing my face in where I'm not wanted.'

'Don't you? Now that's a very interesting viewpoint about the Kilmarnocks. It isn't the impression I've been given so far.'

'You shouldn't believe all you hear, Inspector.'

'Perhaps not. Did you spend the evening with your wife and Miss Markham?'

'I stayed with them for a short time, but I finally decided to have my evening meal at the Dog and Duck, where I have a Friend,' announced Mr Dizzard with dignity.

'Is that the barmaid?'

'It is.'

'I imagine a girl like that knows all the local people and can tell you the village news.'

'I imagine she could. Providing I was so interested as to ask her.'

'Quite so. In fact, not to put too fine a point on it, she has a considerable reputation as a scandalmonger.'

'I am not interested in scandal.'

'Very commendable. And when you had finished your meal?'

'I took the last bus into Loxley and the last train to London, leaving at 8.40. The man at the ticket office will doubtless remember me as I was the only person on the platform at that time. And then beddy-bye for me, laddie.'

'Does your former wife reimburse your expenses on these trips?'

'She gave me a small sum. It doesn't go far these days; nobody wants you when you're old.'

'So you work the bus queues.'

'I don't know what you're getting at Inspector, if that's what you are though I'm beginning to doubt it. I've already told you

125

the place was crowded. I naturally had to wait a while for the bus.'

'Rather longer than was necessary, perhaps. Useful things, bus queues, especially when you're a long way from home. People are apt to be quite a considerable distance away before they discover they are rather short of funds themselves.'

'That's a bloody lie.'

'I'm not accusing you of anything, Mr Dizzard,' said Baxter mildly, 'merely making an observation, like juggling and conjuring being a useful training for light fingers. An observation. As you say, it's a free country.'

Unexpectedly Mr Dizzard laughed. 'That's a good one! If ever I heard pure guess-work that takes the cake! I should save your breath, Inspector, if I was you, because you can't pin anything on me. I wasn't born yesterday you know.'

'No.' Baxter got up. 'Well, thank you for answering my questions. I don't think I need trouble you any further, but it's a pity, isn't it, when you think about it. If you think about it.'

The old man did not deign to reply to this. He struggled to his feet and extended a mauve and trembling hand. 'I'm a gentleman, Inspector. They can't take that away from me.'

'They can, but I'm not going to. All the same, Dizzy, if I might give you a friendly word of warning; watch it.'

Dizzy, as always, had the last word. He pulled down his long upper lip and shut one eye. 'Hinspector!' he said roguishly, 'Hi reely carn't himagine what you can be a-thinkin' of.'

The cabbagy staircase seemed like a breath of Spring. Ted Baxter took a deep breath as he heard the door bang behind him.

23

Mrs Annie Dobbs (83)

Harriet left the car outside Ted's empty house and finished the journey into the village on her bicycle. The first thing she noticed as she approached the green was a bus marked PRIVATE standing at the stop. A cheerful-looking young man in a peaked cap swung himself up into the driving seat and started the engine. The Old Age Pensioners' Outing was over.

Harriet pedalled across to a stout little old lady who was labouring along with an unwieldy basket. Out of the top poked a Thermos flask and a bunch of red berries.

'Oh thank you, dear. It is rather heavy. They give us tea but I always have a bit more of me own as well. And then there's my purse and my drops and my glasses and my woolly and everything but the kitchen sink.'

And your teeth, added Harriet to herself as she responded to a cheery smile. 'You had a nice day for the outing, didn't you.' She tied the basket to her carrier and walked along beside her.

'Ooh it were lovely, Miss Charles. We all know you; living in a village in't it! Well I'm Mrs Dobbs and I hope you'll be very happy here I'm sure. Yes, as I was saying, we all sang: Miss Cotman knows lovely songs, but what dreadful news we was met with at the bus-stop!'

The old lady stopped and looked at Harriet with round eyes. 'Colonel Rillington were there and he whispered it to the ladies but Mrs Metcalfe goes straight into tears and she cries out, "Oh, poor poor Bobby. Where is he? Does he know?" and so of course it weren't two minutes before we all knows about it. Not that we couldn't have know'd it pretty quick anyway.'

'What ever did the others say?'

'What Miss Cotman says you'll never guess. "Oh no, I might have known," or something like that! Dunno what she could have meant because it was the last thing anybody might have known, weren't it, but you never know what folks'll say when they've had a shock, and Mrs Ashford she was wonderful, never made no fuss and took it all in hand, calm and helpful like. Soothing, you know, and got us off bus and all. Just as usual really. Thinking of everything. "I'll cancel the fête," she says to Mrs Metcalfe, seeing how upset she was, "Don't you worry yourself about that." Gives her a little pat on the arm and smiles ever so nice really though she is rather quick sometimes. Like that girl when I had me legs done. Very kind she turned out though I was put off of her while I was unpacking me things. Sharp, you know. I can't believe it, I just can't seem to take it in.'

Lively interest mingled with conscientious gravity on Mrs Dobbs's rosy face. 'I says to my friend, I just can't believe it somehow, knocks you up hearing something like that. Such a lovely lady too what did you good just to look at her.'

'I know. I'm so glad Miss Cotman was able to come after all. She must have been a comfort.'

'Yes we was surprised too. Said her time away was a wash-out, and her friend she was s'posed to be meeting there had broke his leg so she'd rather help with us. Got back just in time. Mrs Metcalfe met her on road and they come along together. We was ever so pleased. Oh, she's a one she is! Old ducks, she calls us! But what was it happened exactly to poor Mrs Kilmarnock, d'you suppose?'

'You probably know more than I do. I've been away all day.'

'Well, we don't know nothing yet 'cept she's dead. All of a sudden like.'

'Perhaps it was a heart attack.'

Mrs Dobbs nodded several times. ' 'Earts,' she said weightily, 'that'll be it for sure. You never can tell with 'earts. Lively as a cricket one minute, gone the next. I could tell you stories you'd never credit about 'earts. ...'

'Awful. I know, so could I. But the outing,' said Harriet determinedly, 'it sounds such fun. Otherwise, I mean. How did it go?'

'Well now, do you know, all this bad news has just about put it clean out of my head it has really, but it was just as usual if you see what I mean. Very good. We always say the Bassington outing brings out the sun. There was Ada Billings complaining of course. If it isn't her corns it's her veins and if it isn't her veins it's her daughter-in-law but it wouldn't be the same without all that would it.'

'What did you do?'

'Well we was a bit late starting off 'cos I met old Mr Faraday at bus with no glass eye. A 'orrible sight. " 'Aven't you forgot something, Mr Faraday?" I asks. "Oops," he says, "forgot again!" "Well, you're not going without it," I says. "Not with me on this here bus!" "No indeed!" says Mrs Metcalfe, what was the only lady helper arrived at that time, and she ran all the way back to his house herself, him being so rheumaticky we'd have waited all day if he'd gone hisself. "In a tea-cup!" he shouts after her. Give her ever such a turn, she says to me when she gets back, hunting through them all on the dresser and then, seeing it staring up at her like that in the very last cup. So the bus had to wait but it were lucky really 'cos then we got Miss Cotman.'

'Well, after that we went for ever such a pretty drive and ended up in a wood. Alf drove us right into the lovely glade, very good he is, and we picked wild flowers, those of us as could. I'm lucky, me legs is fair. But some of us can't walk far and some just sit in bus and look out of the window but we all enjoy it in our different ways. Miss Cotman too. That give us a laugh that did!' It gave Mrs Dobbs a good laugh now. 'Ooh it were a sight, Miss Cotman picking flowers, looked all wrong somehow, but she filled that old shopping bag of hers up all in a minute, keen as mustard. Not like Mrs Metcalfe; artistic she is. Walked all over the place looking for just the right touch of this and that for the ones left in bus. Right off into the woods. Funny little things sometimes what you'd never think of picking, but looked wunnerful all together. And there was Mrs Ashford as well. Knows just what she wants to press into little trays and that for charity. Very good they are. Happen I'll get one next week and give it to my Ireen for her birthday, or one of Mrs Metcalfe's. Oh dear, I suppose they won't have that fête now at all. Isn't it awful the way you forget.'

For a moment the old lady walked on in silence and then she couldn't help chuckling again. She shook her head. 'Oh, Miss Cotman and her flowers, if you could call them that, any old thing! Scratched her wrist real bad but never a squeak, tough as old boots! You ought to put a bandage on that I says. You got to pay for your pleasures she says, quick as pie. She's a caution she is. Mind you, she's not everybody's cup of tea, but you can't please everyone. Made old Mr Mathers cry once I remember, and "That's enough of that, Grandpa!" she says, slapping him on the back like a ton o' bricks and she's a good weight in't she; lucky he didn't fall to bits. When all's said and done he is over ninety. Now *he's* more Mrs Metcalfe's sort, if you see what I mean. Mrs Metcalfe takes him to Mrs Mathers' grave regular in car, but Miss Cotman won't have it. Morbid she says it is, and he's got to be taken out of hisself, but Mr Mathers gets fussed if you say that. Shaky like, and then he gets more forgetful and that fusses him more, you know how it is.'

'I know.'

'Well, nobody suits everybody, that's what I always say, and they're all very kind ladies in their different ways. Mrs Ashford's tiny, in't she! Smarter looking than the others. Perteet I call it. Arms like sticks, couldn't kill a beetle with a hammer but she twists the doctor round her little finger!'

Mrs Dobbs nodded sagely, "O' course he's that sort. Very easy with prescriptions and that, very kind. Asks you what you want, never argues. Bit vague, mind. Tried to give me Ireen's tonic once. Mine's pink. Still, we all know what we're used to and we tell him if he's forgot. My Fred had the dark brown for his chest. Wunnerful it was. Day in, day out, he always had it, come what may, before he was took.'

'It's nice to see people enjoying themselves, isn't it,' suggested Harriet, after a respectful pause. 'If one person's keen on something then everybody wants to do it. They might not have thought of it by themselves.'

'That's it!' agreed the old woman eagerly. 'I always look forward to picking the wild flowers. P'raps it's getting something for nowt but I think maybe it's just seeing the others doing it. But I'd got so many things in my basket you see, so I asks Miss Cotman could I borrow hers and right away *she* wants to pick them too! It's 'uman nature, that's all, jumping from 'uman to 'uman. I would learn the pianner when I was young just 'cause we had one at our school and me friend had lessons, and nothing would quiet me till I had those pianner lessons too. Course I soon got tired of it on account of I wasn't no good at it, just like Miss Cotman would get tired of fiddlin' about trying to make little mats and suchlike like the other ladies do. But I was just the same, wouldn't be left out of the fun you see, when I was a girl.'

'One never likes being left out,' said Harriet.

The old woman laid a soft and wrinkled hand on her arm. 'Well, nobody isn't left out here, my dear, bar one or two what wouldn't do nowhere. It's a real nice village though I say so myself.'

'Who else was on the outing?'

'Well, there was the driver of course, a very nice young man, and those three helpers I told you about, and the rest was OAPs like meself. They're a very cheery bunch though Bert Goggins got a fancy for coming and nobody liked to put him off bus. We was sorry for him 'cos he'll never make a real OAP. Won't make next week by the look of him. Still, we regretted it. Worse than usual and that's saying something. Muttering and grumbling to hisself. I'll tell you they was saints to keep him on at Hall as long as they did. Always one degree under and he's never in Dog and Duck now'days. So where does he get it? You can't turn a blind eye for ever can you. He's had enough chances to sink a battle-ship and enough drink too, and now he's telling against them what was so kind to him in the past. Wicked I call it. "Boozing in shed?" he says. "Nonsense!" he says, half-seas over I need hardly say, "I can't get into shed, can I, when there's others in it," he says, "what I could mention if I had a mind to!" The whole bus heard him, and he gives ever such a 'orrid leer. Dear knows what somebody like you must think, listening to talk like that. It's all on account of that shed having a bad name 'as put it into his head. When it were a summer-house a 'undred years ago they say as there were goings on an' they never forget nothing!'

The old lady shook her head with a look of real distress. 'Now, what I want to tell you is that there in't nothing in it now. I like a bit of gossip meself but not when it's malice aforethought. Nobody in their right mind would take no risk if they was married to Mr Kilmarnock, so don't you take no notice of what you hear, if 'tis those silly stories. He's a nasty piece of work, is Goggins, and rough with it. His father was gardener there before him and that's why they kep' him so long I expect, but enough's enough. Now, I only told you all that, dear, to warn you 'bout Albert Goggins.' She stopped. 'Here we are. Thank you ever so much, I can manage now. I'm a lucky woman to have so much kindness and me legs too.'

Mrs Dobbs pushed open the door of her tiny house. 'Yes, nobody locks up round here. If you can't trust folk where are you? Nowhere, that's what. And Mr and Mrs Kilmarnock have never done anything to be ashamed of and never would. Everybody in this village knows that, and don't you listen to nobody what tells you different.'

24

About Colonel Walter Rillington, MC (63)

There was still a small crowd of people on the green when Harriet returned from Mrs Dobbs's, but she did not join them. The first impact of the news of Fiona's death had passed and anybody who had something to hide would have had time by now to don the mask. She could hear the buzz of awed, excited voices across the still air as she let herself into Rose Cottage.

It was empty of course; she could hardly expect Ted Baxter yet. She sat down at the table and wrote a report on her visit to the Spurs' conference and her talk with Mrs Dobbs, and then: 'Rosemary Ashford, Caroline Metcalfe and Cotty. Reported reaction to news which awaited them after attending OAP outing from 12.0–4.30. Tears from Caroline (expected), helpful concern and efficiency from Rosemary (expected), "I might have known" from Cotty (unexpected).'

She would have an hour or two to wait. Harriet decided to visit Botswana.

As she walked up the road towards the Clancys' bungalow, turning over in her mind various ways of persuading either or both of them to tell her what they had been doing the night before, and rejecting them one by one, she saw a familiar tall, gangling figure walking slowly along in the ditch ahead of her, fair head bent, shoulders hunched, hands thrust in pockets.

Andrew Metcalfe turned swiftly as he heard her footsteps. He was wearing a grubby tee-shirt and now revealed a bottle printed on the front. The rest of his rib-cage was covered in black continuous writing. Harriet had managed to read LIPSMACKINGTHIRSTQUENCHING when Andrew hid it from view by brushing back his long hair with a nervous gesture. His thin face was very pink.

'Hullo,' he said ruefully. 'Caught red-handed again!'

'Why, what are you doing?'

'Well, that's the thing. I – I'm ashamed of it really. It's so t-trivial after this awful business of Fiona. When Uncle Walter told me about it I asked if ... b-but I might as well. I mean I can't do anything about that really can I. Everybody feels awful of course and Thomas looks at them owlishly and goes on and on as if ... but of course he would, wouldn't he, when you think, mind just as much. I-I mean he's only a child but it sounds really weird I do see. I-I don't mean he ... but he was particularly upset this morning, not being able to hear him and he was on his own. Thomas. I've been thinking of trees, but then I thought well, what about d-ditches. I-I sent him in the opposite direction and suggested he looked in the trees and I started off this way. A car could have hit him you see and knocked him into the ditch.'

'Oh I see. You mean *Pusskin*.'

'Ya. I can't help feeling, you see, that he may be, p-probably is, well, you know, dead. So I started looking in ditches by the side of the road, like I said, and f-first of all I met Cotty and felt really stupid shuffling along in the ditch like that but she was really nice about it and suggested up here because of it being such a deserted stretch. I-I mean nobody walks along it unless they're going to visit Biddy or the Clancys do they, and the driver might just throw him into the ditch, even if he saw him. I mean, what else could he do? He wouldn't know where he lived, would he.'

'Oh dear. I do hope you won't find him like that. But one hears so many wonderful stories of cats surviving in strange places.'

'L-Like that story of Uncle Walter's about the cat in the engine room living off the grease on the machines. He knows about animals, Rex is really good. He brought him out this afternoon and gave him Pusskin's collar to sniff, but he sent Thomas off. Said it was too much of a crowd for the dog to work properly.'

'Where did you look?'

'On the common. Rex got really steamed up once and we thought he was on to him. Just near you, that was, but it turned out to be a rabbit. Shot out under his feet. Poor Uncle Walter was quite put out. I-I wouldn't mind having the rabbit actually though, for the s-spleen. Rex got all rabbit-minded then and Uncle Walter said he would have lost interest in the collar so we gave up.'

'What did you do then?'

'U-Uncle Walter decided to meet the bus and sort of gently break the news to Mum and co, and promised to give Rex another go tomorrow if necessary. I went home and tidied up a bit – the lunch – be-before Mum got back from the OAPs. Thomas was still a bit down in spite of what Uncle Walter had said. He really put himself out for Pusskin, much more than I would have expected, perhaps to take our minds off Fiona's d-death. It was really kind of him, but he does ask a lot of questions.'

'What sort of questions?'

'Oh you know,' said Andrew maddeningly, 'about everything really. Any old thing … what Mum was doing last night for instance. So I told him how she fixed her tights onto the netball posts from Thomas's school because she couldn't find a rag. Really weird they looked, stuck out of the back of the station wagon.'

'Dear Caroline – just like her. Which school?'

'Melchester secondary mod.'

'Oh dear, just the opposite direction from Loxley.'

'Ya, well as she was in the car I suppose she thought she might as well. B-but then he went on and asked what she did after *that*! As a ma-matter of fact I said she was at home with me but she wasn't really. I was late out of school and then I met Maureen Clancy,' he blushed scarlet, 'and walked back with her.'

There was a short silence and Andrew laughed, momentarily deflected. 'There was a big Daimler outside their house – "Old Beaky-face," she said, didn't seem to think much of her, weird sort of friends I expect that bloke's got. Well anyway, Mum wasn't actually there when I got home. I mean, not exactly. There was the car and the posts lashed inside with tights attached but she herself was, in actual fact, out. I suppose with Thomas, but I didn't quite tell him that. Not completely.'

'One doesn't necessarily want to tell everybody everything.'

'Ya. Uncle Walter, for instance, as far as Thomas is concerned. I-I didn't want him to seem too obsessive. About Pusskin and that. Or bring Mum into it ... of course we all know Uncle Walter thinks Thomas is off his rocker. I didn't want to make it worse,' he added simply.

'But Andrew, Pusskin wasn't lost yesterday evening, was he?'

'No.' Andrew looked away. 'It's just ... you know ... well, sort of ... I dunno ...'

Harriet put a stop to this with sudden inspiration. 'Of course Colonel Rillington is very manly, isn't he.'

Andrew laughed, suddenly relaxed and articulate. 'I'll say.'

'Can't you imagine,' said Harriet, warming to her theme, 'young Walter sitting in the back of the stalls, the one little boy who was staunchly booing Tinkerbell; *hardly* mad about fairies!'

The mention of Tinkerbell brought Harriet back to the job in hand. She picked up a stick and poked about in the undergrowth. Andrew had his back to her when he said casually, 'Gnomes actually, in this case.'

Harriet did not falter as she parted the long grasses. 'I believed in them myself,' she said.

'He may have wanted Mum to go to a certain place I think.' He laughed again and turned to face her. 'I dunno. Where they lived or something. He never tells me these things. He knows I wouldn't be so sympathetic; I-I'm all for making him grow up. At least. More. Mum understands of course, and Uncle Walter

134

would do anything for her, but there are some things he simply can't conceive of, and you bet gnomes is absolutely one of them. So I didn't say anything about that, especially when it was just when this really awful thing might have been happening to Fiona. It would have made it seem more trivial – and silly – I mean, how could I have told him what I actually thought she was doing!' He looked at Harriet with honest blue eyes. 'He's kind to Thomas but I'm sure he secretly thinks he ought to be put away or something. He's so military, so quick. Everything's got to be cut and dried with him. B-bit different to most people? Must be potty; into the bin with him. He's a nice bloke, mind you, but he's just got that attitude.'

'I understand,' said Harriet, adding, 'You must be a great comfort to Caroline.'

Andrew looked up quickly, reminding her sharply of his mother. 'Oh, I'm afraid ... I-I sometimes feel ... I'm just another worry to her.'

They walked on, eyes down, scanning the ditch together. 'Not that Mum could possibly have known that Fiona was being killed last night, of course,' went on the boy, wrinkling his brow anxiously as he tried to make himself clear. 'But it didn't seem the right time to talk about anything else.'

'That was very sensitive of you. And very sensible too. Well, I'll keep an eye open for Pusskin of course.'

'Fiona could have found him at once if she'd been alive. If she'd wanted to, being so good at organising things. But she was another one who thought Thomas was peculiar. Bobby didn't. He thought he was all right. But I did hear Fiona saying he ought to go to some school or other that she knew of when I was taking round the drinks the other night. I came up behind her. You hear a lot, doing that.'

'Who did she say it to?'

'Dunno. Somebody. Not Mum anyway.'

'I do hope your mother didn't overhear it. Kind though it was meant to be she might have taken it to heart. However casually said.'

'It wouldn't be all that casual coming from Fiona. She was probably half way to fixing it all up already, with one of her influential friends.'

Harriet laughed. 'She couldn't do that! I think your mother is – protective about Thomas though.'

'Very! Much more than she was with me. Of course she'd lost our father by that time. No, I shouldn't think she heard. Why should she have? But I wish she didn't worry so much about old Thomas. He's a bit behind in lessons but I think he's really quite self-sufficient in his own way; quite happy. He goes along at his own pace and doesn't mind what other people think about it. Most people *do* mind, you see, and feel they must be just like the other boys. When you think about it he may be right. I wish I could make her see that, but she doesn't really listen. She's far away, wondering where he's got to now!'

'She's probably rather embarrassed when he plays in other people's gardens but I'm sure everybody quite accepts him doing that sort of thing now. I know I did, almost at once.'

Andrew said soberly, 'Sometimes, though, I see her looking at him, and I think Mum looks quite ill.'

25

About John and Maureen Clancy
(53 and 21)

Harriet rose from the ditch and continued briskly up the road in the direction of Botswana, where she intended to loiter.

She vaguely hoped to come across one or both of the Clancys in their front garden. Not that it looked as if they spent much time there. It was the very antithesis of Little Farthings, being entirely composed of overgrown laurels and rhododendrons in dismal conditions of terminal dankness. However, the owners must presumably use their concrete drive every now and then and if she saw either of them she had decided to embark on a casual conversation so unyielding and tenacious that they must feel obliged in common courtesy, she optimistically hoped, to invite her into the house.

If she did not meet either of the Clancys outside then she would have to think of some reason to knock on their front door.

Before she could pursue this line of thought any further she was interrupted by a shrill yapping. A small orange peke flung himself ferociously against the gate of Pine View. Biddy was more welcoming, and hurried down the brick path to greet her.

'Come in, dear, do! Don't take any notice of *him*,' she snatched up the little dog and pressed his flat muzzle against her own powdery cheek. There was something graceful about the gesture which reminded Harriet that this soft, plump little lady had once been a dancer.

'Come in, please,' she cajoled, as Harriet hesitated. 'If you were going to call on the Clancys you can save your legs because you've missed them, they're not there, and there's nobody else till you get to Melchester. Come and have a bit of a gossip!'

Harriet allowed herself to be swept into a cosy little sittingroom and deposited on a soft, plump sofa. Flowers, large, shiny and overblown, ran riot over covers, curtains, rugs and pictures, and there were many soft, plump cushions in sweet-pea colours. The little dog settled himself in the exact centre of one of them, palsied with suspicion, and fixed her with black, bulging eyes.

'Oh dear, oh dear!' Biddy leant back in her chair and patted her heart. 'What a dreadful to-do. It's nice to see you, dear, it is really. Ann's gone to her mother and I'm all alone, thinking away. Really, I hardly know if I'm on my head or my heels! Everybody's talking about it but I suppose poor Bobby doesn't even know *yet*. Rosemary says nobody could find him and James just had to leave a note on the hall table to stop him looking for her. What a home-coming!'

Biddy's blue eyes filled at the thought of Bobby eagerly opening the front door only to find James's note. 'Of course, it's an upset for everyone. Even John Clancy seemed rattled and he's usually so expressionless, don't you think, dear?'

'Yes. He looks rather guarded, somehow.'

'They're so peculiar aren't they, both of them. I was taking Tweaky Poo for a run just now and there they were in front of their garage as I passed by, throwing suitcases into their car. I heard him ordering her about though he lowered his voice a bit when he saw me. Shifty. I'm sorry for that girl, I am really. He's such a rude man. Makes my blood boil it really does, seeing a fellow treat his wife like that. She may not be exactly brainy but we can't all be Einsteins can we.'

'She does seem almost simple in a way.'

'Scared silly,' explained Biddy impressively. 'Terrified out of her wits, Harriet, that's what's the matter with her if you ask me. Anyway, there they were, so I said something about how kind it was of him to clear up that horrible shed at the Hall. After all, say something nice when you can, I say, and it *was* kind of him, wasn't it, must have been a dreadful job. I wouldn't have thought he was the type to put himself out for anybody but it all goes to show.'

Harriet hesitated a moment and then said, 'As a matter of fact I heard him talking to the doctor, outside my gate. He wanted to help them; I mean they didn't have to ask him. He said he didn't mind doing it because he was perfectly well used to the sight of blood.'

Biddy stared at her, round-eyed, her hands on her cheeks. 'No! Oo-er! Harriet! Now you know what I mean when I say he's creepy. Honestly, he might just as well have said the *taste* of blood while he was about it, I wouldn't put it past him. Sinister!'

'Anyway I must confess I was dying to hear all about it. It's awful but one is, isn't one. But he simply didn't answer me! He just dragged that pathetic little creature into the car quite roughly and said something about how late she always was for everything and then the penny dropped about the suitcases and I realised they were going on a visit or something, and without stopping to think I said "Oh, what a shame you've got to be away just now. You'll miss all the inquest and everything!" It was the first thing that came into my head, and do you know, it seemed to be the most unfortunate remark? They both just stared at me with ever such old-fashioned looks. She looked scared to death and I can see his eyes now, boring into mine. Hypnotic, I call it. I did feel awful I can tell you. Of course,' admitted Biddy disarmingly, 'if I *had* stopped to think I mightn't have said it I suppose, but you can't help feeling these things, can you. I mean to say, it isn't as if we were living in the middle of Chicago, is it. The only excitement in my little life is Dizzy coming down like a wet weekend to depress me out of my mind and tell a lot of tarrydiddles about me to that dreadful girl at the Dog and Duck.'

'I shouldn't worry. We wouldn't be human if we weren't interested.'

'I'm so glad you feel that, my dear, I am really. Anyway I'm not one to take offence, I never have been, life's too short. So I looked in through the open car window and asked if they were going to be away for long and did they want me to feed their cat.

138

It's a nuisance, coming into my garden and eating the birds, but it's a dumb animal when all's said and done, and Maureen gave a little gasp and said she'd forgotten all about it and yes please, and they'd only be gone about a week. I mean they did seem in such a fluster about the whole thing, Harriet; fancy forgetting about the cat. Well he was just starting up the engine when she squeaked out, "Oh John!" just like that, and he snapped, "Whatever is it now," and she said "I've forgotten the letters. They're on the table in the hall," and honestly he gave her such a look out of those eyes! I was sorry for her I really was. So of course I said, as she'd given me the key, "Oh do let me post them for you, I'm just going past the box," and do you know, he even hesitated at that, suspicious to the last, and she said "Oh, please do, Biddy," and he said "Oh, all right then." Can you beat it! Not exactly old world courtesy. But still, you've got to laugh really haven't you.'

'Very odd.'

'You can say that again. So off they went in a cloud of dust, I do think it's so wrong to drive a car like that don't you? He's a queer one and no mistake. Not that I can talk about funny husbands; they don't come much funnier than mine! You know, I just wondered if it might be somebody dunning them for money or something like that. After all, what do they live on? He doesn't seem to have a job or anything, does he.'

'Thomas says he's writing a book.'

'Oh, does he? Well, he is then. That child knows everything doesn't he all about the private affairs of the people in this village; he could probably tell James a thing or two! He's a born snooper, Thomas is. Comes out with some priceless remarks sometimes. Of course he doesn't understand half of what he sees.'

'It can be a rather *dangerous* thing to be,' said Harriet slowly. 'An uncomprehending snooper.'

Biddy looked at her quickly. 'Oh yes, I see what you mean. The private affairs of John Clancy *are* probably pretty murky. I don't trust that man. And of course Thomas wouldn't have the sense to steer clear of someone like that.'

'No. Thomas seems very adventurous in his way, almost foolhardy. Except ...'

'Yes?'

'I think he's frightened of blood.'

But Biddy had already clapped her hand over her mouth with a cry of dismay and jumped to her feet. 'My goodness me! Would you believe it, I've forgotten to post those blessed letters now, and I promised faithfully to do it right away and catch the post! Never mind, no harm done. I'll do it in a minute. Lucky they're not here to see! To tell you the truth, Harriet, I had just popped in to have a good look at them when you came along,' she said frankly, putting on her reading glasses and fanning the envelopes out towards the light. 'I didn't like to hang about there in case they suddenly came back. They're so unpredictable. I would have liked to have a better look round, but it's those eyes.'

She shivered. 'See?' said Biddy. 'He's folded them all the same. Nasty cheap envelopes. Mean! I might have known it. So it's his own fault, isn't it, that we can see through them? Just "Yours sincerely," and then "next week", and this one you can see a bit more, "towards the end of next week," and look, this one more still "... let you know towards the end of next week." '

'Oh Biddy!' exclaimed Harriet, in fascinated disapproval, 'I'm glad I'm your friend and not your mentor. I should have had to do something about you.'

'And look who they're to!' cried Biddy. 'All over the place! The Rev Clarence King from Bimbridge, Lady Beek-Faye, what a silly name, from Melchester, Mrs Lindwall, she's over twenty miles in the opposite direction, and *he's saying the same thing to each one of them!*'

Curiosity got the better of Harriet and she took the envelopes in her hand. 'But Biddy, he might be saying anything.'

'But what? They're not businesses, or shops, and he doesn't know them all that well. Yours sincerely every time.'

'Perhaps he's giving a party.'

'But you can't just say "Towards the end of next week" on an invitation. You'd have a funny sort of party, wouldn't you, never knowing when they were coming or going! And anyway,' she wound up triumphantly, 'Whoever heard of the Clancys giving a party, even a daft one like that. Why, nobody in Bassington has ever set foot in the house except Thomas, uninvited. Though there's others, but never more than one at a time.'

'Others? What like?'

'Just men and women, oldish usually, with big cars. But honestly, Harriet, believe it or not, there's something funny about them too. Sometimes, if I'm working in my front garden and they drive up I smile, you know, how one does, they never smile back, or say anything, nice day, or what a lovely garden. They just scurry up that awful concrete path with their heads down. Furtive.'

'Oh Biddy, you're imagining things.'

'No I'm not. It's just downright odd. You mark my words. Like everything else about those Clancys.'

26

Bobby's return

'I called in on the boys for a moment – at the police station I mean – when I got off the train,' said Ted Baxter. 'Good of me, wasn't it,' he added smugly.

'Marvellous! Whatever did you say, after all this time?'

'I said I was in a hurry.'

Harriet stared disbelievingly. Ted Baxter grinned. 'Well, I was. It's all right. They took it for granted that like everybody else I would have heard about it by this time, so I didn't go into all that. No point yet; I still haven't got any definite evidence, but we naturally *talked* about it. Dr Ashford notified them just before we left. I didn't stay long but I did tell them that I was coming along to see you and I gave you the all-clear – known you for years, taught my daughter, wonderful headmistress, absolutely trustworthy, etc. As the discoverer of the body I must admit they've been on the blower to you.'

'Oh Ted,' said Harriet reproachfully. 'It was your fault I wasn't here.'

'You couldn't have told them any more than the others could,' repeated Ted Baxter patiently.

'I know but I feel guilty. Do they think it was an accident?'

'They've got no solid reason to doubt it officially. Of course they probably realise I'm interested now.'

Harriet looked at his eager face, years younger than when she had met it on the train. 'Yes,' she said drily, 'I imagine they must.'

Quick and business-like, they worked side by side at her sitting-room table, their reports and conclusions spread out before them, neatly labelled.

'Caroline Metcalfe is unaccounted for during part of the evening,' said Baxter at last, slipping in a final paper-clip.

'Yes, but if she's guilty why go to Melchester for the netball posts just *then*? You can't do a thing like that to time! I know schools; she would have to find somebody with some sort of key who would be goodness knows where, and a man to help her lift them into her car and secure them. It would be very awkward trying to do it by herself.'

'Possibly.' He sighed, 'I don't know what to make of all this I'm sure.'

'Nor do I,' said Harriet sadly, looking at ROBERT KILMARNOCK.

'Yes, there are some discrepancies.'

Harriet pushed JOHN CLANCY towards him, with a meaning look.

'A doubtful character, I grant you. The usual channels will help us there, but I can think of at least half a dozen totally innocent reasons for his sudden departure, and I'm quite sure he could.'

'But the letters!'

'Another six totally innocent reasons,' repeated Baxter equably, without raising his eyes from MRS DOBBS.

'But Ted, those letters might tell us something. Do you know a Lady Mary Beek-Faye?'

Ted Baxter stared. 'Yes. She's a well-known figure in the local horsey world. You can't miss her because she's about seven feet tall and dressed in floating stuff. I don't know much about ladies' fashions but Lady Mary looks wrong to me. Married to a colossal fellow who rides a sort of cart-horse and swears blue murder. He's the MFH, a bit fruity even for the hunting field, a real rough customer. A gambling man with an eye for the ladies and a boozer's face. Not exactly my cup of tea. He's known as Old BF in some quarters.

'His bacon is saved by her money I'd say. Just. She's rather a pathetic lady really; I don't know how she stands it. Just the opposite in all respects. Vague and bloodless and ineffectually well-meaning. Why?'

'I think she may have been visiting the Clancys between five and six last night.'

Ted Baxter raised his eyebrows. 'The Clancys? I shouldn't have thought they had much in common. Still, you never know.

She was alone, was she?' He scribbled down a few words. 'Might be handy for his alibi.'

'If necessary.'

They exchanged a look.

Harriet glanced thoughtfully down at COLONEL WALTER RILLINGTON. He took more interest in that kitten than I expected him to. I thought he was one of Thomas's detractors. I don't really know very much about Colonel Rillington though; he's so controlled. The question is, what sort of person would commit this sort of crime?'

'You think that the character fits the deed?' Baxter nodded his agreement. 'A man who lives his life in a hurried, botched-up sort of manner, acting on impulse and covering up his mistakes as well as he can at the last minute, may well produce the same type of murder, should he do such a thing, while a tidy-minded killer is more likely to commit a premeditated crime; a careful, thought-out affair. But the difficulty is to decide what kind of crime we have to deal with. What is this one?'

'Oh surely, horribly untidy,' said Harriet, remembering the dreadful scene with a shudder.

'Ah!' said Baxter. 'The trick is that a tidy mind may decide to lay a smoke screen of higgledy-piggledy details round a very neat crime. It's much more difficult the other way round.

'There's a lot of interesting stuff here but it's still inconclusive,' he went on, turning over the pages and adding a word or two here and there. 'There's many a murderer goes free for lack of evidence. We may have our suspicions. ...'

'Oh, we must avoid those vague suspicions!' cried Harriet. 'If only we could find the murderer before anybody else knows there has been a murder at all!'

'Well, so far this one appears to be foolhardy to the point of madness. The seizing of a sudden opportunity, with no time for a moment's hesitation. Your walk home with Mrs Ashford, for instance, couldn't have been foreseen. No, this could hardly be the crime of a thoughtful, careful personality.'

'I suppose not. Unless ...' said Harriet slowly. 'Unless it didn't *matter*.'

She handed him a list of names she had been writing down. 'Untidy,' she suggested.

Baxter read:

MAUREEN CLANCY
BEATRICE COTMAN
ANDREW METCALFE
CAROLINE METCALFE
AUGUSTUS DIZZARD
JAMES ASHFORD
ALBERT GOGGINS

He nodded. 'The others, from their appearances, outlook and habitat, I have judged "Tidy",' went on Harriet in professional tones. '"Do you agree? That is, John Clancy, Rosemary Ashford, Biddy Dizzard, Colonel Rillington, Thomas Metcalfe (in his way), Miss Markham ...'

But at this point she was interrupted. 'You've forgotten me,' said a third voice. 'I'm a tidy one.'

Both Ted Baxter and Harriet leaped to their feet in a concerted effort to hide the tell-tale papers.

'I've just seen James's letter,' added Bobby Kilmarnock, as he stood swaying in the doorway with a face like chalk. 'It said to ring him so I did. He told me you'd found her. He wanted to come over but I said I'd come and see you.'

Harriet reached him first and led him unresisting to a chair by the fire. Baxter dived instinctively for the corner cupboard and put a glass of brandy into his hand. Bobby sipped it obediently and looked up at Harriet with the ghost of his old polite smile. 'Sorry to barge in like that but the door was on the latch. I should have rung ... may I ask you?'

'Of course.' Gently and carefully Harriet told him that Fiona had been killed instantly. She told him about the broken shelf.

There was a long pause when she had finished. Bobby looked at Baxter without surprise and Harriet introduced him as an old friend. 'I happened to see him this morning,' she said, stretching the truth a little. 'And so he got involved in this awful tragedy.'

'That was a lucky chance,' said Bobby simply. 'It must have been the most appalling shock for Harriet, so soon after she came here to live. Like a blow on the face ...'

He stopped abruptly.

Harriet said swiftly, 'It's so good of you to think of me, when we are all full of anxiety and concern for you.'

Bobby's blue eyes were friendly. 'It's all right. I know how she died, and that from now on I'm going to say the wrong thing and other people are going to think they're going to, and we're all going to be jumpy and over-sensitive, but we mustn't let it *matter*. We must accept it as one of the dreary after-effects of an ... outrage ... of this kind.'

Harriet smiled back. He's without guile, she thought. He trusts everybody. At least ...

Bobby said, as if in answer to her thoughts, 'I never trusted Goggins.' Then he told her that he had been prepared for something awful when he saw the cancelled strips over the poster for the fête as he drove into the village. 'I knew, you see, that Fiona never let anybody down.'

There was a knock at the door. Harriet glanced at Bobby who nodded. 'They're all bound to know by now.'

It was Caroline, all eyes and staring freckles.

'Oh Harriet, is Thomas with you?'

'No, it's Bobby.'

Bobby had already jumped to his feet, and Caroline took him in her arms, holding him fiercely. 'Is there anything in the world that I can do?'

'Just be there, dearest Caroline.'

In a moment Bobby turned to Harriet. 'I left after breakfast yesterday. Please tell me what happened from then on.'

Harriet explained about the preparations for the fête and the arrival of the urgent proofs from New York.

'Yes, I see,' said Bobby. 'Fiona always prided herself on doing that sort of thing right away.'

'She took them with her to the hammock and from time to time one of us went out to ask her a question about the fête.'

'And she was just as usual?'

'Absolutely. Although ...'

Bobby spun round on her, 'What are you trying to say?'

He would have to know sometime. Harriet told him about the anonymous letter. 'It contained a sort of threat. I gave it to James but the police may have it now.'

'But Fiona didn't seem upset at all?'

'Not in the least, she never mentioned it. It struck me as more silly and pompous than frightening.'

Bobby listened intently as Harriet told him about the rest of the afternoon, adding 'I expect James told you that it was at least 12 hours before I found her.'

'He said about the lawn mower. But she never mowed the lawn. Why should she? I don't think she knew how to start the damned thing.'

'I wondered if she might have been looking for something else that she needed very much. She didn't ring you up, did she?'

'Actually, she might not have been able,' said Bobby slowly, 'to contact me. I lunched at the Garrick with an old friend of my father's. I don't think I told her about that, and then I bought some shirts and things in Piccadilly, and so on. No, she might easily have missed me.' He looked at Harriet as one who appreciated an intelligent woman. 'How could the *lawn mower* kill Fiona?'

'It was lying on her chest, and – and I think James thought it might have struck her upturned face first,' answered Harriet uncomfortably. 'It was the heaviest thing, that's all. There were others that could have been just as dangerous, falling from a height like that.'

She looked into blue eyes which valued her real opinion and had a sudden longing to give it, but instead she described, in the least gruesome way possible, in answer to his questioning, how the shed had looked. 'I'm thankful Thomas didn't find her. He and I were both out there very early this morning, while it was still dark, and we got as far as the entrance to the courtyard. He was over here looking for his lost kitten.'

'Pusskin? Did you find him?'

Harriet shook her head. 'Just his collar in my front garden. Thomas showed it to me after breakfast this morning. It was lucky I was there to stop him coming in again. I'd just discovered Fiona, you see ...'

Bobby looked less bewildered, almost eager, as he talked about the boy. 'Poor little Thomas. He must have minded a lot to go after him in the small hours.' Then he slumped back in his chair, long legs out-thrust. 'I thought that shelf had the usual sort of junk on it. Dusty old packets of slug-death and weed-killer.'

'Not any more,' said Caroline. 'The big things had been put up there, out of the way. To wash the floor perhaps.'

Bobby looked at Caroline with a strange expression on his face. 'Why the lawn mower?' he repeated.

'Try not to think about that part of it, Bobby darling. It's all over now, and she didn't suffer at all. We shall probably never really know which object actually killed her.'

'Why go to the shed at all?'

'Perhaps, being such a tidy person, she wanted to rearrange it.'

'She would have done that after Goggins had left.'

He took a deep, uneven breath.

'Yes, I see,' said Caroline. Her eyes sparkled with tears but she spoke matter-of-factly. None of them looked at Bobby as he sat, still urbane, still elegant, his sleek head in his hands. Caroline studied her own, so square and workworn, as they lay curled upwards in her lap. Finger by finger, she examined carefully the contours of her nails. 'We may never know exactly why,' she went on doggedly, 'Fiona decided to go down to the shed.' Thick pale lashes shadowed ashen cheeks. 'Do let's – agree now to say nothing which can never be proved and might cause trouble.'

Bobby was silent.

Caroline looked up, her face belying her stillness. Not still with an inner calm, thought Harriet, but still like a cat hiding in the long grass. Still with an effort of the will. Unnaturally and watchfully still.

But then, weren't they all? Ted, impassive but not cold, looking as nearly invisible as is possible for a big man in a small room, had his elbows on the table obscuring, she noticed thankfully, CAROLINE METCALFE.

And she herself, looking so steadily at the leaping flames of the little fire, with every fibre of her body strained to catch the faintest nuance amongst her companions.

Into this silent atmosphere of watchful pause and tension came a shockingly loud and jangling interruption. Heads jerked up, eyes widened, and nerves jumped as the electric bell shrilled out, together with a heavy thump against the front door and a muttered 'Bugger!' as Cotty staggered in. 'Left your door open!' she cried accusingly, and 'Have you seen ...'

At the same moment the telephone began to ring.

As though waking from a trance Bobby started up. 'Cotty!'

'Bobby!'

Harriet turned her back to them and picked up the receiver. A pleasant voice at the other end asked for Detective Chief Superintendent Baxter. Behind her Harriet heard a confused medley of greetings, condolences and introductions. She said

147

quietly and quickly, 'Harriet Charles speaking.'

'Is he with you?'

'Yes of course. How lovely to hear your voice.'

After a short pause the voice said that it was lovely to hear hers, and gathered that she was not alone.

'No, no, not in the least.'

'I'm not quite in the picture this end. Could you take a message?'

'Oh, that's quite all right.' Harriet allowed a second before she added, 'Lunch would be lovely. A good gossip.'

A trace of humour crept into the other voice. 'Perhaps the good gossip could come *later*. We'd be very grateful if you would keep this *strictly* under your hat,' the voice lowered still further. 'Please tell him that the p.m. will take place tomorrow. Sunday. We've brought it forward a bit. Right? I thought he'd like to know, as he's taking such an interest.'

'Yes, absolutely. I do understand.'

'Thank you. Good-bye.'

There was a small click at the other end, and Harriet said enthusiastically, 'My dear, of course you can't. I'll see you on Thursday week. All news then.'

Had she sounded quite right, she wondered, for such a crisis-ridden occasion? The room seemed very small as she turned towards the group by the fire. Bobby had come over and was standing beside her. 'That reminds me,' he said. 'I must ring John Clancy. I hear he has been very kind.'

Harriet told him the Clancys were away.

'Oh, I'll just speak to Walter then. I asked James,' said Bobby carefully, 'to leave all the − people, and arrangements, till tomorrow. I'll stay in my own house alone, peacefully, for one night more. Before they come.'

They looked at him anxiously. Of course the poor boy was not himself. 'Nobody will expect you to be sensible, or take decisions, after such a terrible shock. Not tomorrow, not for weeks,' said Harriet at last.

Bobby stood, looking into the fire, surrounded by an almost visible miasma of sympathy. 'I know,' he said. 'Everybody will be very kind.'

He was at the door when he swung round with his characteristic grace and said to Caroline, 'Give my love to Thomas. Don't forget. Tell him I'm *sorry* about Pusskin. It's rotten luck feeling strongly about something when everybody else is feeling strongly about something else.' He looked into her eyes intently. 'James said it was an accident. No question of that. I just wondered how − it came about exactly.'

Her voice quivered. 'Of course.'

Harriet saw him to the gate. 'You've been wonderful,' said Bobby, looking down at her with a faint smile. 'James said so. No fuss. One does appreciate that.'

Harriet looked up into the clear blue eyes, once so quizzical and now so grave. And something more. They were apprising her. What did he want? What was she to do? She waited, amongst the sweet herbs that had struggled up through the weeds at their feet. Now he glanced back with the same questioning look to where the tall, fine figures of Cotty and Caroline stood in her doorway.

The air was very still. Bobby lingered on, until at last he murmured softly, 'Will you tell Ted Baxter I was glad to see him?'

Harriet turned sharply, but Bobby had left her.

27

Saturday evening (early)

Bobby's high gates clanged shut. As Harriet turned to go indoors there was a pattering of feet behind her.

'Oh Harriet!' cried Biddy breathlessly, 'I couldn't just stay up there all on my own, not knowing what was happening. I feel something in the air. I'm sure I'm psychic. I never ever thought I'd miss those Clancys but I do, and Ann's gone to her mother as usual. It's all so awful. Can I come in and sit with you, just for a little while?'

'Of course. You must stay the night if you'd like to.'

As Biddy entered the room Caroline told her that the accident theory was now definitely confirmed.

Ted Baxter cleared his throat. 'It's not quite as simple as that, Mrs Metcalfe. The matter cannot be finally settled until after the verdict, at the inquest.'

'But won't that be just a matter of form?' Cotty turned towards this mysterious and authoritive friend of Harriet's. 'Depending on James's evidence? Isn't it bound to be "Death by Misadventure" or whatever?'

'Dr Ashford's evidence will be valuable, but the result of the post mortem must also be considered. That will probably take place next Tuesday or Wednesday.'

'But why a post mortem?' cried Cotty, Caroline and Biddy in unison.

All three women now stared at Ted Baxter with dismay, *Who are you?* written so clearly on each face that Harriet confessed, 'Ted knows. He's a retired policeman.'

'Of course I'm not officially concerned,' Ted assured them, 'But I am aware of the general procedure.'

Caroline's chin came up proudly. 'I see. I suppose ... usually. But surely there is no need for that in this case. Can't we insist ... ?'

'I'm afraid a post mortem is obligatory after any accident at all, Mrs Metcalfe. Mr Kilmarnock will know that; it won't be a shock to him,' he added soothingly.

There was a stricken silence until Biddy voiced their general thoughts. 'But ... Fiona!'

Ted looked sympathetically round the room. 'I wish we could avoid it too. I know it's not a pleasant thought, especially when the victim is young and beautiful, but I can assure you, great respect is shown for the dead and as I say there is no way round what is, unfortunately, the law of the land.'

There was a pause.

'Losing Fiona,' said Caroline meditatively, 'Is like the sun setting over the whole village.'

'I remember thinking she was like the sun myself,' agreed Harriet, relieved that the conversation had changed direction. 'On that first evening at Cotty's when I met you all. And how the sun eclipses the moon until it sets, and then the moon comes into its own again.'

'Moonlight sonatas,' said Biddy, vague but romantic.

But Caroline's eyes, large and tragic, returned to Ted. 'But can't ... ?' she began again.

'You mustn't feel too badly about the p.m., Mrs Metcalfe. Actually Mrs Kilmarnock was pretty badly knocked about, especially on the face. Harriet naturally didn't say much about that with Mr Kilmarnock here but you could say, I suppose, that the – desecration has already been ...'

Ted Baxter turned suddenly in his chair. Harriet followed his glance and said, unperturbed, 'It's only Thomas.'

The boy stood outside, ghostly in the dusk, nose flattened like a pudding against his usual window. Caroline jumped to her feet, wrenched it open and dragged him inside, as though Harriet's garden was full of savages. It seemed a relief to her pent-up nerves to cry ferociously, 'Thomas! How many times have I told you? I won't have you creeping about in other people's gardens and houses. Why, it's practically breaking and entering! At a time like this, snooping about frightening everybody to death. ...'

Thomas stood his ground, his large myopic eyes fixed on his mother's face, waiting patiently to get a word in. 'I *wasn't* snooping!' he now said aggrievedly, 'I was looking for Pusskin. I *told* you. And Harriet doesn't mind.'

'I don't,' said Harriet quickly, pouring oil on this sea of troubled emotions. 'Not a bit.'

Caroline turned a scarlet face on her. 'You're very kind,' she said, 'but he really mustn't do it, Harriet. It's not a joke. It's embarrassing and ... even dangerous. It's a silly babyish trick, going into somebody else's house before breakfast and going upstairs. Frightening people,' she repeated.

'I don't. I never go upstairs. The Clancys' window was open so I just went a little way in and saw the papers by his typewriter. I never said I went upstairs. But nobody ever *listens* to me.'

Harriet remembered his bedraggled figure the night before. His mother's thoughts had evidently turned the same way. 'That's bad enough,' raged Caroline, 'but I wasn't talking about the Clancys.'

Thomas looked bewildered at this onslaught and Harriet said gently, 'Actually, Thomas, how *did* you know Fiona was asleep, if you never went into her bedroom?'

'Because I saw her. I thought perhaps she was camping, like we did in the cubs. Trying it out, to see if she liked it like I did in the garden. I say things a million times and nobody ever ...'

Cotty laughed, quite like her old self. 'Give him his due, we all saw Fiona fast asleep in the hammock. The trouble is, we're all absolutely overwrought. It's been such a horrendous day. Poor old Thomas; he's just in time to bear the brunt of it!'

She laid a kindly hand on Thomas's shoulder, 'Come along. Don't mind us.' Harriet looked gratefully at her handsome but unglamorous face, as they all got up and moved towards the door. Thomas had one last grumble. 'She must of been jolly cold, but all grown-ups are potty. At least I sleep in my own bed. But everything *I* do is wrong. I know a whole lot more than anybody else but I can't open my mouth without seeming wrong, when I'm right. All I was doing was looking. He just isn't anywhere. He never goes off on his own.'

'Cats do, as they grow up,' said Cotty. 'He'll turn up.'

'He wasn't grown-up and she wasn't in the hammock. She was in the shed.'

'Come on. I'm starving.'

'I'm frightfully sorry,' said Caroline through frozen lips, 'I think I'm going to faint.'

She flopped on the sofa. Thomas turned to Harriet with a look of alarm and asked with a rising voice, 'What's the matter with her?'

'She's worn out, Thomas. She didn't really mean to be so cross with you.'

Caroline was shivering violently. Biddy fluttered round her while Harriet and Cotty left the room, one to fetch a milky drink and the other a warm covering. Cotty was looking thoughtful. 'Thomas and his kitten! In the middle of all this drama!' Her voice was cheerful and capable as usual. What a godsend she was, with her finding of the matches, the saucepan, the milk and the glass. Harriet stood for a moment in the kitchen with the rug over her arm, admiring this efficient bustle.

'You never know how they'll take it,' she agreed.

Caroline drank the milk and stood up, wobbling but 'perfectly all right'. Thomas would look after her.

Ted Baxter took her arm. 'It's been a hard day for everybody, Mrs Metcalfe,' he said as he escorted them to the door. 'I should have an early night. See that Thomas is safely tucked up in bed too, and lock up.'

Rillington came in, took Ted Baxter in his stride, and said, 'What's the matter with Caroline? I've just seen her, in the road, with Thomas, looking as white as a sheet.'

'She felt faint,' said Harriet, 'but she insisted on going home alone. Biddy, you will stay here tonight, won't you?'

Walter Rillington spoke for her. 'I expect she'd rather get

home. There's nothing like one's own bed after a shock. I'll run you there, with Cotty.'

Biddy was grateful. Rillington's calm authority had steadied her nerves and now the thought of supper by the fire and her own warm bed tempted her.

Baxter looked at them all, wearing exactly the right expression of concern that a responsible man should if unexpectedly confronted with an emotional situation amongst strangers. Rillington smiled at Harriet. He looks much the most relaxed, she thought, remembering the Germans. I don't understand him yet.

'You've done wonders,' he said, and then in another tone, 'I do hope Caroline will be all right.'

'I know she was devoted to Fiona but all the same, I was surprised when she nearly conked out, she's usually so strong,' said Cotty. 'Like a battle-axe with those children of hers. Or do I mean a tigress? Poor old Thomas, I feel damned sorry for that kid sometimes. Of course she'd do anything for him but I do think she ought to let him go a bit. Off the hook. Let him stand on his own feet.'

Rillington shook his head. 'I think he stands on them too much. He's got a screw loose somewhere and dear old Caroline can't face it. Keeps pretending he's perfectly normal and then gets all hot and bothered when he doesn't act like it. Of course it's hard when it's your own boy.'

'I know he's unusual but I do think perhaps he is sometimes rather misunderstood,' suggested Harriet diffidently. 'He's only a child after all, who has lost something he loves.' She thought of Fiona's poem. 'And after all, why should he and Fiona mean all that much to each other? They were so very different, and to him, Pusskin may be much more important than she was.'

There was a murmur of assent and some desultory conversation. Everybody said how tired they were, but nobody seemed to want to leave Harriet's friendly sittingroom.

Eventually Cotty yawned. 'I'm off. Come on,' she announced, as she flung on her big tweed cape with a flourish. 'Can't keep my eyes open.' In spite of which, thought Harriet, she made a splendid figure standing there in the firelight beside fluffy little Biddy. Bright-eyed, upright, tall and strong, like an eagle with its chick.

Ted Baxter gave the colonel a few moments to settle his two passengers. The night was very still, and Cotty's deep voice and

Biddy's high one floated in at the window. When he heard the car start off down the road he removed the cushion he had thoughtfully manoeuvred onto the 'case histories'.

'A close shave,' he said with a grimace. 'We've read them and we've written them. Now let's put them in the fire.'

Harriet nodded, and he squatted on the hearth, feeding them into the flames. 'What is Mrs Metcalfe so frightened of?' he asked casually.

'Frightened?' repeated Harriet slowly. 'Well of course it's been a dreadful shock for everyone and she was very fond of her cousin, but I don't know about frightened. I should have thought that Caroline had rather a lot of courage, actually.'

'Oh yes, I agree with you. She's got a strong face. All the same,' Ted Baxter got up and knocked out his pipe. 'She's frightened. Well, I'd better be getting along I suppose. There's nothing more we can do tonight.'

Suddenly Harriet did not want her stalwart friend to go. Like Biddy, she disliked this time of day, so gloomy and dim. And what an exhausting affair this particular day had been! She sighed. If ever one was going to be lonely it would be tonight.

But one was not going to be lonely. Miss Harriet Mary Charles, OBE, MA, straightened her shoulders.

Baxter said comfortably, 'Not that there's anything very special to be getting along for, but I wouldn't like to turn into one of thse poor old fellows who shave once a week.' He shook his head, and Harriet shook hers. Or worse, she thought, thinking of Dizzy, much, much worse.

But Ted Baxter would always be so reassuringly all right, with his bristling hair and good, alert expression. Not much to look at, she decided, looking at him, but neat and tidy and satisfactory, like the colonel was. Not so stylish. Baxter was frank and uncomplicated, like a dog, while Rillington was stealthy and mysterious, like a wolf. And they were both managing very well on their own.

As she was going to.

'Good night,' she said cheerfully.

Before Ted Baxter left he poked the last curling ashes into fragments. COLONEL WALTER RILLINGTON, MC and JAMES ASHFORD, MD crumbled blackly into oblivion. The last to go was ROBERT KILMARNOCK, JP. Harriet watched it gravely.

'Yes,' said Baxter, 'I'm afraid he may not have been at the

Garrick Club for lunch yesterday, unless he drove. But it's quite a short walk from St James's and the parking is difficult round there. He was rather elusive altogether yesterday, with that car of his. But don't worry, there's many an explanation. There!' he said, straightening up and looking down at her with one of his rare grins. 'Finished! Up the chimney and out of your mind for tonight. There's nothing more you can do now, you've done enough for six already.'

'Rest in peace, in fact,' said Harriet lightly.

'No.' Baxter suddenly looked formidable. 'That's exactly what I don't mean, and if I may give you some advice, build up your fire and settle down in front of it. Draw your curtains, don't look out into the garden; it's spooky after a death. Go to bed early with a hot water bottle and a favourite book. Lock your door. Look after yourself. These affairs are upsetting, you know. A shock. More than one thinks.'

She smiled at him and went to open the door. 'And you. You've been marvellous.'

She stood there as he started up his car and drove away.

Then she turned back into her little hall. She felt warmed, consoled, pleased at Ted Baxter's fatherly concern for her. Pleased to be told what to do.

Not that she had any intention of doing it.

28

Vigil

Harriet was standing in her darkened hall with her coat on when she heard the gate click and saw a shadow pass her window. She waited for a few minutes and then silently opened her kitchen door and approached the tall thin youth who stood with his back to her, looking slowly about him.

The touch of her hand produced a sharp flinch and a muttered 'Wha – wha ...?'

Surprise had rendered Andrew so doubly incoherent that Harriet was able to draw him unresisting inside, and to look at him accusingly. The bony planes of his face were visible in the half-light as he blinked and swallowed apologetically. 'Just came to tell you that Mum's feeling much better. Th-thought you might be worried about her.'

'Thank you, Andrew dear. That was kind of you to come and tell me.'

And it was kind, if that was what he had come for. But now he seemed strangely disinclined to go away again, staring down at his thick-booted hostess with a hunted expression. 'Are you – are you going out, then?'

'Why not?' demanded Harriet. 'You're out, aren't you?'

'That's different. I'm a man,' said Andrew, looking about fifteen. 'Actually I-I think I'll stick around with you.'

But Harriet strongly advised him against this idea. Wasn't his mother in need of his support? After all, she had seemed upset. Not that a state of upsetness was surprising in the circumstances, but ...

'And Andrew, don't tell anybody about me, will you.' The light from her bedroom illuminated the top of the stairs. She could not think of any reason to give him for lurking below in the darkness, and merely added humorously, 'I was told to stay indoors and go to bed!'

But Andrew, when she finally escorted him out, glanced round over his shoulder. 'I-I think you should actually,' he replied seriously. 'S-stay indoors and go to bed I mean. If I were you.'

The night was cool and clear. Harriet stood for a moment outside her back door, avoiding the square patch of light on the grass beneath her bedroom window. She could see right down to where the distant river wound its way along the valley. Each shrub, each tree, was outlined in silver.

Carefully she made her way past the bushes and brambles, keeping to the shadows, and wedged the little gate open amongst the tall grass. Now, looking back, she could see the shed with its cobbled yard, and behind that the dark shape of the Hall, with one lonely lamp burning downstairs. What was Bobby doing at this moment, she wondered. Sitting with his head in his hands beside the empty fire? At his desk? Drinking? Trying to eat? Nobody knew. And he had so clearly indicated, this night was his own.

There was a lilac in Harriet's garden which had grown over the years into a fair-sized tree. It had a hollow beneath it with plenty of room for Harriet and now, with infinite care, she eased herself down into it, her back against the gnarled trunk and her outline obscured by suckers. It was an ideal vantage point for her garden, parts of that next door and of the commonland beyond them both.

Settled here, prepared for a long vigil, she started to think.

Had the police already been there that afternoon, scanning the neat and tidy shed for for the automatic check-up that follows an accident? Before tomorrow's post mortem? Other eyes might be searching then, with a narrower scrutiny, as hers searched about her now, but with machines, dogs, guards, ropes cordoning off, all the paraphernalia of the modern murder hunt.

If she was proved right would they come headlong, straight from the mortuary, wondered Harriet idly, or would they take their time, collecting the ropes, dogs, etc? After all, there was not all that hurry; nobody but she and Baxter knew it *was* a murder hunt.

Or did they?

Surely all those little sounds she kept hearing were not the usual nocturnal activities in these parts?

Could she not hear soft, murmuring voices from behind the wall? Men's voices in the garden of the Hall. But who would disturb Bobby at such a time?

Harriet shifted her position slightly and wished she had brought a cushion with her, but it was no good thinking about that sort of thing already. She was in such a strained, tense position trying to make out the words next door that it was quite a relief when she realised that they had ceased. Admittedly their place was taken by other little sounds, rustles, movements and living silences, but now Harriet was determined to relax and try to clarify her mind.

Suppose Biddy had casually revealed what she might have heard through the window about the cherry? Suppose somebody had heard the other end of her telephone call? Somebody that the official sounding words from the police station would strike fear into the heart of.

Somebody might hear *about* them, who was not necessarily in her room at the time.

Biddy, Cotty and Rillington driving home together. What had they said? Had they rung anybody else up afterwards? Had they all stayed put?

'Harriet pretended she was talking to a woman but it was really a man. I could hear his voice.'

Quite innocent, and then the casual questions ...

'Perhaps she's got a lover.' 'Who, her? Shouldn't think so, didn't sound like it. All pompous and long-winded.' 'Did you hear what he said?' 'Oh, something about bringing something forward a bit.' 'Bring what?' 'Sunday, something about Sunday.' 'Tomorrow, you mean?' 'I don't know. Sounded like a.m., or p.m. And a hat. Under your hat.' 'Odd, perhaps she's a spy or something. ...' '

Etc. Etc.

And then there was that bit about the knife. Somebody might have heard that too. (*Had* Biddy walked straight on? If not, she was not one to keep her own council!) Anybody. Thomas for instance – Harriet's heart gave a horrid lurch of pity and fear – with that habit of his of standing outside the window. And any caller might have walked up to the front door, heard the voices inside, and then walked quietly away again.

And then there were the wives. *Mrs* Ashford, *Mrs* Clancy. Presumably their husbands would have told them all about the shed and what they had found in it. They were hardly likely not to mention such a dramatic event, were they?

And then there were all the other people that those wives might talk to, especially Rosemary Ashford, and there was no limit to the amount of people those people who had been talked to might talk to, especially Biddy Dizzard.

In person, or on the telephone.

And then there was no limit to the trouble that could be caused by the wrong person finding out some insignificantly significant little thing. Something for instance that was destroyed, or tidied away, or changed by those three men, possibly in all innocence. Some vital piece of evidence that might mean nothing to the speaker and everything to the listener. Somebody might guess what it meant and be in danger. Somebody might know what it meant and be dangerous.

Old Dizzy, for instance.

Or Goggins.

Round and round went Harriet's thoughts as she cowered amongst the twigs and prickles, and slowly the time passed.

Far away down the valley an owl hooted, and the lean pale shape of a hunting cat passed unnervingly close beside her. There were the little rustles and squeaks she had come to know. But still there were others. She had expected to feel alone tonight. Had braced herself for hours of solitude.

At Little Farthings a door opened and shut, and Colonel Rillington spoke soothingly to Rex. Harriet turned up her collar against the night chill and felt a beetle fall down the back of her neck. The voices on the other side of the brick wall had long since ceased but a solitary figure now stood by the herbaceous border, looking out over the landscape and drawing on a cigarette. She could see the glow at the end, brightening and fading. An old rhyme came into her head: *Boys and girls come out to play, the moon doth shone as bright as day. Leave your supper and leave your sleep ...*

But there had been no supper to leave. And hardly any lunch. No wonder her mind was wandering! Gingerly Harriet felt in her pocket for the banana she had brought out with her and started to peel it.

Now Bobby had finished his cigarette and was pacing restlessly about his garden. Every now and then he came into her view, looking taut and yet fluid, like a panther in a cage. How beautifully he moved! Had he moved like that in the army? In his special division? On some deadly mission?

Strange to think of that sort of thing now. Harriet remembered Walter Rillington saying his godson was a marvellous dancer though not much good at games. Bobby and his 'rabbits'; that was more like him! Harriet's mouth twitched as she imagined those boys, always the specials, but an earlier variety of special this time, brimful with youth and high spirits, running and shouting and laughing. Always laughing.

How unsuitable that she should connect Bobby with laughter of all things, at this most tragic time. But she did. Even now that basic joyous quality still clung to him. Even now, on this awful evening, even now Harriet seemed to discern it as she watched him strolling away.

She did not see him again but neither did she feel she had the garden to herself. Once or twice she thought she heard a whisper. She removed the bulk of her weight from a really lethal thorn. The minutes ticked by and became an hour, two hours. Still the leaves rustled.

Come with a good will or not at all.

Rustle, rustle, pause, rustle. Was that a twig breaking? Harriet was reminded of long-ago games of grandmother's footsteps. How frightened she had been then, in spite of the giggles, as the soft footfalls crept up behind her!

Ridiculous!

How absurd were the things that frightened children! The dark. Hide and seek. Ghosts. Burglars.

Murderers.

And how good it was to be now grown-up. Too old, too experienced, too tough, to be frightened of such things any more ... and armed this time with her foreknowledge; they weren't expecting her, but she was expecting *them*!

Except ... Harriet felt suddenly colder still ... Andrew had seen her, spoken to her, indicated to any unseen watcher that she was there, in her garden instead of her cunningly-lighted bedroom. That unseen watcher, those unseen watchers, could have noted that she never again crossed the lighted square of grass outside her back door. Had never returned to the house. Might be watching her now, waiting until she was *really* alone.

But these were morbid fancies because really nothing seemed to be happening at all. Harriet finished a lump of cheese, the last thing she had with her, and began to feel thirsty.

It was a twig that had broken because here was another one, unmistakable this time and a good deal nearer. Perhaps it was Pusskin! Harriet's heart lifted at the thought of restoring the little creature to her friend. If only it was. If only it could be, and somehow all her fears be proved groundless. But this sound could never be that of a cat. Light and stealthy was the footfall, but human.

'Don't speak.' It was a command. Colonel Rillington slipped down beside her and put his mouth to her ear. As his body pressed against hers Harriet became aware of the fragrant scents of clean linen, soap, warm skin, added to those of the garden around her.

'Whisky,' he breathed.

'An answer to prayer,' she replied, taking the paper cup and putting it to her lips before handing it back for him to take a swig and return, like a schoolboy at a midnight feast. 'What are you doing here?'

'The same as you I expect, it may be a long time yet.' If it was possible to whisper breezily the colonel was doing it. 'Why don't you let me take your place? You go back into the warm.'

'Thank you, but I'll stay. I don't think it will be long now; they won't want to waste this moonlight.'

'Let's hope so, I'm getting stiff. I was sitting in my shrubbery and I decided to call on you in yours. We can get cramp together.'

The colonel refilled her cup and she now drank from it gratefully. The spirit radiated its pleasant effect after Harriet's frugal fare. Grandmother's footsteps receded from her thoughts.

'Prickly place you've chosen,' whispered her neighbour after a while. He topped up her whisky and put the flask back into his pocket.

'What about yourself?'

'No. I want my hand steady.'

'Do you know – have you any idea?'

Walter Rillington looked at her with his pleasant wolfish smile, shaking his head slightly. She could see the clarity of his eyes as the warmth of his body invaded hers; a pleasant antidote to the pins and needles in her feet. 'No. Not really. But they'll come back. I was there this morning and I've been here, roundabout, all day.' The teeth flashed in the darkness. 'Little do they know that I'm here now! They'll come, to make sure, and perhaps ...'

'To collect it?'

'Possibly.'

After that they did not speak.

The intensity of Harriet's gaze sometimes made her believe something moved in the scrubland before her, before a blink would send the scene back into its deathly stillness. Now, surely, she and he were truly alone.

And then, at long last, there was a faint movement beside her and Harriet followed the colonel's alert, pointing finger, to where a familiar figure had stepped out into the clearing in the ragged circle of trees beyond Bobby's garden, looking to left and right.

'That's our bird, I fancy.' Rillington's voice was quiet and flat.

But Harriet was speechless. Thunderstruck, she stared ahead and swallowed, as if she was gulping down a large, unpleasant pill.

The colonel silently rose to his feet. One could no longer imagine such a man groaning at his digging. 'Goodnight, Harriet,' he said softly.

Harriet hardly noticed his going. She remained, heedless now of all her physical discomforts, as though turned to stone.

It was Caroline.

29

Saturday evening (late)

So it had been Caroline all the time. Caroline who loved Bobby. Harriet had known that, of course, ever since she had first seen the two together at Cotty's party.

Caroline the passionate. Caroline the single-minded. Caroline the actress, the show-off at school. And incidentally Caroline the deprived, for whom marriage to Bobby could restore the life she had been brought up to and give opportunity and understanding to the children she loved so much. Yes, loved: above all, Caroline the loving.

But those who love can also hate. Caroline concealing that hatred under the guise of gratitude and admiration, bending over the graceful figure in the hammock, smiling and affectionate. And then, Caroline the quick, the impulsive, the brave (for Caroline was brave in spite of her disclaimers, no doubt about that), seizing her opportunity. Smilingly and affectionately doing something ... dreadful, before coming back across the lawn to rejoin her friends, with plenty of time now to drive into Loxley and to collect all the goalposts she wanted in Melchester. All the time in the world. Just as though nothing had happened.

Yes, all that Harriet would have to believe.

And now, having somehow managed to do so, she must sit here, cold, damp, but smugly safe in her own garden, watching Caroline incriminate herself, pledged to report back to Ted Baxter all that she saw. She, Harriet, must set the wheels of justice in motion and let it take its course.

Lost in her horrifying thoughts, drained of speculation and surmise, she scarcely noticed the footsteps behind her. Nothing really mattered now.

'I thought I should find you here,' said Cotty. She had lowered her voice but it still had the ring of authority, of command. A good voice to hear in a tight place.

'Oh Cotty, thank goodness you've come.'

Harriet smiled up at her friend, with a tinge of remorse, and, on an impulse, seized her gloved hand. 'Thank goodness you've come,' she said again.

'Have we both hit on the same idea?'

'I suppose so. It's the only time, isn't it. There was only tonight.'

'Exactly. Nice to have company. I think we deserve a bit of this.'

Cotty was pouring whisky into the little silver tops of her leather container.

'But I've just had some.'

'Who from?'

'Walter Rillington gave it to me before he went home.'

'Never mind, it won't hurt you. We may have a long wait yet.'

Cotty knocked hers back with her usual cheery gusto and Harriet, after a moment's hesitation, followed suit. Certainly the damp chill, the constant expectancy, the straining of the eyes and the stiffening effect of motionless crouching was taking its toll. Some further warming up would be welcome.

Cotty manoeuvred her rather bulky figure down beside her. 'What on earth is Caroline doing out there?' she murmured in surprise. 'She looked so queer in your house. I thought she was going back to bed.'

'I don't know,' Harriet replied uncertainly, reluctant to cast the first stone. 'Perhaps she couldn't sleep.'

'She certainly seemed quite peculiar this evening. Not herself at all.' Cotty glanced round suddenly, 'Harriet, you don't think ...'

'Of course not!' Harriet tried valiantly to put conviction into her voice. If Caroline had to be given away it would be to the proper authorities only. And after all there was no *proof* yet. All Caroline had done so far was to stand there, looking very much alone and rather lost. And now she was sitting on a tree-stump in the middle of the circle, facing the way she had come and resting her chin on her hands.

'I just thought it was rather a doubtful sort of accident. I expected Goggins, or Dizzy. Someone like that. At least I hoped.'

Harriet nodded sadly. Goggins or Dizzy: yes, indeed! 'I do

163

understand. Some awful old thing that wouldn't have mattered so much. I know we're all supposed to be equal in the sight of God but I never can quite feel the same.'

'I should think not!'

The two women huddled together companionably amongst the lilac suckers. What a strange sight they must make, thought Harriet. It was all so strange. Nothing seemed to be going according to plan. Why didn't Caroline get on with it?

Harriet was grateful to the talkative Cotty for being silent now, just when she wanted to collect herself. Anxiety, shock, alcohol, the long and extraordinary day she had lived through, all seemed to combine to make Harriet feel sleepy and stupid. Her feet were numb and her eyelids started to droop. Perhaps Ted was right – it was all too much of a strain for an old thing of sixty. She should have tamely retired to bed as he had advised. It had been conceited of her to think otherwise.

Now a shadow stole down the garden beside them, elaborately furtive, slipping from bush to bush as Harriet herself had done. She started up, but Cotty put out a restraining hand. 'No. Wait.'

'But it's only Thomas. He's going towards the common. Supposing he sees. ....'

'We came to watch, Harriet, to find out. There's no going back now.'

'But Thomas doesn't count. Oughtn't we to ...'

'Hush. Everybody counts.'

But Thomas had not seen his mother. His whole attention was given to surreptitiously crossing the bridle-path beyond Harriet's ditch, red indian style. In this way he succeeded in reaching the dark group of birches where he vanished into the shadows. Caroline remained immobile.

'She looks like Rodin's Thinker,' observed Cotty, amused, but Harriet did not answer, so deeply was she concentrating upon her own whirling thoughts.

Doggedly, muzzily, she brought them back to where they had been interrupted. A happy afternoon at Bassington Hall with laughter and jokes, and Fiona making some amusing remark about Cotty's treasure-hunt. Cotty's deep answering chuckle. If only Harriet didn't feel so fuddled!

Back. Back to Caroline killing her cousin and then walking lightly back across the sunny garden, saying that she had gone to

164

sleep, so that nobody would discover the truth. Coming in through the french windows laughing and talking as usual before driving all the way to Melchester to fetch the posts for Fiona's fête, before making the children's supper, before accompanying Thomas to his gnome place because he had asked her to. Because for some reason today was a special day for gnomes.

Horrible: just as if nothing had happened.

Well then, what was Caroline doing, wasting her time like this, looking so perplexed? Given all the above there was nothing to look perplexed *about*. She must know where to find what she herself had hidden.

Harriet shook a head which felt thick and woolly and then stopped because it made her giddy. Once again she made her brain retrace its steps.

What had Fiona said about the treasure-hunt? What had the joke been? Had they actually heard the joke?

Back to Caroline walking gaily across the lawn to rejoin her friends. Happy and carefree she had seemed then. Not cold and anxious as she looked now, sitting alone down there in her nightdress and dressing-gown. Happy and carefree, just as though nothing had happened.

Just as though nothing had happened. She always came back to that.

No wonder, for, as far as Caroline was concerned, *nothing had happened.*

Oh, what a time to yearn so passionately for her warm bed, just when she wanted all her wits about her, just at the climax of all her efforts.

Just when she was at last certain of the truth.

Stiffly, Harriet turned and looked at her companion. Cotty was ready for her. For how long had those large bright eyes been so steadily fixed upon her, from only a few inches away? Those observant, slightly protuberant golden eyes, set towards the sides of her head like a hare's. Like the mad march hare in Alice's tea-party. Little Alice playing with the black kitten before she went through the looking-glass. Such a dear little fluffy kitten.

A black fluffy kitten with a bell round its neck to protect the birds. Sewn firmly to his collar by somebody who could not bear to see a living thing hurt.

165

'Wha-wha-' Harriet struggled over the difficult words. 'What did you do with Pusskin?'

'Poor little Pusskin. He suffered from anaemia so I threw him in the nettles, right there, just beyond your garden,' said Cotty easily. 'Nobody goes into the middle of a clump of nettles, do they. Not unless they have to. And when they do have to he won't be there. Not when the police come. Not bloody likely! In actual fact, of course, not bloody at all.'

Cotty laughed heartily at this. 'But definitely flat. A little black pancake. He came in useful, didn't he. He didn't live in vain! *Who would have thought the old cat to have had so much blood in him?* I'm not totally uneducated, you know,' she remarked conversationally, 'though I may not have all your damned Oxford degrees.'

'I alwaysh knew you were clever, Cotty.'

Cotty nodded amiably. 'It's annoying isn't it, when other people turn out to be clever too. Or even cleverer! But that's life, I suppose. Poor old Harriet, you have missed out on that, haven't you, with your spectacles and your Latin and your Greek? It's such a shame. Just those half-baked children whose parents could afford to get shot of them. Think of it, Harriet! Somebody wonderful! Imagine it, if you can. Wanting you. A man! It's so unfair to think I've felt more truly alive in the last week than you have in sixty years!'

'You're right!' said Harriet in a rush, getting the words out at last that she had been struggling with for some time. 'I mean, it wash clever. To move body to toosh – toolsh – when you seemed to be at Shpurs. I can't shink how. You did it.'

'No, you wouldn't, would you, so I'll tell you, shall I? I just got up in the night and drove back here! Simple! I'd already hidden Mabel you see, in the trees about half a mile away from the Spurs. They're always too busy with each other at first to notice much outside the grounds. I popped up there on Wednesday as soon as Bobby told me he was going away. He tells me everything. I came back by train, disguised of course in case they recognised me at the station. Just a turban made out of my towel, and sunglasses. Purple lipstick. This and that. It was easy. They never did.'

'Not *now*, Cotty. They'll – they'll remember *now*, when they're ashked. The turban. The shunglashes.'

'But they won't get asked, will they,' said Cotty gently, as though to an idiot. 'Nobody will think of asking them. Why should they? Funny old girl; I really am sorry, you know, about all this. It's been quite a day, hasn't it. I know you're sleepy but I shall have to go myself in a minute so try to attend. Do watch that boy going up that tree after giving us his famous stalking act! Yes, that's him half-way up, testing every branch, didn't you notice him? It's a pity about your eye-sight, isn't it. Poor child, was there ever anybody so slow! Never mind, Caroline hasn't seen him either. Pathetic, isn't she, waiting in the gnome place, expecting him to turn up at the witching hour! Perhaps she thinks she'll see some fairies. I'm afraid she'll be disappointed at what she will see. Of course you've only got to pick up that big black note-book beside his bed to find out *all* Thomas's precious secrets.

'It'll all be there, painstakingly copied out, about me going into your garden this morning, or trying to, and Fiona lying in the shed before I did the doings. All ready for somebody to piece together; most interesting for them I'm sure, but they'll miss that because I shall nip in and get it back when the hoo-ha starts.'

Slowly Harriet focused her eyes on Cotty, as if through a dark and distant cloud. Cotty looked back at her with a straightforward, friendly concern that was somehow more frightening than anything she had done so far. 'How are you feeling? You look a bit pooped. You ought to give your hair a comb. It's untidy. You're usually so particular about that sort of thing, aren't you. One of your inhibitions I suppose. Still, there's nobody to see you but me, is there, so never mind. Now, where was I? Oh yes. I drove back. Keep awake, this is worth listening to. Seventy miles sounds a lot but it doesn't take long in a reliable car on a motorway. I had Mabel tuned up as soon as I bought her, not that I suppose you'd recognise the sound of a tuned-up engine would you, not unless I did it in Latin or Greek.

'Anyway, I left her a few hundred yards away and walked through here, to avoid disturbing Krysta more than I had to. Luckily it was terribly easy. I tipped Fiona out of the hammock onto a blanket. Like a sack of potatoes. I realised the advantages of the hammock straight away. I had all the luck, didn't I; I've always been a lucky person. Once she was on the blanket it was no trouble getting her into the toolshed, with those marvellous legs of hers all trailing about and banging into things. I'd got a hammer with me in my bag, and gloves as well. I'd thought of everything, but of course I've had it on my mind for months. You look rather sick; don't be it over me, will you. Bobby would have hated Fiona by the time I had finished with her; he's always so fastidious, isn't he. That's one of the things I love about him. One of the things he loves about me is my vitality, my fitness, my strength.

'I told the Spurs at breakfast that I'd had a bad night; true enough though actually I enjoyed it. I left nothing to chance. I even said the food had upset me in case I'd been heard leaving my room. And of course you can always rely on some old hypo saying it had upset them too!'

'I. Shall. Tell. Bakshter.'

'My dear, I'm afraid you must try to get it into your head. You really won't be telling anybody one single thing. Why did you think I was telling you all this? How are your legs feeling? I remember my old Mrs Brown complaining about her legs. They went off to the land of Nod before she followed them herself for good and all, poor old duck. About time too. She wouldn't have blamed me for what I did I'm sure. Ridiculous, a big household like that for one old biddy. Oh Harriet, you do look funny with your mouth open like one of Walter's goldfish! Come on, buck up, what did you think I lived on? Air?'

'Thomash'll tell him.'

'Thomas won't be telling anybody anything either.'

'C-Cotty. I *beg* you.'

'Beg away.'

'I shall shtop you. Killing him if itsh. Lasht thing I do.'

Cotty opened the large eyes to their fullest extent. 'What do you take me for? As if I would hurt a child! No, no. He's going to kill himself. Look.'

Helplessly, Harriet watched as Thomas let himself carefully onto the ground, switched on his torch, and started to search amongst the heather below the tree.

'I'll give you a hint. I told him I'd seen that bloody – sorry, damned, kitten stuck up the tallest birch tree. It was kinder really than telling him the truth, wasn't it. I mean, he wouldn't have liked the truth very much, would he. I said I wasn't a very good climber, so he'd have to get it down himself. Threw a pebble at his window. Kids like that sort of cloak and dagger stuff don't they! I'd forgotten what an assiduous mother that fool Caroline is. Even when he did manage to escape she somehow found he was gone and blundered along to look for him. Even she realised it was a bad night for him to be out in. Funny how many people cottoned on to that! Even a cretin like Thomas wasn't likely to start all over again looking for a black kitten in the middle of the night, so she opted for his other passion and went to the gnome place. Fairies; I ask you! Really, he deserves what's coming to him.'

Cotty shook her head. 'That boy's too secretive for his own good,' she said regretfully. 'If only he could have *told* someone. Ah!'

Thomas stooped to pick something up. Harriet's desperate warning came out only in the strangled murmur she had grown accustomed to. Frantically she tried again to rise on cotton-wool legs. Cotty easily pulled her down with one hand and leaned forward expectantly, keeping her fingers on Harriet's arm. 'This is going to be interesting.'

Thomas suddenly recoiled and Harriet heard not the explosion she had expected but a thin, high scream. Caroline jumped up, looked wildly round, and then started towards her son.

The boy turned blindly and Harriet heard his thudding footsteps as he tore down the hill in headlong flight, faster than she had ever imagined he could go, but clumsy as ever, uncoordinated, tripping over the tree-roots and recovering himself, arms outflung, gathering more and more speed, out of control. Towards the path by the tennis court. Towards the direct route. Towards home. Then he saw his mother.

It was a man's voice, loud and harsh, which barked out his name with such authority that the child swerved and fell, face downwards in the heather. A burly figure raced down towards him, past Harriet, over the ditch, shouting as he ran, 'Don't move, Mrs Metcalfe; Stay where you are!'

Baxter reached him first, Bobby a moment afterwards.

Cotty's tightly clenched hand now released its hold. 'God rot their souls,' she said calmly.

Harriet's mind reeled. Her heart had moved from her chest into her ears and threatened to deafen her altogether. A mist rose before her eyes. From a vast distance, conjured up by a tremendous effort of will, her own voice whispered, 'I don' unnerstan'.'

'You don't understand quite a lot, do you, my dear, but I can't continue your education now. There are too many people about. As your protector seems to be otherwise engaged I shall do the other thing.'

Cotty's gesture was swift but it was as if in slow motion that Harriet saw the glint of the slender knife as it rose in the moonlight before her and started on its deadly downward curve. At the same moment there came a loud crack from behind her, an acrid smell, and a moment of dead silence during which Harriet made yet another futile effort to clamber through waves of blackness onto feet she could not feel.

It seemed quite a long time after the hiccupping grunt that she took the full weight of Cotty's body.

As if in a dream she heard again the sound of running footsteps, nearer at hand this time, a torch shone full on her face and then away. The garden was full of familiar people whose hands were pulling, pushing and lifting. Harriet, flat on her back, stared groggily up into anxious, torchlit faces. Cool, appreciative grey eyes looked into hers. 'Drugged I think.' It was Walter Rillington's crisp voice. 'But unhurt.'

The last words Harriet committed to memory that night were his. 'I may not be of much use these days, but thank God I'm still a fairly decent ... no, in all due modesty, a *very* good shot!'

30

The men

A lot of unpleasant things had happened to Harriet but they were all over now. Apart from a headache and a sore throat of laughable unimportance she was warm and comfortable, in the mortal world, amongst the scent of flowers.

Cautiously she flexed her toes. Yes, both legs were in working order.

From the window behind her high bed a beam of sunlight fell on Bobby's face. He stood looking down at her with eyebrows raised. Harriet nodded reassuringly, and raised her own in return.

Boddy told her vaguely that everybody had come and done everything and been everywhere, adding that he wasn't supposed to be here at all. Hoarsely, Harriet begged him to tell her more.

'Well, I guessed it was murder when I saw old Ted Baxter. If he was paying you an informal call he would have pushed off, wouldn't he, instead of so silently remaining? The lost kitten made me wonder, and then I'm afraid I couldn't help overhearing some of your telephone conversation and realising that if it was all going to get so official tomorrow we might reasonably expect the murderer to return while the coast was still clear, to tie up any loose ends.

'So I kept watch and after a while Ted joined me; asked if he could use my garden if necessary, and so on.' A hint of his old smile appeared. 'A tactful way of letting me know that he was keeping an eye on me, husbands being usually No 1 suspect! The rest you know, only too well.'

Harriet opened her mouth, but a nurse had taken Bobby indignantly away.

The next time she opened her eyes she felt perfectly well. A chair creaked beside her as the occupant leaned forward and put a hard hand on hers.

'Ted! I can't understand what happened. I never tasted anything that hadn't been tasted first!'

'Nor did I.' Two voices spoke in unison. So Walter Rillington was there too. Harriet looked round. *And* a policeman. Had he been there all the time?

'That's all very well, but what happened to *me*?'

'You have to open both those little twin flasks before you can drink out of the tops. One had a tiny piece of scotch tape stuck to it. You got the other, with the ground up Mandrax.'

'But the taste!'

The detective-sergeant now spoke. 'There's none to speak of. And to a lady like yourself, with other things on her mind. ...'

Laughing was so delightful, but Harriet stopped suddenly. What did they intend to do about Colonel Rillington?

Rillington answered that one himself. 'I'm hoping they're fairly slack down here.'

Harriet did too, and the sergeant looked properly blank, as

Rillington said nostalgically, 'Well, if they're not I shall have one moment of glory to mull over in my cell. It wasn't all that easy … getting one without the other in the middle of the night amongst a lot of lilac suckers with a single bullet. She had to go,' he said firmly, for the benefit of his uniformed companion, who had allowed a gleam of indulgence into his eye. 'I'm not pretending I enjoyed it, but if I'd winged her she would still have done poor Harriet in. A bit potty, you see, given to senseless lying. I mean to say, she could have stopped for a chat without pumping a perfectly healthy throttle.'

'Given to lying,' corrected Harriet, 'but that was setting the scene for Mabel going wrong, all ready for some mythical garage to put right. After all, we don't have all that many trains down here.'

'And who would think of checking which garage?' said Ted Baxter. 'Though there's plenty of checking going on now.'

The policeman caught his eye and took out a note-book. 'Do you feel well enough to answer a few questions, Miss Charles?'

'Certainly,' said Harriet grandly, lying back on the pillows with her mind as clear as a bell.

Mellifluously, she told him about the Spurs. How Cotty had never taken leave of her old friends, had obviously intended to return before she had been missed. Would have done if Mr Faraday had not forgotten his glass eye and if she missed lunch well, she *had* complained of an upset stomach at breakfast!

The stubby pencil hovered uncertainly over the paper, but Harriet swept on regardless. 'The alibi would have held.' Her eyes widened. 'And she might *still* have got away with it if it hadn't been for Colonel Rillington. Who would have connected her with any of it?'

'Two stabbings in two days,' remarked the young man stolidly. 'Might have taken a bit of accounting for.'

'My little job perhaps,' said Rillington grimly. 'Since they would both have been done with my knife and I was on the spot each time. Of course I could have explained about sitting alone in my shrubbery with my binoculars and my rifle, but I daresay Miss Cotman could have thought up a better story for herself than that.'

'Possibly she could have, sir.'

'It was bad luck she was stampeded into trying to stab me,' said Harriet. 'After taking all the trouble to drug me.'

'You fought very strongly against the effects.'

'It's better if you get them conscious,' added the sergeant professionally.

'Cotty was resourceful, wasn't she, and she was clever. She told me so herself and I agreed with her. Clever but careless. What a stroke of luck that the police never had a chance to see that shed as she left it!'

'A terrible mistake.' Walter Rillington took the blame squarely. 'But I swear James never suspected a thing. It was just removing the body and so on as quickly as possible, for Bobby's sake. But you can't fool me with two different kinds of blood. It was much older in the eye-socket and on the blanket for instance than the stuff on the floor. I never saw the stab wound but I did notice when I came to put it up again that the shelf had been sawn nearly through. Annoying for her to find she couldn't budge the thing without. The brackets were rusted into the screws and more or less immovable. They would have supported a couple of elephants as they were, and spoiled the whole effect! And talking of elephants, by that time I had missed my knife.'

'But you didn't say anything?'

'I'm a soldier, not a doctor.'

There was a pause which nobody attempted to fill, during which the colonel gazed coolly out of the window.

'Gossip,' tried Harriet.

'Stupid insinuations that one doesn't believe.'

'Of course not, but one may remember them. Initiated by Cotty but passed on by somebody else?'

'Poor Biddy, she was rather distressed about it. Naturally I assured her that it was absolute poppycock,' said the colonel heartily. 'A girl like Fiona would have chosen something a bit more swish than a toolshed to meet a lover in, wouldn't she!'

'And what about Mr Clancy?'

The sergeant grinned, and Baxter said, 'He ought to have suspected something. Being a medical man.'

'Of course,' Harriet remembered the breathless words outside her window. 'Run away with one of his patients I suppose and of course at his age one is quite likely to be already married.'

'He was writing a book on personality disorders,' said Baxter.

'It's a pity nobody ever *does* listen to poor Thomas, Harriet said. 'He could have told us that.'

'They'll be listening to him now. But Clancy was keeping mum about anything he noticed. Maureen may well have mentioned the fact that she was the last to leave.'

'She probably looked rather over-excited and silly too, when she got back so late from that work-party,' said Harriet. 'If Andrew's expression was anything to go by I rather think she may have – flirted with him a little.'

'And she was hardly likely to tell him about that; she lived in considerable awe of John Clancy. No, it would have worried him, that look of hers. In his line of country you don't miss much as far as facial expressions go. He knew her to be unbalanced; what about a little off-hand murdering for kicks? and whichever way you look at it he was responsible for her. No wonder he worked like a demon after he had sized up that shed!

'Apart from that John Clancy wasn't keen on appearing in the public eye from his own point of view. He therefore writes to his patients, postponing their appointments until after the inquest, and makes a quick getaway, trusting that the whole thing will be over by the time he returns, with Fiona conveniently reduced to ashes and no more awkward questions.'

'Coping with Maureen must have been only one of his anxieties,' said Harriet.

'Yes. Life can't have been too easy for him, though he'd kept a hard core of devotees which he was naturally unwilling to lose.'

'I'm glad it won't be necessary to check his alibi,' said Harriet. 'Psychiatric patients often dislike being known as such, don't they, especially in a country place, if they have a certain position.'

'Quite so. Miss Cotman's party must have been a nightmare to him, when he realised that the wife and children he had not run quite far enough away from were the very same unfortunate family that Fiona was about to give a home to, right under his nose. A most unpleasant and difficult situation; no wonder he left early! Added to which, with the police called in, a handwriting expert might get to see that anonymous letter.'

'The wording was so obviously his,' said Harriet. 'I wonder if his book is written in the same style, and if he will remember to change the dedication before it is published.'

'He may not need to. That little dolly drop of his can't be much of a companion for a clever man. Maybe he will settle down again with Olly and Polly and Co, if they'll have him.'

'But meanwhile he's landed with quite a reasonable motive for doing away with Fiona. It was only we who knew he was actually in the clear.'

'Well, it's all water under the bridge now,' said Ted Baxter. 'I reckon that queer looking place of his will be up for sale within a month. Too much investigation has been done on Mr Clancy already. I doubt whether we'll be meeting Olly and Polly either.'

'I'm not so sure about that,' put in Rillington. 'Bobby's a very kind man, you know.'

A very kind man. For a startled moment Harriet considered what that kindness had been inadvertently responsible for. Then she said, 'And now, of course, the police have been there.'

'Ah. You can find so much when you know what to look for. Signs ... kitten's fur and – the distribution.'

'At one time,' said Harriet quietly, 'actually stamping on the little body to. ...'

'We think she did. On the floor of the shed.'

She turned to Ted. 'And you never mentioned the kitten to me at all.'

'No. It wasn't very nice, Harriet.' He looked down at the floor. 'But the thought did strike me when you told me that Thomas had lost him, just before we met that ambulance. You had already given me such a very graphic description of that shed.'

'And you?'

'Yes,' said Rillington. 'And of course the possibility that it might be still on the premises. I mean, if the whole thing was going to pass off as an accident, why not just chuck it away? It's the instinctive thing to do with something unpleasant. I nearly got Rex to pick it up, and then I realised: leave it, and wait.'

'How clever we all were!' exclaimed Harriet. 'Even Bobby, who never saw the evidence but knew his wife so well.' She hesitated. 'And ... Pusskin himself?'

'All disposed of. You must have come very close to discovering him. And finding Miss Cotman too.'

'I really knew there were three of us that night, not two!' Harriet sighed. 'I even dreamed about them.'

'But it was probably your presence which caused her to fling the kitten's body away in a panic and provide us with our only real evidence and a bit of luck for the colonel.'

'In fact things might have been difficult for Colonel Rillington if she hadn't,' said the young policeman.

'But he was devoted to Fiona and anyway he's much too cool

and efficient,' cried Harriet indignantly. 'Oh, it wouldn't have been like him at all!'

'Try that in a court of law,' suggested Rillington, smiling.

*   *

'Not that Colonel Rillington was quite prepared to *leave* it to a court of law,' confided Baxter when they were alone. 'Andrew was on a look-out too. Bright boy, that. And Mr Kilmarnock was asking me some searching questions. He's a very clear-sighted man.'

Harriet was pondering on Cotty's brinkmanship. Her ebullient behaviour under the beady eye of Mrs Dobbs. How she had bounced back from her difficulties.

'She really was a very remarkable woman,' she said. 'If the OAPs had not removed her for a number of hours. ...'

'Leaving us free to pursue our enquiries,' said Baxter happily.

'And give everybody time to come to the same conclusion, each thinking they were the only one to guess the murderer might return.'

'I was wondering whether Colonel Rillington, or Andrew, or Mr Kilmarnock, or Mrs Metcalfe, or even Thomas, was going to collect that kitten,' said Baxter. 'They were all prowling about, nobody knowing which was the hare and which the hounds. Not like Miss Cotman, sitting cosily talking to you in such an apparently friendly way.' Ted Baxter shook his head in vexation. 'That stopped me suspecting *her*. But Colonel Rillington had you under observation all the time. Very keen eyes. He knew you'd seen that shed as it was and, very sensibly, he trusted nobody. When you were in mortal danger I wasn't even looking.'

'Of course not,' said Harriet. 'You would be watching Thomas and his mother. What was happening there?'

'A thin wire,' said Baxter drily. 'Where else should the panic-stricken Thomas run but down that ordinary, straightforward path, towards home? He would hardly do his favourite detour under your fence and through your nice jungly garden this time.'

Harriet's eyes darkened in horror. 'But why was Thomas so *terrified*?'

'Miss Cotman simply left the gloves and the hammer under a bush – they were not very pretty – adding a notice saying 'BEWARE!' Just the thing to intrigue a small boy. As soon as he

176

picked up the notice he saw what it concealed. It must have been a surprise for Miss Cotman when Mrs Metcalfe turned up, with that sixth sense of hers. Would she reach the wire first and spoil the whole plan? Going uphill it would hardly incommode her. Not that it would have actually killed the boy. Another botched job. You really need a motor-cycle for that kind of thing. Nasty though.'

'So Cotty might have actually seen Thomas run onto the wire *in front of his mother*.' Harriet remembered the eager fingers pressed into her arm. Although she was warmly tucked up in bed, she shivered.

Baxter nodded. 'As you say, a remarkable woman, but a wicked one.'

'Are you going to tell them about the wire?'

'I don't expect so. We just removed it. I doubt if Mrs Metcalfe will ever see the police files.'

'Supposing it had all gone as Cotty planned it?'

'A newcomer is found dead in her garden. A heart attack, perhaps, followed by exposure? Nobody knows the previous state of her health. After Thomas's death there will be plenty of opportunity for Miss Cotman to quietly collect kitten, notice, gloves and hammer – a nice heavy parcel for the river perhaps – before sleeping the sleep that even she must be requiring by now. There is nothing to connect her with the wire.'

'As it is. ...'

'As it is, of course, you're alive and so is he, and we have them all.'

31

The women

'But to think that we were the ones to give her that double flask!' exclaimed Rosemary Ashford. 'She was really very helpful during that 'flu epidemic when the family were with us.'

'And to think that I was fast asleep in bed the whole time,' began Biddy once again. 'You could have knocked me down with a feather.'

'We couldn't, not if you were lying down already,' replied Rosemary unfeelingly. 'But you know, once the shock was over *I* wasn't altogether surprised.'

'Come off it, Rosemary!' Caroline's face had regained its usual glow. 'You'd never admit it if you were!'

'No, honestly, I mean it. I've met people like Cotty before. The bossy nurse. Oh, I know you're going to say I was one of them and you're right,' she added disarmingly. 'But I mean the sort of bossy nurse that gives savage blanket baths and is marvellous at the Christmas party. Admired by all but I never trusted them. They liked seeing people suffer. That was why they chose nursing in the first place.'

'I know,' said Harriet. You had to hand it to Rosemary; she often got it right. 'Cotty was under-matron at rather an old-fashioned school, you see, during my first term there as a teacher. Two girls reported sick and she told them to go and get on with it in that bracing way she had, and when they both nearly died I caught a curious expression in her eyes. It was as though, amidst all the general pain and anxiety, Beatrice, as we called her then, was actually enjoying herself.

'But of course she always was very cheerful and energetic. Never at all *lazy*, the usual cause of such incompetence! So I told myself that she might have just been run off her feet at the time. The real matron returned from somewhere or other, the girls recovered and were removed, Beatrice Cotman disappeared and I hardly recognised her when I met her again.'

Biddy's china-blue eyes had been getting rounder and rounder, almost like those of Tweaky Poo, who was clutched tightly in her lap, suffering her affection with immutable dignity. 'But Harriet,' she gasped. '*Why* did she do it?'

'That was one of the reasons,' said Harriet, 'for this tea-party.'

'It's a jolly good one,' said the appreciative Caroline, helping herself to another cucumber sandwich.

'Apart from thanking you for your kindness towards an interfering newcomer.'

'Of course you had to interfere,' said Rosemary crisply. 'You were the one who lived on the spot, was connected with the police, understood Thomas, knew all the suspects and discovered the body.'

'And anyway,' added Caroline practically. 'Think of the alternative.'

'That's what I did think of,' said Harriet.

A slight feeling of constraint now descended on her, and she put some coal on the fire. 'And I wanted to see you without Bobby.'

'I shan't say a *word*,' promised Biddy heroically.

Harriet smiled. 'But of course even the modest Bobby must know by now that Cotty was emotionally involved.'

'In love with him, you mean,' said Caroline flatly.

'I'll begin at the beginning,' said Harriet. 'I heard so much about Fiona Kilmarnock; how beautiful she was and how wonderful in every way, that I hadn't bargained for the attraction of her *husband*! Nobody had mentioned that, and of course Bobby himself is quite ignorant of it. He has the born charmer's look of attentive appreciation, but it's genuine. He really does love people; he really is interested in them. He loved and was interested in Cotty. He loved and was interested in all his friends.

'And he was repaid in kind. While Fiona was admired, flattered and desired Bobby was loved. His detractors (a bitter, envious old fellow like Dizzy, for instance), were few and far between. Most people would do anything for him.'

Harriet gazed thoughtfully into her cup. 'And Cotty did. The effect of Bobby's attractiveness upon her can only be described as cataclysmic. Not only did she fall wildly in love with him but she was wonderfully, joyfully, passionately *certain* that he felt exactly the same way towards her. It was rather splendid that, in its awful Brünnhilde way.'

'But why,' objected Caroline, 'if he wasn't.'

'They say that murderers are conceited. Cotty had no doubts. She was convinced that only Fiona stood between them.'

Harriet broke off and then said, 'The tragic part was that she wasn't a very feminine personality. Not like you three. Never likely to inspire the passion of her dreams. It was a dream world she lived in, you see. Rather a vague one, because she had forgotten a lot of it. Lies do get so muddled, don't they. The truth is easier to remember.'

Caroline said, 'And there was nobody round here to substantiate what she said.'

'Occasionally one might turn up, I suppose, like me. I knew that a school like Greengates would never have employed a male gym-teacher, for instance, especially like the one she invented.'

They all remembered some of Cotty's stories, with varying

degrees of compassion. Harriet said, 'I'm glad she died then, sharply and cleanly in her hour of triumph, instead of being publicly humiliated and confined for life. Whatever was wrong with Cotty, and there were terrible things wrong, she was ... vital. Free. And I believe it would have been life. You see, she was already an established murderess.'

There was a gasp.

'Oh yes, she told me so, and gave me the remains of the same Mandrax that her previous employer had been prescribed. They found the old bottle, from a Suffolk chemist. They would have investigated all that sort of thing, if she had lived. Perhaps she had received other doubtful legacies from other old people. Cotty was forceful and persuasive and, of course, only too easy to become dependent on.

'Of course it's easy to say all this now but I was a rotten detective. I still didn't really suspect Cotty.'

Harriet looked at Caroline. 'It was only when I was forced to suspect you that I realised the truth. You would have had to kill her before you fetched the netball posts. Before you took Cotty to the station. You couldn't do it between the two journeys because how could you possibly know exactly when we would leave, or I return?

'Cotty's personality fitted the crime but she had a watertight alibi. Caroline saw her off in that non-stop train. But now, as I considered Caroline for the part, Cotty's alibi fell to the ground. I realised that Fiona could actually have been murdered in *public*.

'If any of us had looked up at that particular moment we might have seen the back of Cotty as she bent over the hammock, talking away, masking any other sound with her loud laugh, and stabbing Fiona through the heart. Perhaps we did see her.'

'But the struggle. Surely ...'

'Cotty knew her anatomy; she had a nurse's training. Also it's difficult to struggle in a free-swinging hammock. She was efficient, even remembering to empty the cup of tea she took her. The fact that it had no lipstick on it seemed insignificant at the time. Afterwards you remember these things.'

'So she might never have been suspected,' said Rosemary quietly.

'Oh, but if *only* I had not bought Rose Cottage! No wonder Cotty hated me. If only that garden could have remained uninhabited for just a little longer, instead of acquiring a new owner who could never be trusted to keep out of it! But at first luck was with her. The well-meant removal of the obvious signs of Pusskin's death was a gift from Heaven. Imagine the unsuspecting police doctor. That stab wound was tiny and the other injuries severe. If another day or two had passed without further examination the time of death would become vaguer and the kitten's blood the same colour as her own. Who would test it?'

'Really,' said Caroline thoughtfully, 'it was quite a simple crime.'

'Which, unfortunately for Cotty, turned complicated,' said Harriet, 'because Cotty, though twisted, was not a complicated person. Starting with the simple idea of pocketing Walter's knife she waited for an opportunity to fake the accident in the shed when Bobby went up to London. When that happened Goggins could take the rap. His carelessness, stupidity and dishonesty were well known. Who would believe it when he told the truth? She would mask the absence of the real weapon with a multitude of others and then pay a little visit to one of her many friends. At a suitable distance.'

'Only,' said Caroline the intelligent, 'it started to go off the rails.'

'Yes indeed. She never told me of the *mistakes* she made, which sent the whole thing spinning off in the wrong direction. But at first all goes according to plan. She holds her breath when the courteous Caroline insists on saying goodbye to her hostess. But no, although Fiona is already dead Caroline suspects nothing and may even be prepared to swear that Fiona is alive at the time of their departure.

'Cotty returns to the hammock about ten hours later, via my garden. It is vitally necessary for her to slip the proofs in at the french window (though she overlooks a page, in the dark) and Krysta is momentarily alerted. She successfully drags her burden out of the dog's sight and into the shed, thanking her lucky stars that there has been so little bleeding, and for the cherry covered dress.

'Now she takes a hammer from her red shopping bag (she dare not use a weapon which will be found later for the actual deed), and brings it down on the beautiful face she hates so much. It lands in the eye, which might normally be expected to bleed profusely. Imagine Cotty's feelings as she realises that it is not going to; Fiona has already been dead too long for that.

'The bold but slapdash plan has now hit a serious snag. Even James at his vaguest is bound to notice the bloodless appearance of the battered corpse before him and realise that death could never have occurred according to the mock-up in the shed.

'Cotty stands there irresolute, considering different possibilities. We don't know how *long* she stands there because I have gone to sleep again, but I think it is some time before she finally decides on stealing the kitten. It is the weakest and most submissive of the animals nearby. She crosses the green and pushes open Caroline's unlocked front door. Perhaps the dog clatters across the uncarpeted hallway. Even he will probably investigate at this hour and have to be reassured. This, or some other sound, arouses Thomas.

'Cotty stuffs Pusskin into her bag and hurries back here, tinkling away until she throws the little collar into my unkempt garden; that useful by-pass between two excellent house-dogs!

'Meanwhile Thomas has discovered his loss. He slips out of the house and listens intently with the sharp ears of childhood. He follows the distant sound of the bell.

'Cotty starts on the shed. There is a lot to do. Colonel Rillington, who notices every detail, might easily have visited it during his construction of the stalls the day before in search of nails etc., and she has not dared do more than discreetly tamper with the shelf before now. Certainly Pusskin is still alive. He has to be. Perhaps she secures the bag with a stone.

'She certainly won't have done much before she hears Thomas's running footsteps. He is in too much of a hurry to be quiet this time.

'Hastily Cotty switches off her torch, seizes the bag and, according to the police, retreats into the shadows by the gateway. From here she sees, to her further horror, the light going on in my room.

'She must be in an agony of impatience as she stands there, with a restraining hand over the kitten's face, willing Thomas to go away and wondering what I am going to do. During this time she is badly scratched. The claws catch the vein in her wrist. She snatches her hand out sharply with a gasp of pain and bleeds sufficiently to mark our shoes when we pass the entrance.

'Slowly, as he always does everything, Thomas searches the garden. Every inch receives his careful attention with Cotty retreating at his advance and peeping out to observe his progress. She freezes when he seems to glance towards the shed. Will he see Fiona? No, he appears unconcerned.

'But he *has* seen her, lying on the rug. The fine night reminds him of sleeping out in his own garden before his camping trip. The injured eye is away from the door. She is just another incomprehensible grown-up to him and he continues his search in the shrubbery nearby.

'I am now forced out myself; I can no longer keep up the pretence of not seeing Thomas's torch. He doesn't notice me leave the house and fails to recognise my unfamiliar hooded figure.'

'He switches off the light and goes into hiding, spying on what he believes to be a wholesale cat thief, while I in turn do my stint at searching the garden, taking up more precious time.

'Eventually Thomas and I confront each other, with long explanations. When we eventually leave the garden Cotty is not sure what we are up to. Only when I am safely asleep in bed will she feel free to continue. Actually I never switch my bedside light off and must delay her further until she decides to risk it, and with trembling hands completes her grisly task.

'The extreme care necessary to set the scene in haste and near darkness is enough to strain even iron nerves. However, she carries it through without discovery, though not without taking part in my semi-waking dreams.

'At this point Cotty, now thoroughly rattled and within an ace of freedom, makes her second mistake. She follows her natural instincts and flings the rather gruesome little object over my fence and into the nettles before making her escape. She relies on it neither being found in a recognisable state nor being associated with Fiona's death. This is the nearest she gets to panic, nothing else occurs to her. All she can think about is covering that seventy miles before her room-mate wakes up. Still she hangs onto the shopping bag with its incriminating contents. She intends to keep the knife – it has proved itself, like the Mandrax, and may again. Remember, Cotty is a killer. The bag, the gloves and the hammer must never be found. Their disappearance can come later, when Cotty has time to think.

'She is out on the deserted motorway with her foot down and the bag in the boot before she begins to reflect. Will that shed stand up to close inspection? She was too agitated to give it all a second look. If it gives rise to any doubt and the *kitten* is searched

183

for and found what about her? Not many other people know all the details of the Metcalfe household that were needed to abstract him. She decides to retrieve Pusskin's body. Only then will she really breathe freely. She has an alibi and nothing to connect her with the crime. She, and the one person she cares about, Bobby, will be in the clear.

'Once again she starts on the tedious double journey, slipping out of the back row in the morning lecture, after a sufficiently provocative remark to make her presence felt. She leaves the car off the Loxley Road, waits until after the OAP bus is due to leave and then hurries along to rectify her mistake, taking that famous bag for what she devoutly hopes is its last journey. When it is safely disposed of with all its contents, en route to Rampton, then, and only then, can Cotty relax.

'But now fate turns against her and she runs into Caroline outside my house. What dreadful bad luck! The very one who had seen her off on the train the evening before! Naturally Caroline is surprised to see her. What can Cotty do but accompany her back to the OAPs, where she is eagerly welcomed.

'She is out of action now for some hours, still lumbered with that bag. No wonder she refuses to lend it to Mrs Dobbs and grabs up armfuls of berries and flowers to cover what it contains and also, as it happens, provide an excuse for the deep scratches on her wrist. Once this is done she acts her usual part to perfection, but Mrs Dobbs has already noticed her uncharacteristic behaviour earlier on and repeats it to me.

'When they return Cotty throws out a dark hint that can apply to anybody, just in case. So much has already gone wrong and in a pinch it may divert suspicion from herself. And now Thomas makes a chance remark which sends her floundering further out of her depth. He claims that he has seen Fiona lying asleep in her shed.

'Normally this might have gone unheeded. He lives in an imaginative world of his own and is apt to make enigmatic statements. But Fiona has since been discovered in that shed, *heavily mutilated and covered in blood*. She could hardly have been mistaken for sleeping by the most absent-minded observer.

'This discrepancy brings a calculating look into Cotty's eyes. It belies the ordinary remark which she is making in my kitchen at the time. She knows Thomas for what he is: an honest child who has lost his kitten and is frightened of blood. His calm announcement shows her clearly that he is the sole witness of Fiona's body, lying in the shed, *before Cotty had got to work on it.* The net is closing in. How soon will Caroline work it out?

'And who will remember that Thomas has already found the little collar, lying alone? We all know that it was never taken off in the ordinary course of events.

'Now Thomas's hours are numbered. He must not talk again. Somebody might listen next time, and he is so horribly accurate about times and details. He is not likely to forget them as he copies them out from one book into another.

'Who will link these statements up and draw the obvious conclusion; that the kitten's fresh blood was used to mask the fact that Fiona died long before she was injured, and that Cotty no longer has an alibi?

'How many people already had?

'Cotty now starts taking wild risks. It is she of course that is really near the border-line, not Thomas. Caroline senses the danger surrounding her son and is sharper than usual with him when he wanders off on his own, though previously he has come to no harm. She lies sleepless in bed, listening to every sound.'

Harriet added, without looking at her, 'For some time she has been needlessly afraid of his being taken away from her and put into a world he couldn't cope with.' She added in a matter-of-fact voice, 'Also, Caroline had another and very terrible fear.'

Caroline had turned her face away from the fire. She said in a low voice, 'So you knew.'

32

Settling down

'I guessed,' said Harriet, 'because of you being that quite usual but curious anomaly; a sensitive *mother* who knows she is right and a sensitive *person* who knows nothing of the sort! For instance, the fact that you know Andrew is a splendid boy and are actually very proud of him does not prevent you feeling a considerable degree of embarrassment over his accent, for instance, or the length of his hair.'

Caroline smiled faintly.

'When I brought Thomas back that night I expected you to say "Where have you been?" but instead you said in a puzzled voice, "What have you been doing?" Had he hurt his feet? Such a fusspot would hardly keep it to himself! But he said nothing about the spots of blood which he had not noticed on his shoes.

'This returned to you with a dreadful force when he told you casually that he had seen Fiona "asleep in the shed". Not only Cotty was affected by this remark. It actually caused you to faint with terror.

'Had you, *could* you, have been wrong all these years about your own child? For him to have looked upon a hideously bloodstained body with such uncaring eyes would have been totally out of character. As it would have been totally out of character for mild little Thomas to batter Fiona to death. But given one impossibility then nothing is impossible.

'And people who behave totally out of character are insane.'

Caroline folded her hands together to control their trembling. Harriet switched once more into the third person.

'But soon Caroline must have recovered her native good sense and started to consider. The two conflicting stories, looked at more calmly, showed her plainly that this was no accident. Thomas was in the vicinity and might have picked up more than enough to put himself at risk. He kept a daily record which was easily available, though she would never read it herself.'

Harriet looked affectionately at her friend. 'Not that I realised what Caroline was going through. I was still trying to work it out. I had guessed Pusskin's possible fate but was not sure who was behind it all.

'I had readily discounted Caroline, who seemed to be no killer. On the contrary she gave tender care to all that needed it; old people, flowers, animals, children ... in fact she was particularly devoted to and wrapped up in her children. She loved them passionately, and I realised that she was a very passionate person; her childhood reminiscences emphasised this part of her nature.

'Gradually I was forced to consider her. She had singleness of purpose. She was not a sentimental woman and would have no false scruples. She was extremely honest. She would not think "I

186

could not do that sort of thing, I am not that kind of person,"
because if she had to she could.'

Harriet looked at the firm set of Caroline's mouth, met the large
steady eyes and spoke to her directly. 'At that time,' she said, 'you
could have been a dangerous adversary.'

'Could I?' said Caroline wonderingly.

'Yes, for how could you ever fail Thomas, who feels totally
secure in your support? He tells you what he tells nobody else
and shares his inmost thoughts with you without fear of ridicule.
You would never break his trust in you and would fight to the
death if it was for him. You knew Fiona was not altogether
sympathetic towards Thomas. He was not of her ilk.'

'So, did you really think ...?' Caroline gazed unbelievingly at
Harriet.

'I was waiting for the murderer to come in view, looking for
something, and you came into view, looking for something. Yes,
my dear, I nearly did. But ...'

'But what? You've just said, quite rightly, I do see – I've never
thought of it before, actually – that I'm capable of murder.'

Harriet smiled benignly. 'Of murder, yes, if necessary, perhaps
you might be, and perhaps we all might be. It wasn't murder that
I was sure you weren't capable of, Caroline, it was just that I was
absolutely and irrevocably certain that *you would never kill
Pusskin*!'

*   *

Harriet lay back in her chair and said dreamily, 'Tragedy strikes.
A rich, gifted, beautiful and altogether highly successful young
woman dies. And there, already, we have four perfectly good
reasons for killing her. The money was actually another strike
against Caroline. Fiona was fond of her, had no other close
relatives and was married to a rich man. While she remained
childless she would probably have left Caroline well provided for.
But somehow I couldn't associate Caroline strongly with money,
short of it though she may be. The very ferocity of the crime
seemed to indicate passion of some kind.'

'Yes, I see that,' said Biddy eagerly. 'But would you say being
gifted is a reason for being *murdered*?'

'Possibly. A gifted person who is recognised can inspire savage
jealousy in the gifted person who is not. Of all the gifted people in

this village – and there are a number of highly artistic people – most were using their gifts in a purely local, amateur sort of way. They might have taken pleasure in this, or they might have resented it. Biddy, for instance, and Ann, had given up careers on the stage. Only Fiona had made her name.

'And with *poetry*, of all things. A lot of people consider that poetry, particularly the modern variety, is either easy or nonsense or both, and view it as they would, say, abstract painting, as something any child could do. Even her most loyal admirer, Colonel Rillington, was doubtful about her poetry!'

'I suppose you suspected us all,' said Rosemary in her direct way.

'Even me?' exclaimed Biddy, all agog.

'Pretty well all,' admitted Harriet cheerfully. 'You seem the antithesis of a cold-blooded killer, Biddy, but you *were* a professional actress! You had no apparent motive but as we saw with John Clancy a fair assortment can suddenly spring up from nowhere. And Ann was an unknown quantity to me, intelligent, brooding looking. She might have had a past. She might have had a motive.'

Harriet looked at Rosemary Ashford. 'And you had all the anatomical knowledge and conceivably might have imagined that you had a motive.'

Rosemary stared at her coolly for a moment and then gave her clear laugh. 'Go on, say it,' she said. '*Jealousy!* Yes, you'd be right!'

'It is remotely possible that you might stab somebody,' continued Harriet. 'The iron determination is there, the – ruthlessness even, but you are too neat and fastidious, too far-thinking and controlled, too organised altogether, for this crime. Even if you did forget the congealing qualities of blood you would never wildly throw the dead kitten away. You are a self-possessed person, unlikely to panic.

'Of course there were some bothersome side-lines too, such as John Clancy's real family.'

'I knew it!' cried Rosemary triumphantly when she heard the story. 'He was just the type!'

'Well,' said Biddy frankly, 'I must say I never guessed all that, but I always said there was something funny about him.'

'And about Maureen Clancy too. I don't suppose he ever knew that she had at least half an hour mysteriously unaccounted for.

That would have really finished him off. ...'

'I wonder what she was up to, all alone in that house,' said Rosemary at last. 'One thing's certain; she never went near that hammock. She was too timid and nervous with Fiona altogether.'

There was a thoughtful pause.

'Make believe!' exclaimed Biddy suddenly. 'That's what I would have done at her age if I'd been her, all squashed down by that awful man. Swanned about while I had that lovely place to myself and dreamed of being a grand lady, pretending that I was Bobby's wife.'

'I never thought of that, Biddy,' cried Harriet. 'We shall never know for sure, but I think you're right!'

'It's having been on the stage myself,' said Biddy modestly. 'It does make you understand about people wanting to act.'

'I even succeeded in almost suspecting the kind and gentle Andrew,' said Harriet. 'He is adolescent, idealistic, clumsy, impulsive, protective, and he knows about ... biology.

'As for Thomas, no, of course I didn't, but he *is* rather secretive.'

'He feels it's a waste of breath if nobody believes him,' explained Caroline.

'Of course. But now, after his important evidence, he is much more likely to be taken seriously.'

'I know,' said Caroline. 'It's one of the – one of the ...'

'Good things that have come out of this whole dreadful affair,' finished Harriet boldly. 'Then there was Colonel Rillington, a little mysterious to me. A kindly, helpful man, but either slightly shy or slightly cold, I wasn't sure which and, as Dizzy pointed out, trained to kill. Quickly and quietly with no messing about and no second thoughts. That was true, though one discounted most of what Dizzy had to say. Even James turned into rather a funny sort of doctor!'

'James?' demanded Rosemary wrathfully. 'What could anybody say against James? He's the nicest, sweetest, most innocent man in the world! That's the troub ... I mean, that's the truth, and if any of you don't believe me well, I'm sorry for you, that's all!'

Harriet laughed. The calm and confident Rosemary had actually gone quite pink in the face. 'Don't worry. He didn't mention his name and even I, a complete ignoramus, took no notice, so I'm quite sure nobody else would! But of course Walter Rillington was not only trained to kill, silently and swiftly, he was extremely good at it. Bobby said something of the sort, in his light, affectionate way.'

She nodded her head. 'Yes, Bobby might have planted that remark. Even Ted began to doubt him. Normally he would never have disturbed a shocked and grieving man in his own garden after he had especially asked to be left alone. No, however attractive, one had to include Bobby on the list of suspects. He had the opportunity and he was a good actor. He might have deceived us about the happiness of his marriage as he deceived us about his alibi.'

'Bobby?' All three women now gazed at Harriet in disbelief. 'But Bobby is so honest,' said Biddy.

'All the same, he didn't tell us the truth about his London trip.'

'But why ever not?' asked Caroline.

'He gave the truth to the police, and a harmless white lie to us. A letter that morning made him change his plans. He spent the afternoon and early evening in a Sussex prison, speaking to one of the prisoners, and also to the governor.'

'One of the prisoners?'

Harriet nodded. 'A distinguished man. At least he was, when Bobby's father was alive. Now he is old, and drunk, and silly. The case has sensational aspects ... no, I swear, I don't know any more than that!' insisted Harriet, catching Biddy's eye. 'But Bobby thought he might be able to help him. He intervened, with some effect it seems.'

'Just like him,' approved Rosemary.

'Yes, you wouldn't hesitate to do what you thought was right.'

Rosemary snorted, 'I should hope not!'

'But some people are different about such things.'

'I shouldn't dare to barge into something embarrassing,' confessed Biddy. 'I'd hate to be cruel, but I might pretend not to know! I suppose it's no good trying to pretend to be what you're *not*.' She paused, and then said suddenly, 'Poor Cotty.'

'Fiddlesticks! Not poor Cotty at all!' exclaimed Rosemary with her usual vigour. 'If you weren't so soft, Biddy, you would have seen that husband of yours off years ago, with police protection if necessary!'

'I imagined that he needed me, in some tangled sort of way,

and one likes, I suppose, to be needed. Even by him.' Biddy stroked the unresponsive back of Tweaky Poo, with two plump little white fingers. Some remaining strand of loyalty to Dizzy stopped her from repeating what Ted Baxter had told her in confidence about that visit to London. 'But I'm afraid that really he – just used me.' Well, she wouldn't be seeing so much of him now. Her blue eyes rounded as she looked at them each in turn. 'It's quite a relief, to realise that I just thoroughly dislike him!'

'It's quite a relief to realise that my life's been given back to me.' Harriet's smile broadened as she met the three answering smiles.

'Another page, of glorious life, in middle-age.'